Rescuing Harley

D1565859

Rescuing Harley

Delta Force Heroes

Book 3

By Susan Stoker

Cover Design by Chris Mackey, AURA Design Group
Cover Photographer: Darren Birks
Edited by Kelli Collins & Missy Borucki

Manufactured in the United States

Table of Contents

Dedication

For David

Chapter One

"**Y**OU ARE OUT of your ever-loving mind."

"I think it's awesome."

Harley Kelso stared at her siblings in disbelief. She wasn't surprised one of them didn't think much of her latest plan, but it was beyond surprising that *Montesa* was the one who didn't think it was a good idea. She was usually all gung-ho in support of Harley in whatever crazy thing she wanted to do. Her brother, Davidson, on the other hand, was almost always overprotective, scaring the shit out of the rare date who came to the house when she was younger and generally vetoing anything that was the teensiest bit on the wild side.

Both siblings were older than her, but ever since she was a little girl, Davidson had been the stereotypical protective older brother to both her and Montesa. He'd taken on a gang of boys who'd been harassing Montesa once, and gotten beaten pretty badly in the process, but his distraction had worked and given her the chance to run away.

Harley would do anything for her brother and sister,

but *this* she had to do, no matter what they thought.

"I know it's not exactly the safest thing in the world, but something's wrong with my graphics, and the only way I can think to fix it is to experience it myself."

"Bull," Montesa countered immediately, then started ticking items on her fingers as she spoke. "One, you could watch YouTube all day and see firsthand what's involved. Two, you could go to the airport and get a pair of binoculars and see what it's all about. Three—"

"No," Harley interrupted, knowing her sister could go on all day if given the chance. "It's not the same as experiencing it myself."

"Where do you want to do it?" Davidson asked.

Glad that her brother was being reasonable, Harley eagerly told him what she'd learned. "Through a professional skydiving club in Waco. The guy who owns it has logged a gazillion jumps already. He was in the military, I don't remember what branch, but he's got all these accolades and stuff on the website. I watched the video online and I've read a lot about it. I'm doing a tandem jump, so it's not as if I'll be going by myself. I'll be strapped in front of a professional. The whole thing will only take like twenty minutes, and most of that is getting up to the right altitude."

Montesa sighed. "You're really gonna do this, aren't you?"

"Yup." Harley knew she sounded a lot surer than

she was, but if she showed even an ounce of fear, her sister would pounce on it and eventually convince her to give it up. "I need to. I've been working on the graphics for the latest game in the *This is War* franchise and every time I code the men parachuting out of the plane, it looks funny. All jerky or something."

"And you think experiencing it firsthand will help you be able to code it better?"

The skepticism in her sister's voice was hard to miss.

"Well, yeah. Look, let's just say for a second that I'm crazy, and don't know what I'm talking about. At the very least, it'll be a cool experience. I've read the club's safety record, it's flawless. No one has died. No one has been injured. The people they have as the jumpmasters have lots and lots of jumps under their belts. It isn't like I'm randomly going to the airport and asking someone off the street if they'll jump out of an airplane with me strapped in front of them."

Montesa sighed and looked up at the ceiling as if hoping for an answer written up there. "I have no idea how we're related."

Harley smiled at her sister. "Me either. We don't look a thing alike and I'm as different from you as I could be."

"I wasn't talking about looks and you know it," Montesa griped, moving her eyes away from the ceiling and back to Harley's, then dramatically sighing again.

"Make an appointment with John, he'll make sure your will is up to date before you go."

Harley rolled her eyes. "Jeez, I don't need to update my will, weirdo. You and Davidson are already gonna get everything I have if I croak. And I'm not going to go to your office and meet with your partner just so you can both grill me some more and try to talk me out of this. Forget it."

Harley loved her sister's law partner. He was about fifteen years older than her, and he'd hired Montesa right out of law school and after she'd passed the bar. He had a small law firm, but he'd obviously seen something in Montesa that he liked. They'd been working together now for about ten years. Harley thought there was more between them than just being law partners, but there was no way she was going to butt into her sister's love life. The second she did, Montesa would be all over her about *her* lack of a relationship. No thank you.

"How about I drop you off then?" Davidson asked.

Harley shook her head, glad she'd already arranged everything. "No can do, bro. It's next Wednesday, you have that conference next week."

"Shit, Harl, why'd you schedule it for a weekday? Put it off until the weekend and I'll be back and can go with you."

"No. I've already got the appointment and have paid

the deposit."

"How much is it?" Montesa broke in.

Sometimes talking with her siblings was like watching a tennis match, but Harley was used to their ways.

"It's only two hundred and fifty bucks."

"Jesus, that's highway robbery."

"No it's not, cut the crap, Davidson," Harley exclaimed. "Think about it. The plane, the fuel, the parachutes, the expertise of the jumpmasters...it's actually pretty cheap."

"Dammit. I hate when you're right, but I still wish I could be there," he grumbled, looking anything but happy.

"Do you want me to get the video? It's an extra fifty bucks. I wasn't going to but…"

"Yes."

"No."

Montesa and Davidson answered at the same time.

"I have no desire to watch my baby sister go splat, or drool all over herself as she plummets to the ground," Montesa said firmly.

"On that visual, I have to agree. Sorry, Davidson, no video. My drool doesn't need to be plastered all over the Internet, because I know if you got your hands on it, that's exactly what you'd do."

Davidson smiled at her, then got serious. "I think this will be good for you. You don't get out much and maybe you'll meet someone there."

Harley stood up from the couch and carried her plate to the kitchen, refusing to be hurt by her brother's insinuation. She knew what she was and what she wasn't. She was a nerd. A dork. She wore glasses and preferred to wear comfortable clothing all the time. She'd never in her life worn makeup, much to Montesa's consternation. It just wasn't her. From a young age, she'd been fascinated with computers and video games, and she'd spent most of her high school years in front of the television playing first-person shooter games with people on the Internet she'd never met.

Her love of all things video games had led to her majoring in Computer Science at a local community college. She then moved out to California to finish her undergraduate degree and went on to get her graduate degree in Computer Science, with game development as a specialization.

It had been tough to move away from home, but both Montesa and Davidson had supported her wholeheartedly. After years of hard work, and an internship with Activision, she'd been hired on full time. The best part of the job was that she was able to work remotely, and had immediately moved back to Temple, Texas, to be near her family.

She'd always been close to them, even before her parents had died. Maybe it was because of their names and the fact they'd been picked on, or because they were close in age, or maybe simply because of genetics, but the three siblings had always stuck together. Davidson was two years older than Montesa, who was two years older than Harley, and neither would let her forget that, no matter how old she got, she'd always be the baby. Harley wanted to argue that at thirty-four, she could hardly be considered a baby, but secretly she didn't mind her siblings being so involved in her life. The alternative was too depressing to think about.

Honey and Jim had been hard-working and hard-playing parents. They were into the biker way of life, and had named their children accordingly. Harley didn't think naming your children after motorcycles was normal, but who was she to say. Her mom was always smiling and wouldn't hesitate to drop everything to help out a friend, or one of her children, if needed. She was healthily plump and never made any apologies for liking to eat and drink whatever she wanted. Jim had been a tall bear of a man. He'd had a slight beer gut, but like his wife, didn't seem to be bothered by it. He'd worn his hair long in the back and had a full bushy brown beard. He'd frequently said he loved the feel of the wind blowing through it as he rode.

The two fell madly in love in their early twenties when they'd met at a biker rally. They'd gotten married six months to the day after they'd met and didn't let society's expectations on what they should do with their lives matter. They loved the biker lifestyle, and made no apologizes for it either. They weren't strict parents, but did insist on their children being respectful. They'd encouraged their children to follow their hearts and passions and do what they wanted to do with their lives.

They'd been on their annual pilgrimage up to Sturgis in South Dakota when a man in a big pickup truck had simply not seen them in his blind spot and changed lanes right into them. Jim had tried to protect his wife, but his bike had collided with Honey's and they'd both careened over the side of the mountain they had been traveling on. Neither had a chance.

It was the worst time in Harley's life, but deep down she was glad her parents had died together. She and her siblings knew there was no way either of them would've been able to handle being alive when their spouse wasn't. She was seventeen at the time, and since Montesa was still living at home, her sister was able to get full custody of her until she'd turned eighteen.

More than once when she was little, Harley had wanted to change her name, but after the accident, she grew to love it. It was a connection to her parents. So what if it was a bit weird? Celebrities gave their kids all sorts of names today that were way stranger than hers.

"I'll call when I get back from the conference and we can do lunch. You can tell me all about it," Davidson ordered, his eyes piercing in their intensity as he looked at Harley.

"I'd like that," she told him immediately. He and Montesa were her closest friends, of course she would tell them about the jump afterwards.

Her brother and sister had brought their dishes to the sink and were getting ready to leave. It was their weekly ritual to have dinner together one night and they usually rotated houses. It had been her turn to host this week, and as usual, she'd ordered out. Tonight was pizza night. Montesa and Davidson complained about it, but Harley knew they secretly loved the junk she ordered for them.

"Please call me the second you get home," Montesa said as she hugged her sister. "I know your mind will be going a million miles an hour trying to figure out how to put what you just experienced into code, but I'll worry until you call."

"I will. Drive safe you guys."

"Love you," Davidson said as he hugged her.

Harley stood on tiptoes to wrap her arms around her brother's shoulders. She was tall at five-ten, but Davidson was easily five inches taller. Montesa put her arms around the two of them and they had a group huddle by the front door for a moment. Much to her consternation, Montesa had gotten her mother's genes; she was the runt of the family at five-six and had a hard time keeping weight off her heavy frame.

"Okay, enough. Go. I'll keep in touch and let you know how it goes," Harley ordered as she pulled back and pushed her siblings toward the door.

"You better," Montesa scolded as she hitched her purse up on her shoulder. She might look like a sweet, slightly frumpy middle-aged woman, but she was a firecracker in the courtroom and had gained a reputation as someone who didn't take crap from anyone. She won way more cases than she lost. Rumor had it that when other attorneys learned they'd be up against Montesa in the courtroom, they'd push their clients to settle, knowing their chances of winning had been lowered dramatically simply because Montesa was on the other side of the courtroom.

Harley watched as her siblings waved once more as they left. Her townhouse was in an area of Temple that catered to the older set. Exactly how she liked it. She craved quiet and didn't worry about her safety much living in the subdivision. Gretel Owens was a widow who lived in the townhouse next to her. She was eighty-three and acted thirty years younger. She had a crush on the man that lived on the other side of Harley, Henry Baberfield. Henry was a Vietnam Veteran who had never been married. According to Gretel, he was a womanizer in his day, but that didn't seem to deter her. Harley had no idea how old Henry was, but could guess he was probably around the same age as Gretel.

Living where she did, tucked between two octogenarians, suited Harley just fine. She was socially awkward and preferred her video games to people. The computer couldn't hurt her like people did. She'd learned a long time ago, however, to not take shit from anyone. So what if she was a nerd? So what if she was an introvert? There was no rule that said every human on earth had to be outgoing and beautiful. And when push came to shove, Harley would bet that most of the people who gave her pitying looks probably had kids who played her video games. It was money in her pocket, and that went a long way toward making her not as sensitive anymore to the looks and comments she got.

Harley shut the door and went back into her office. She had a ton of questions she wanted to research about skydiving and how it all worked. She only had a few days to get everything together before her adventure. As much as she'd talked her brother and sister into accepting what she was going to do, deep down, Harley wasn't sure she really *should* do it. But Activision had recently hired a new batch of developers and she didn't want to be left in the dust. She had to do something to impress her boss, and making the troop drop in the latest *War* game was just the thing. She wanted it to be visually stunning and make the player feel as if they were actually parachuting down onto the battlefield.

It was a great idea—she just had to have the courage to go through with it.

Chapter Two

H ARLEY WAS A lot less nervous than she thought she'd be when Wednesday finally rolled around. She'd dressed in the recommended loose-fitting clothes, which was what she normally wore, so it worked out well. Jeans, long-sleeved T-shirt with the *This is War* logo on it, and a pair of sneakers. Trying to act as if she signed up to jump out of a plane every day of the week, Harley strode into the Waco Skydiving Club with far more confidence than she felt.

Not sure what she was expecting, Harley was surprised to see only one person who looked like he worked at the club milling around. There were six other people clumped together chatting happily near a table in the back, obviously all friends. Her heart dropped.

The last thing Harley wanted to do was go through this experience with a group of people who knew and liked each other. She already felt like enough of an outsider in her everyday life.

"Hey, you must be Harley. Welcome! Come on over here and we'll get introductions done with before we get started with the legal stuff."

The man who'd spoken had a goatee and a slight beer belly. His hair was blond and slightly mussed. The jeans looked worn but comfortable and he wore a T-shirt with the words "Waco Skydiving Club" across his chest. He reminded her a lot of her dad, and that made her relax a bit. It was as if he was there looking over her.

"Thanks, Dad," she whispered, then took a deep breath.

She walked over to the group, and seeing them all laughing and talking together made her already shaky confidence take a nosedive and she was once again ready to scrap the entire idea, but the man who resembled her father didn't give her a chance to even open her mouth.

He addressed the entire group. "I'm Tommy and I started this club about eight years ago. There are a lot of active duty and retired military guys around here, as you know, who were looking for a way to have some fun in their down time. We follow the US Parachute Association rules and regulations and we keep a close eye on the weather. If there's even a chance of it turning, we won't jump. Safety is our number one priority here. So with that out of the way, why don't we go around and you can introduce yourself and say why you're here today."

Harley felt like she was in the fourth grade again. She'd been the new kid in school and she had to stand in front of the class and tell everyone who she was and her favorite subject in school. Science apparently wasn't the right answer because from that day forward, she'd been made fun of and picked on, not only because of her odd name, but because she was a science nerd.

"I'll start," a good-looking man with a deep voice said. "I'm Joe and this'll be my fifth jump. I did my first a couple of years ago and was hooked." He nodded to the woman at his side.

"Oh, okay, I'm Sarah. This will be my fourth jump. Joe convinced me to go with him after he'd gone his first time, and even though I was reluctant, I decided to go for it. Now he won't let me live it down that he's been one more time than me."

Everyone around the beautiful couple tittered. Harley mentally groaned. Great. Now she was not only going to have to do this with a group of friends, but she would bet everything she owned that she was the only newbie there.

Her fears were confirmed when the rest of the group also chimed in with the fact that they were repeat jumpers. When it was finally her turn to introduce herself, she kept it short and sweet, wanting nothing more than to get on with it.

"I'm Harley. This will be my first time. It's good to meet everyone." Just because she didn't like to be in groups, didn't mean she didn't know the rules. Be polite. Smile. Look interested.

"Hey, Harley, cool name. So you're the only virgin here, good to know," Tommy boomed out, his words echoing across the room.

Harley blushed and bit her lip. She knew the man was talking about the fact that she was the only one who hadn't jumped out of a plane before, but it suddenly felt as if he knew the one sexual encounter she'd had when she was in college had ended in embarrassment. Harley supposed she was technically still a virgin, even though the guy had shoved his fingers inside her and broken her hymen. It had hurt, and she'd jerked her knees up, nailing him in the balls. Needless to say, that had ended the night, and the pseudo-relationship they'd had.

Harley went through the motions of laughing along with the others. Thankfully Tommy didn't dwell on his little joke and continued, "Okay, most of you know the drill. We'll get your IDs and weigh you so we can pair you up with the best tandem master. We've got snacks and coffee and water, but I don't suggest guzzling too much liquid. Once you get strapped in, you won't be able to use the restroom for at least an hour or so."

He eyed the group up and down and nodded. "Looks like you're all dressed appropriately, thank you. Harley, since you're wearing glasses, we'll want to make sure we have a pair of goggles that fits over them. Remind me later if I forget, okay?"

Harley nodded, stupidly embarrassed that she was

the only one wearing glasses. It wasn't anything to be embarrassed about, but she still was. She'd tried wearing contacts, but staring at the computer for hours at a time dried her eyes out and gave her awful headaches. It was simply easier to wear glasses.

"Once everyone is settled, we'll watch a couple of videos. The first will describe the process you're about to go through. From how the parachutes are packed, to fitting the harnesses and what you'll do once it's time to jump. Then we'll get the legal stuff out of the way and have you sign the waivers. There's another video about the dangers of jumping out of a plane, just so you know what you're getting into, then if you're all still interested, we'll take payment and get you suited up. Any questions?"

Harley had about a million, but when she looked around and saw the rest of the group looking bored, she bit her tongue. This was why she didn't want to go with a bunch of people who'd done this before. She was nervous as hell and wanted as much information as she could get, but instead of relying on other newbies to ask questions, she was on her own.

Keeping her mouth shut for the moment, she followed behind the others and settled into a chair in the front row. She wanted to be able to see and hear the television clearly. The other couples immediately started talking amongst themselves, but Harley's complete attention was on the screen.

"So? What do you think?" Tommy asked his friend, Beckett "Coach" Ralston, as they stood inside the small office at the Waco Skydiving Club looking out at the group of civilians who would be skydiving in a few hours.

Coach shrugged. "Looks about like the group we had yesterday." Jumping out of a perfectly functioning plane wasn't exactly Coach's idea of a good time, but he'd taken two weeks of leave after the kidnapping of his teammate's girlfriend and daughter. Emily and Annie were fine, but Jacks, the vindictive ex-soldier who had orchestrated the entire incident, hadn't been so lucky. He'd spent a few days in the hospital recuperating, and was now currently a guest of the State of Texas. Jacks would be going on trial in a few weeks, and Coach hoped he'd spend a good chunk of time behind bars.

Coach and the rest of his Delta Force team were taking some time off and Tommy had been in a bind. One of his regular jumpmasters had broken his leg. He had a replacement coming, but the other man couldn't get there for another month. Since Coach had the time, and nothing else planned, he'd agreed to come and help his friend out.

Coach and Tommy had met a couple of years earlier. He'd heard about a new technique for packing a parachute and had wanted to try it out. He'd researched and found that the Waco Skydiving Club had an excellent reputation and was already using the new procedure. Coach had gone out to check into the organization, and they had clicked from day one. Tommy was older, and more redneck than Coach was used to, but he was a great guy with a heart of gold. There was no way Coach could turn down his plea for help.

"The three couples have all jumped several times before, we've only got one virgin this time," Tommy told him, raising his chin, indicating the tall woman sitting in the front row of chairs intently watching the safety video. She was the only one paying attention, sitting with her eyes glued on the screen, and apparently tuning out the chatter from the rest of the group behind her.

Coach chuckled. "As if I couldn't figure that out on my own."

"Yeah, kinda hard to miss."

"Think she's gonna go through with it?" Coach asked, knowing Tommy had a good eye for who might chicken out when the rubber met the road.

"Oh yeah. She might be new at this, but she's got determination oozing from every pore of her body."

Coach narrowed his eyes and examined the woman, wondering what it was that Tommy saw in her. She wasn't anything special to look at. She seemed tall, but slender. He couldn't really tell since she was wearing a baggy T-shirt, but her legs looked miles long in her jeans, without many curves. Her hair was shoulder length, a light brown color, and hanging loosely over her shoulders. She was currently biting her lip and jiggling one foot, watching the television nervously, pushing up her glasses, which kept sliding down her nose.

"She'll be with you," Tommy told Coach. "She's tall, and she won't fit comfortably against the others."

Coach knew the man was right. At six-five, he was a couple inches taller than any of the other jumpmasters. The woman could go with someone else, but it made more sense for her to be with him since she seemed to be the tallest woman of the bunch. She'd fit against him better since they'd be strapped together from hips to chest. If he was paired with the smaller women, their feet wouldn't even touch the ground once the harnesses were strapped together.

Coach nodded at his friend. "I figured. What's her story?"

Tommy shrugged. "Don't know. She didn't say much in the introductions. Just that she'd never jumped before."

Coach was always fascinated with the reasons why

people decided to do a tandem jump. For some it was because they'd beat cancer, others because they wanted the adrenaline rush. A few had only agreed to accompany their partners because it was something they'd wanted to do. But for some reason, Coach figured none of those explanations fit the woman completely engrossed in the safety procedures.

He turned to Tommy. "I hope she doesn't back out. It's a beautiful day. I'm actually looking forward to jumping today."

Tommy's laugh boomed out through the small office. "Good. I knew if I could get you out here and have you jump enough, you'd see the beauty in it."

Coach smiled ruefully. "It's not like we see much beauty when we do this for our jobs."

"I know, that's why you needed this," Tommy retorted immediately, obviously having a good idea what it was Coach did for a living, even if they'd never talked about it.

Coach rolled his eyes. "Okay, fine. I'm enjoying it. Happy?"

"Immensely." The older man looked through the glass again. "Looks like the videos are almost over. I'll get them to sign the waivers and take care of payment, then it'll be time for them to meet everyone. You ready?"

Coach nodded. "See you in a few."

He watched as Tommy strode out of the office and went over to stand next to the television, ready to stop the video as soon as it was done. Coach's eyes went to the woman in the front row. He'd been with his share of women over the years, fewer now that he'd reached thirty-five. In the days when he'd first joined the Army, he'd been like most young soldiers, taking home anyone who showed an ounce of interest.

Once he'd joined the team, however, he was more interested in working hard, staying alive, and making sure his teammates made it home in one piece as well. When he got home from missions, all he wanted to do was relax, not deal with the intricacies of picking up a woman in a bar or even having a long-term girlfriend. His days of dating women he met in bars were long over. It'd been years since he'd been in a relationship, and he could count on one hand the number of sexual encounters he'd had since that time.

But there was something about the woman drinking in every scrap of information that flitted across the television screen. She wasn't his type. He liked smaller women who he could dominate easily. He liked the feeling of being bigger and stronger than any woman he took to bed. He liked being in charge. Coach figured it was a side effect of being a Delta Force soldier. He wasn't an asshole in bed, or out, but he spent so much time ordering people around and having them do his bidding immediately and without question, that it had become ingrained in his psyche.

And he definitely liked curves. Lots of them. He was a tit man, and he'd been known to spend hours worshiping a woman's breasts. He preferred a woman to be natural; there was just something so wrong about seeing a woman naked with boobs that didn't sag at all. He liked long hair on a woman, didn't matter what color it was, and he definitely liked his women to have some sort of intelligence. Ditzy women who only wanted to sleep with a soldier, and didn't care what kind, weren't for him.

After observing the woman who'd stood up and followed Tommy to the other side of the room to pick up the waivers she needed to sign, Coach decided she really wasn't his type at all.

But that didn't keep his eyes from straying to her ass as she walked. She was tall and slender, but perfectly proportioned. Her legs were long and her hips were wide. She swayed sexily as she walked, even when she didn't know someone was observing her. Coach's eyes widened when she put both hands on the small of her back and stretched, arching her back, working out the kinks that had formed while she'd been seated on the metal chair.

She was standing at the back of the group, her profile to him. Coach sucked in a breath. When she arched backward, her T-shirt tightened against her chest and he could see that she indeed had some curves hidden under her oversized shirt. Her tits weren't huge, but against her slim frame, they stood out like little apples.

She curled her hands over her upper arms and rubbed them, her eyes glued to Tommy, who was explaining how the equipment they'd be using worked. Coach remembered that the air was turned way down in the outer room, to combat the rise in temperature that the customers usually experienced when they got nervous.

The woman's nipples were prominent under her clothes, and Coach could clearly see them against her shirt, even from across the room. God. Damn. Yes, he was a breast man, but nipples were his weakness, and it looked like this woman had a pair he'd like to get his hands on.

She turned away then, holding out a hand to grab the pen Tommy was holding toward her, and Coach shook his head. Jesus. He was ogling the woman as if she was a stripper writhing against a pole. It was rude, and unprofessional, and…

Coach's thoughts dropped off.

She'd leaned over a table in the back of the room to sign the release form and her ass was fucking perfect.

Coach spun around and wiped a hand through his short hair. Jesus, he had to get a grip. The last thing he wanted to do was go out there with a hard-on to meet her. They'd both be embarrassed, and since she had to be strapped up against him, it would be extremely obvious and awkward.

Coach took a deep breath and tried to think of anything that would make the blood pooling in his dick evenly distribute itself throughout the rest of his body. He thought about his teammate's new daughter, Annie. He'd heard from Blade, another member of his team, about her first rappelling lesson.

Fletch refused to teach her, he was way too protective of the first grader, so Blade had volunteered. He reported that the little girl was absolutely fearless, squealing in delight when she'd pushed off of the training wall at the gym on the base. Coach smiled. Annie was a delight and he couldn't be happier for Fletch. He and Emily were perfect together; her daughter was simply the icing on the cake for Fletch.

Coach relaxed, feeling his erection deflating now that he wasn't thinking about how the mysterious woman on the other side of the room was just the right height for him to bend over and take—

No. He couldn't go there. One of the drawbacks of being attracted to smaller women was that he wasn't able to comfortably take them in many positions, at least not without a lot of work on his part. Coach hadn't minded before, but now, he was visualizing how much easier it would be to take her from behind, or even standing upright in the shower…and liking it. He just may have to rethink his "type" of woman.

Coach groaned and shifted his dick in his pants, willing it to calm down again. Fuck. He had a job to do, and he had to get himself together in order to do it.

Finally, feeling like he had himself under control, Coach turned to the office door. He had to get his mind in the game. He couldn't be distracted, not when he was about to throw himself out of a plane and go hurtling toward the ground. *Especially* not when he had a woman strapped to his chest. Hurting himself was one thing, but hurting someone else, a woman who was probably someone's sister—and hopefully not someone's girl-friend or wife—was another thing altogether.

He opened the door and walked toward the group, smiling in what he hoped was a friendly way. Showtime.

Chapter Three

HARLEY WAS HAVING second, and third, thoughts about this whole thing. The safety video scared the shit out of her. There were so many things that could go wrong it wasn't even funny. The plane could crash, the parachute might not deploy, the reserve chute might fail...she was crazy for even thinking she could do this. This wasn't her. She was Harley, the chick who sat on her butt all day.

She was in the middle of her internal freak-out when a man appeared in front of her. She tilted her head back to look at him. He was tall. Freakishly tall. And he was hot. He was wearing a buttoned-down blue shirt, which should've looked weird, considering where they were, but it didn't. She couldn't see what kind of pants he was wearing because he had some sort of overalls covering them, obviously his jumpsuit. A harness was sitting low on his hips, the straps dangling between his legs as he stood there.

"Hey, my name is Beckett Ralston, but my friends call me Coach. I'll be your jumpmaster today. Do you have any questions?"

Did she have any questions? Uh, yeah, only about a hundred.

"Hi. I'm Harley."

"Harley. I like it."

"Yeah, um, my parents had a thing for motorcycles." She kept the explanation short and sweet, her mind going in too many directions to get into it at the moment.

He held out his hand to her. "It's good to meet you."

Harley shook his hand.

"I appreciate you volunteering to be my first-ever customer."

Harley's eyes shot up to his. "What?"

He chuckled and grinned, his eyes dancing. "Sorry, jumpmaster humor. To put your mind at ease, I have no idea what number jump this is for me, but it's well into the upper hundreds. Relax, Harley. You're in good hands. I'm not going to let anything happen to you."

"Oh, well. Okay." She bit her lip.

Coach's thumb brushed over the back of her hand once in a barely there caress before he let go. "Go on."

"Go on, what?" Harley asked, resisting the urge to wipe her hand on her jeans. Her skin felt like it was tingling where they'd touched, but that was impossible...wasn't it?

27

"Ask me the questions I can see burning behind those beautiful brown eyes of yours."

Harley pushed her glasses up on her nose for what seemed the millionth time and considered the man in front of her for a moment. Coach was much taller than she was, but he didn't use his height to intimidate her. He had short dark hair, but not buzzed like a lot of the military men in the area had. And he smelled delicious. Many men doused themselves with cologne, but Coach used only a small amount, or he used scented soap. Whatever it was made her want to bury her nose into the space between his neck and shoulder and inhale.

She wondered if he had some Greek blood in his veins, because he had the kind of dark skin and facial features that reminded her of men from that area. His nose was a bit too big to be considered handsome, but his square jaw, high cheekbones, full lips, and the hint of a five o'clock shadow made him look more...manly than most men she encountered on a daily basis.

He stood a respectful distance away from her and crossed his arms over his chest. He had broad shoulders, and his body naturally tapered down to his trim waist. She could see he was very buff under the blue shirt; his muscles rippled with each of his movements, pulling the material taut. Harley immediately began to design a character in her head who would look just like the man standing in front of her. He'd make an excellent soldier for one of her games. She could imagine him taking down the enemy and saving the girl from the bad guys at the same time.

No one could ever dismiss this man as not being…dangerous, but it seemed somewhat banked. As if he could function perfectly well in polite society, but the second he was provoked, he'd pounce.

Harley tore her mind off of what Coach looked like and tried to bring herself back to his request. She did have questions, lots of them. Coach waited patiently for her to work through the thoughts in her head, and she appreciated him not rushing her. Most people found silence awkward, and jumped in to ask another question or to clarify whatever it was they'd asked, but apparently not this guy. He looked as though he'd stand there forever waiting patiently as she got her thoughts in order.

A memory came to her and she smiled.

"What was that thought?"

Harley jerked, forgetting he'd been watching her so intently. "Oh, well, you remind me of a dog we had growing up."

"Really? This I gotta hear. I'm not sure I've ever been compared to a dog before, at least not in the first five minutes of meeting someone."

Harley blushed, and looked away from his intense gaze, cursing her habit to blurt inappropriate things without thinking about what she was saying first. She hurried through the story, trying to get it over with. "It's nothing bad, it's just that we had a dog who was as gentle as could be, and would never start a fight. I felt one hundred percent comfortable with her being around kids, even toddlers. She'd let them poke and prod her, and even pull on her ears, but if another dog snapped at her, she was suddenly all-in, snarling and fighting as if she'd been born to do it. I always likened it to a kid dropping his bags and going whole-hog in a playground brawl." Harley shrugged self-consciously. "That's all."

Coach chuckled, and luckily didn't look offended in the least. "That's a pretty good observation. I'm harmless, Harley. I don't go out of my way looking to get into it with people. But I also won't stand around and take shit from anyone, or let any of my friends take shit from others. So I guess I *am* like this dog of yours. When provoked, I'm one hundred percent all-in and will defend myself, or my woman, against someone else."

Holy. Shit.

Harley nodded and wanted to change the subject. There were many times in her life when she'd wished for divine intervention to save her from awkward situations, and this was one of those times.

She looked around, seeing the other couples greeting their jumpmasters. The noise in the room had risen with every additional person who'd entered. Some were headed over to an area on the back side of the room, which had harnesses spread out on the ground. "So…I do have questions."

"I'm happy to answer anything you can throw at me. I promise to be honest with you, and if I don't know the answer to something, I'll tell you rather than making something up."

His answer surprised Harley, but she sighed in relief. She hated when people tried to pretend they knew something when it was obvious they had no clue.

"Come on, let's go over there and get you fitted, and you can ask me what's been whirling around in that pretty brain of yours while we do it."

Ignoring the "pretty" comment—it was obvious this man wasn't hurting when it came to picking up women—Harley let her questions fly as they headed over to the harness-fitting area. "What happens if the main chute doesn't open? Will the reserve one automatically go off? Do the lines ever get tangled? What if the wind is blowing really hard, does that make it harder to steer? How *do* you steer? Is it like a car where if you turn right, you'll go right? Or is it the opposite? What's the material of the parachute made out of? Will it hold us? How much can it hold? We're both pretty tall, does that matter? What if I decide right before we're about to go that I can't do it? Will you make me? What's it like when you're falling? Is it peaceful? Is it loud? Is it hard to breathe? What's the highest someone can jump out of a plane? Is it harder to steer when you're higher up?"

Harley took a breath to ask more questions, when Coach stopped her with his hands up as if defending himself from blows.

"Hang on, woman! Give me a chance to answer those before you lob more at me. I'm good, but I'm not *that* good."

Harley blushed and ducked her head. Dang it. She'd just been so anxious to learn as much as she could about the process, she'd just spewed out all her thoughts without thinking...again.

She felt Coach's finger under her chin, tilting her head up to him. "Don't be embarrassed. I love that you're so interested in this. I'll answer all of your questions, but maybe hit me with only a couple at a time, yeah?"

Harley nodded. "Sorry. I have a tendency to be intense when I'm interested in something. Just tell me when you've had enough."

"I don't think I'll ever get enough of you, Harley."

Coach's words were low and even, and Harley could only look up into his hazel eyes in bewilderment. Was he...flirting with her? *Her?* Harley Kelso, the techie nerd? No way.

She opened her mouth to say something, she wasn't

sure what, when a voice called out from across the equipment laid out on the floor in neat rows.

"Hey! It's great the beanpole has a giant to jump with today."

Harley turned and saw Sarah, one of the women she'd met earlier, standing with her friends and laughing at her less-than-witty comment.

The words were said in a teasing tone, but they still hurt. Harley had heard that kind of thing her entire life. She knew she was skinny and did her best to put on weight, but some days, when she was engrossed in her work, she simply forgot to eat. On top of that, she had a naturally high metabolism, so no matter how much she seemed to eat, she never gained a pound.

She'd learned a long time ago, however, to just ignore the mean remarks. Most of the time they didn't bother her anymore, and sometimes she even thought of a good comeback. But before she could open her mouth, Coach took a step in front of her and put his hands on his hips as he stared down the other woman.

"That was an extremely rude thing to say," he barked out, clenching his teeth. "I don't care that you just insulted me, but I won't have you taking a dig at anyone else. Any of the jumpmasters here would be perfectly suited to jump with Harley, but its best to pair people up who are close in height. So you're right, it *is* a good thing I'm here to jump with her today. Apologize."

Harley froze where she stood. Coach's back was ramrod straight and he stood in front of her with his legs shoulder width apart, as if he was ready to take a physical blow for her. She could see his shoulders rising and falling as he took quick, even breaths. He was honestly offended on her behalf. It was impossible to believe. Almost as impossible as the thought he might be flirting with her.

Harley put one hand tentatively on Coach's back, both in thanks and to try to soothe him, and said in a soft voice, "Its okay, Coach. It's not a big deal. She wasn't wrong."

He ignored her, and crossed his arms over his chest, waiting for Sarah to apologize.

"I-I'm sorry, I didn't mean anything mean by it. I was just trying to joke around."

Coach didn't respond, only nodded and turned back to her, dismissing Sarah. Harley saw him take a deep breath and forcefully try to relax his shoulders.

"If the main chute doesn't open, the reserve one will. And before you ask, the reserve chute is inspected just as the main one is, it's the law. Additionally, the Waco Skydiving Club has AADs—Automatic Activation Devices—on every parachute. If, for some reason, the main chute isn't deployed, and the reserve chute isn't pulled before a preset altitude, usually around two thousand feet, it mechanically opens the reserve automatically without you or me having to do anything."

Harley nodded, perfectly happy to put the embarrassing situation with Sarah behind her, and allowed Coach to put his hand on her lower back and lead her over to the end row of harnesses.

"As for steering, it's fairly uncomplicated. The lines are attached to the back right and left sides of the parachute. To turn left, you pull down on the left line. To go right, you do the same on the right side. Once we're in free fall, I'll show you where the straps are and I'll even let you steer for a while, so you can get a feel for it, if you want." Coach kneeled down on the ground and fiddled with one of the harnesses, but he didn't stop answering her earlier questions.

"The chute itself is made out of a nylon cloth, and it's very strong. It can hold much more than just our combined weight. Free fall is exhilarating. I won't lie, you might have a tough time breathing at first, until you get used to it—and it will be loud. We won't be able to talk until the chute deploys. We'll be falling around a hundred and thirty miles an hour when we first leave the plane, but once I deploy the drogue chute, the smaller chute that slows our speed, we'll slow to around a hundred and fifteen or so. When we hit fifty-five hundred feet, I'll pull the cord. Once I get my harness and parachute all the way on, I'll show you where the ripcord handle is. Then when we're out of free fall, you'll be able to hear me and it's like floating."

He stood up holding a harness in his hands and his eyes met hers. "What did I miss?"

Harley was impressed. He'd segued into answering her questions after the embarrassing confrontation with Sarah without missing a beat. "How high will we be jumping from and what's the highest altitude someone can jump out of a plane at?"

Coach held the harness out for her to step into. She did as he indicated and he answered her newest question as he worked to make sure the fit of the contraption was correct.

"Since it's nice today, and there are seven jumpers, the pilot will probably take us up to around thirteen or fourteen thousand feet. HALO jumps can be done up to thirty thousand feet."

"HALO?" Harley asked, assuming he wasn't referring to the video game. The word sounded familiar, but she wasn't sure what it stood for in his world.

"Sorry, I forget civilians don't know all the acronyms. Stands for High Altitude, Low Opening. It means jumping out of a plane way high up, but not opening the chute until close to the ground. Soldiers use it when they're trying to get into an area undetected. If the plane stays high enough, the ground radar can miss it, and waiting until the last possible second to deploy the chute means there's less of a chance tangos will greet the soldiers when they land."

Harley grabbed onto the harness that Coach was trying to tighten around her. She turned to face him. "You're a soldier." It wasn't a question.

Coach nodded nonchalantly. "Yeah."

"But you're here."

He grinned. He was kneeling on the ground, as it was easier to shift the harness up her hips and tighten the straps from that height. "Yeah, I had some time off and Tommy's a friend. I'm helping out."

Harley's eyes lit up in excitement. "Cool."

Coach's hands gripped her hips and he turned her away from him again, so she wasn't looking at him anymore. "I take it you like soldiers?"

"It's not that," Harley hurried to explain, not wanting him to think for even a second that she was the kind of woman who got off on going out with soldiers simply because they were soldiers. "I'm not a barracks bunny. It's just that I'm here today because I'm trying to perfect code for a war video game I'm designing. I can't get the parachute scene to look right. I thought if I experienced it myself, I'd have better luck."

"Ah, and the soldier thing?"

Harley flushed, glad she wasn't looking at Coach. "Well, I just figured…" Her voice trailed off. What had she figured? That he'd answer the million questions she had and put up with her dorkiness long enough to help make her code more realistic?

"You're cute. I'll answer whatever questions you have, Harley. No problem. Now, what else did you ask earlier that I didn't answer?"

Harley smiled. Coach was being very polite. And he thought she was cute. She didn't think she'd been categorized as cute since she was two years old. She was practical, and tall and willowy...but not cute. She probably should've been offended, but she simply couldn't dredge up the energy to care.

Besides, Coach would probably run screaming in the other direction if she really asked everything she wanted to. Ideally, he'd be right there next to her as she worked on the code, but that was a pipe dream for sure. She'd have to soak up all the answers she could right now. "What if I freak out and decide that I can't jump at the last minute?"

Coach stood up behind her and she felt him tug hard at the harness around her hips. It pulled tight against her jeans and she staggered against him and took in a startled breath. He leaned over her, which was easy for him to do since he was so much taller, and fiddled with the straps over her shoulders. "You aren't going to freak out. I'll be right there with you. I've done this hundreds of times, Harley. I'll keep you safe. Promise."

"But if I don't want to do it? Will you force me?"

Coach turned her then, putting his hands on her shoulders and leaning toward her. Harley forgot about the other people in the room. She stared up into Coach's serious face as he spoke.

"I would *never* force you to do anything you don't want to. I might push, and try to convince you, but if you really decide that you can't jump, we won't. Once we get in the plane, you won't get a refund, but you don't have to take the jump. Are we clear?"

Harley nodded, relieved. She didn't want to chicken out, but there was always the possibility. Coach's words went a long way toward making her feel better about the whole thing.

"All right then. How does this feel?" Coach tugged on the harness once more, his hands curling around the straps that ran up and over her shoulders.

Up until now, Harley had been keeping her mind away from the fact that Coach was hot, smelled delicious, and was standing closer to her than any man had in years. But his knuckles brushing against her chest as he grabbed hold of the straps reminded her of the fact that she was attracted to him. She felt her nipples bunching and tried to hunch her shoulders forward to hide the fact.

He let go with his right hand to pull on the strap that was connecting the shoulder straps across her chest. Again, his knuckles brushed against her, between her breasts this time, and she almost gasped at the sensation. She was embarrassed as all get out, knowing her damnable large nipples had to be showing through her comfortable cotton bra as she imagined how his hands would feel against her bare skin.

"I-It feels tight. Restrictive," she stuttered out.

He nodded, as if pleased, and thankfully ignored her wobbly voice. "Good. The harness *is* uncomfortable, I won't lie. It's like rock climbing or repelling gear. It's designed to keep you strapped to me, nice and tight. We'll be connected in four places, two at your hips and two at your shoulders, but we won't do that until right before we jump. When the chute goes off, plan on having a wedgie." Coach smiled, but continued, "When I tell you, you can stand on my feet while we're under canopy and adjust it a bit if it's too uncomfortable."

Harley gulped and nodded, not wanting to think about wedgies and pulling the harness out of her butt when she was attached to him. She wished he'd take his hands off her, but at the same time, wished he'd never let go.

"We want your harness snug. There's no chance it'll come loose while we're in the air, but you'll feel better if it's tight. I think it's good." Coach took a step back, dropping his hands almost reluctantly. "We've got about fifteen or so more minutes before we load up. Do you have more questions for me?"

Harley took a deep breath, happy Coach had put some space between them. Suddenly the thought of being strapped to him seemed way too intimate for two people who had just met. Maybe if she talked to him some more, asked him more of the questions she had burning in her brain, she'd get over her stupid attraction. It was worth a shot.

"Yeah, I do have more questions."

"Come on, we can sit over here," Coach told her, showing her a bench against the wall.

Harley nodded and went over to where he indicated. She could do this. She had to think about work. She got her thoughts in order and began to think about computer code and how she'd make the opening shot in the new *This is War* game the best ever.

Pushing her glasses up again, she asked, "What about the landing? I mean, I saw it on the tape, but it looks complicated with two people."

"The days of hitting the ground like a sack of flour and rolling are over. The chute acts sort of like a glider, and the shape of it allows for an easier landing. It's a bit more complicated with two people, but I'll do most of the work. When I tell you, all you need to do is pull your knees up, and let me get my feet on the ground first, then you'll just put yours down and help us stay upright. It helps that we're close to the same height."

"What if I screw it up?"

Coach chuckled and put one arm on the back of the bench, looking completely relaxed. He didn't seem worried he was paired with a klutz. "You can't screw up the landing, Harley." When she looked askance at him, he put his hands up in surrender. "Hey! I'm not lying. Look, when you get to the ground, it doesn't matter how you got there, just that you're there in one piece, right? So if I overcompensate, or if the wind blows right when we get close to the ground, or you have a sneezing fit, it doesn't matter. We'll just topple over and take the brunt of the landing on our sides. I'll steer us, but basically you want to hit the top of your thigh, then hip, then side. Roll into it and it's not a big deal."

"We won't suffocate by the parachute wrapping around us?"

Instead of laughing, Coach merely shook his head. "No. It might come down over us, but it's lightweight, not heavy canvas, so it's easily removed."

Harley bit her lip and watched as the others finished up their preparations. They were all smiling and happy and didn't look like they had a care in the world. She couldn't help but be nervous. Not only was she scared, but she wanted to memorize the entire thing so she could do the video game justice.

"You'll show me the thingy to make the chute open?" she asked after a moment.

Coach put his hand over hers and his voice got serious. "Yes. I said I would. But I need you to trust me up there. I can't have you freaking out and going for the ripcord handle before we're at the proper altitude. Let me do my job. You're safe with me."

Coach's hand was warm and so much bigger than her own. Just having him touch her made her less nervous. A *little* less nervous. She was being a big baby.

"I won't. I do trust you, it's just...I'm nervous. And I deal with being nervous by learning everything I can about the situation I'm about to go into." Harley shrugged. "You should've seen me last year when I went whitewater rafting in Colorado with my brother and sister. You would've thought I was preparing for the national exam on how to be a whitewater guide or something. I swear that poor college kid was glad to see us leave at the end of the day. I tipped him big, but still, I know I drove him crazy."

Coach smiled, but didn't remove his hand. "I don't mind. It's refreshing. It'll be much more fun for you, I think, now that you know what I'm doing as we go. What other questions do you have?"

Harley relaxed even more and thought about what else she might need to know for her game. Coach was being very nice and patient with her in answering all her questions. She'd lucked out in getting him as a jump-master.

Ignoring the fact he was still holding her hand, and

trying to push her embarrassment down about having so many things she wanted to know, she threw caution to the wind and took him at his word...and asked another question.

Chapter Four

COACH TOOK A deep breath and tried to calm down. First it'd been the other customer's snide dig about Harley's size. The story of the dog that Harley used to have rang true in his mind. He was fairly easygoing, until someone went after a person under his care. And Harley, whether either of them wanted to admit it or not, was under his care. And not just because he was her jumpmaster for the day.

There was something about her that reminded him of his little sister. Jenny had been three years younger than him and shy. Extremely so. He'd spent his childhood watching as she'd been made fun of and picked on. He'd done everything possible to look out for her. Once she'd turned twelve, however, she'd fallen into a deep depression.

Coach had done what he could to try to protect her from the malicious taunts at school, but his love and protection had been no match for the bullies. A group of mean girls had taken it upon themselves to tear her to shreds, and had been remarkably successful at it too.

Bullies pushed Coach's buttons more than anything else. It wasn't a conscious decision on his part, but seeing what his sister had gone through had made him more sensitive to the issue, and more determined to make sure it didn't happen to anyone around him again.

It was no wonder he'd reacted the way he had when Sarah had taunted Harley. He didn't care that the woman was also making fun of his own size, he'd long since come to terms with his height and strength. But no one made fun of a woman around him. No one. Not ever.

Harley hadn't even commented on his extreme reaction to Sarah's words, but had let him lead the conversation and answer some of her questions. He was grateful. Coach didn't like thinking about Jenny's childhood; how what she went through had turned him into the man he was today.

While Harley reminded him of his sister, she was also very different. Yes, she was shy, and a little socially awkward, but she had an inner strength that Jenny never had. Harley hadn't shrunk away from the mean comment from Sarah, but Coach knew that if he wasn't there, she would've probably just ignored the other woman and tried not to let the words get to her.

But he *was* there. And Harley had put her hand on him, letting him know she was okay. The light touch of her fingers on his spine had calmed him down a bit. She hadn't freaked out, withdrawn, or screeched back an insult.

Answering her seemingly unending list of questions, Coach ran though the mechanics of how the parachutes were packed and how exactly the AAD worked. He'd memorized all of the details while training to be a Delta Force soldier, so he could recite them backward and forward in his sleep. He'd been blessed with an eidetic memory, he could remember everything he'd ever read, and most things he saw, so it was easy to pull facts out of his overactive brain to try to teach Harley everything she wanted to know.

He finished getting himself rigged up after a few more questions, explaining how the jumpsuit he was wearing made the harness and parachute fit better. She watched carefully as he buckled each strap and he showed her the altimeter, which would be strapped to his hand so he knew exactly when to pull the cord to deploy the parachute. He didn't really need it, having jumped enough to know instinctively when he was at the right altitude, but he didn't tell Harley that, she was already nervous enough.

Tommy brought them two pairs of goggles, and Coach helped fit a pair over Harley's glasses. She seemed embarrassed to be fussed over, but Coach ignored her protests and made sure her glasses weren't smooshed on her face under the protective eyewear.

Watching Harley soak in the information he gave her was beautiful. She wasn't humoring him, it was as if she was cataloging everything he said and storing it away in her mind. It had been a long time since he'd met a woman who genuinely was interested in what he had to say. He made a mental note to look her up when he got home and check out some of the other games she'd worked on. If she paid this much attention to detail on all her games, he had a feeling they were kickass.

Coach had been doing fine dealing with his attraction to Harley, answering her questions while fitting her harness and being professional, until he'd turned her around and saw how her nipples had peaked when he'd tugged on the straps over her shoulders. He'd had a hard time not lowering his head and kissing the hell out of her right there.

But then he'd seen how embarrassed she'd been by her reaction to him. She'd hunched her shoulders forward to try to hide it. Coach was used to women flaunting their assets around him, not being embarrassed about them. It endeared her to him that much more.

As he answered her very intellectual questions, Coach got a better picture of who Harley was. She was smart; she'd have to be in order to be coding video games. She wasn't flashy or even comfortable in her own skin. She had no makeup on her face, which made her look fresh and clean, rather than like someone who was trying too hard. She was willing to do things outside her comfort zone, if only to gain knowledge.

And she had no idea that she was pretty. None. She wasn't categorically beautiful, but the longer Coach spent with her, the more attracted he was.

All in all, he liked what he'd seen so far. Coach kept his eyes on her brown ones, not lowering them to her chest, as much as he wanted to.

"What kind of plane are we jumping out of today?"

Coach cleared his throat, trying to keep his mind off her tits and on her question. "You're in luck, Tommy went out of his way to get one of the newest and most comfortable GC Caravan Supervan 900 airplanes. There are only around fifty of them in the world."

"What makes it so special?" Harley asked, leaning forward and resting one of her elbows on her knee with her chin in her hand.

"It's been modified specifically for skydiving, and the thing that's the most important is that the exhaust is on the opposite side of the door we'll be jumping out of." When Harley opened her mouth to ask the obvious question, he hurried on. "That's important because it gets rid of the carbon dioxide in the cabin, so everyone is more comfortable when the door is open. There're two benches that run the length of the plane, and it's actually pretty cushy as far as these kinds of planes go. We'll sit in the order we're jumping."

"Order?"

"Yeah, we'll be last. I hope you don't mind."

Harley shook her head. "No. Actually, I prefer that. I can watch the others and learn from them."

"You want to go over the positions again?" Coach asked.

"No, it seems pretty straightforward. You'll clip me to you, we'll scoot forward toward the gaping hole in the plane, then we'll shove out. I'll arch my back with my knees bent and my feet up between your legs. My arms will be out. When you tap me on the shoulder, I'll grab hold of the straps at my chest to brace myself and the chute will open. It'll jerk me up and my feet will fly upward. I have to be careful not to kick myself in the face." She smiled as she said the last.

Coach laughed. "Yup, you sound like a pro."

"What if I screw it up?" Harley asked in a low voice, looking around to make sure none of the others were listening.

Coach put his finger under her chin and forced her to look at him. "You aren't going to screw it up."

"But if I put my arms in the wrong position, or—"

"You're not going to screw it up," Coach repeated firmly. "Other than taking out a knife and stabbing me in the middle of the jump, or cutting your harness off, nothing you do will mess me up enough that I can't get the chute open. Okay? Stop worrying. This is supposed to be fun you know." He dropped his hand from her face reluctantly.

"Humph, fun. Yeah. I should've listened to my sister."

Coach smiled at her cute mutterings. He wanted to ask her about her sister, about her family. She'd mentioned them earlier and he found himself wanting to know more about them…about her.

The words came out before he thought better of them. "Wanna get something to eat afterwards?"

"What?" Her head whipped around in shock.

"Food. You'll probably be hungry when we're done."

The look she was giving him was blank. Coach couldn't read her at all.

Finally, she asked tentatively, "You want to go out with me after we've jumped?"

"Yeah, Harley. Very much."

"Why?"

Coach smiled. He hadn't worked this hard to get a woman to go out with him in a long time. He liked it. "Because I like you. Because you're interesting. Because I'm sure when we're done you'll have a million more questions to ask me."

She looked at him for a beat before nodding. "Yeah, I probably will. Okay, if you're willing to help me out with my work, I'm game."

Wanting to make sure she knew it wasn't just to help her out with her job, Coach clarified, "I'm willing to help you out. But I also want to get to know you better."

Harley sucked both lips in and then licked them before saying in a soft voice, "Okay. Then yes, I'd like that."

"Good. Me too. Ready to jump out of a plane?" Coach stood up and held his hand out to her.

Harley swallowed hard, but nodded and put her hand in his. "Not really, but ready or not, it's time. Let's do this."

Coach didn't drop her hand after she was upright. He simply turned and followed behind the others as they made their way out the door to the tarmac and plane. For the first time in a long time, Coach was looking forward to the jump. He couldn't wait to experience it through Harley's eyes.

Chapter Five

HARLEY TOOK A deep breath and tried not to hyperventilate. The trip up to the coordinates they'd be jumping from didn't take very long, maybe around fifteen minutes. The others were chatting with each other as they climbed to the proper altitude, but Harley couldn't hear a word they were saying over her own beating heart and the roar of the plane's engine.

She only knew they arrived at the right place when one of the other jumpmasters stood up at the back of the plane and gave a thumbs up to everyone and turned to his customer. Harley couldn't remember the woman's name to save her life, but she happily turned her back to the man and he hooked her harness to his own.

Two other employees opened the door on the back right side of the plane and Harley took a deep breath at the rush of air that whooshed through the cabin. Coach had been right though, it didn't take her breath away as she figured it might, that fancy engine was apparently doing its job.

Harley watched with wide eyes as the first pair of

skydivers launched themselves out the door. She held her breath, not able to take her eyes away from the blue sky she could see going by.

Was she really going to do this? She was insane. Seriously. Why hadn't she listened to Montesa? She could've watched this from her computer, safe at home, what was she thinking?

"Breathe, Harley."

The words were spoken right next to her ear, and Harley let the breath she was holding out with a whoosh. She turned to see Coach leaning into her.

Coach didn't bother to watch the others prepare to jump, his entire concern was for Harley. She was obviously scared to death, but so desperately trying to hide it. Her eyes were wide and her pupils were large black dots, dilated as if she'd just visited the eye doctor.

He put his hand on her leg, feeling it jiggling up and down in her nervousness, much as it had been doing when she'd watched the safety video. "That's it, breathe. You've got this. Remember, I'm going to do all the work. All you have to do is trust me. I wouldn't do this if I didn't think it was safe. I'd never hurt you."

She nodded jerkily, but didn't take her eyes away from the door.

Coach touched his finger to her chin and turned her head until she had no choice but to meet his eyes. It was loud in the cabin, but he hoped she could still hear him.

"You can do this. It'll be over within fifteen minutes. We'll be on the ground and then we'll go get something to eat. You can ask me all the questions that will have built up between now and then. Yeah?" Coach knew he wasn't saying anything she didn't know, but he hoped his words would shake her out of her terror.

He saw Harley swallow hard once, then again, before she nodded. Licking her lips, she said in a voice that was in no way convincing, "Yeah, I got this. No problem."

Coach smiled. He couldn't help it. She was funny and adorable at the same time. Picking up her hand, he put it on his chest, next to the handle that would release the parachute, keeping his hand over hers. "To the right of your hand is the ripcord. It'll be under your left armpit. Once we hit around five thousand feet, I'll pull it with my left hand."

"If I move weird, will I set it off?"

Coach shook his head, happy that he'd been able to get her thinking about logistics again, rather than her fright. "No. It has to be pulled down with a hard tug. You can't make the chute go off prematurely just by bumping into or touching it."

He felt the pair next to them jostling forward. It was getting closer to their time. "I'm glad I'm the one who gets to experience this with you for the first time, Harley."

55

"Kinda like popping my cherry, huh?"

It was obvious she hadn't thought about the words before they'd slipped out, because her face flamed red and she closed her eyes in embarrassment.

Coach choked back a guffaw, not wanting to make her any redder than she already was. "Something like that, yeah. You ready?"

Harley nodded enthusiastically. Coach figured it was more to try to get her mind off what she'd just said than the fact that she was really ready to go.

Coach pulled the goggles, which had been resting on top of her head, down to cover her glasses, making sure they were comfortable, as he'd done on the ground. He then rose from his spot on the bench, not letting go of Harley's hand. He used his free hand to prop himself up against the plane and to keep his balance. "Let's do this, Harl."

The nickname came out without any thinking on his part, but it felt right. He helped her stand. Her legs were, not surprisingly, a bit wobbly, and he led them to the back of the plane. He turned her so he could hook up the four-point harness. Coach tugged on each of the attachments, showing her that they really were secure, but smiling when she tried to turn her head and look at them anyway.

Coach put one hand around her and rested it on her belly. He felt her suck in a breath at the feel of his hand, but she settled under his touch. He moved them in tandem so that she was facing the door…and the sky.

He nudged her forward until they were standing at the door. He leaned down and spoke right into Harley's ear, the wind making it almost impossible to have a conversation this close to the door. "Hold on to your harness straps now, Harl. I'll count down to three, just as we practiced. On three, I'll push off and we'll be flying. Don't close your eyes; you'll miss the best part."

Coach saw Harley nod and she gripped her harness tightly with both hands. He could see her knuckles, white against the black of the strap. Taking the time to reassure her once more—he couldn't stand to see her so scared—Coach pressed his hand against her stomach for just a moment, then moved it up to brace both of their bodies in the doorframe.

"One. Two. *Three!*"

On the count of three, Coach did just as he'd warned Harley he would. He pushed and they were airborne.

HARLEY WANTED TO close her eyes. So badly. But didn't. If Coach said this was the best part of the flight, she wanted to experience it, even if she was scared. This was what she needed to make the parachute sequence in the video game more realistic.

She saw the ground, then their bodies flipped in the air and for just a moment, she saw the plane above them. It gave her the feeling that she was actually falling, but as soon as she saw it, Coach flipped them again and they were facing the ground once more.

Remembering her training, Harley spread her arms out and bent her knees. She tried to get her breath, but it was hard. Falling at over a hundred miles an hour wasn't that conducive to breathing, that was for sure.

For twenty or so seconds—Harley couldn't be sure how much time had passed—the jump was exhilarating and exciting, just like everything she'd read it could be. The wind was intense, but the goggles on her face allowed her to keep her eyes open and not miss anything. She felt Coach along her back, strong and secure. She saw him checking the altimeter on his hand out of the corner of her eye. The ground looked extremely far away, and it almost didn't feel like they were moving at all.

It was loud, the wind rushing past her ears made it impossible to talk, as Coach had warned. She could feel her heart beating hard and she felt jittery, as if she'd downed several highly caffeinated drinks. It was exhilarating and scary at the same time.

Just as Harley was settling in to enjoy the experience and try to catalog it in her mind so she could program the jump correctly in the video game, something caught her eye. It was moving quickly toward her and she ducked instinctively, not even knowing why or what she was ducking from.

Everything happened so fast, Harley had no idea what *had* actually happened.

She felt wetness on the back of her neck and seeping down under her shirt, and Coach suddenly felt different along her back. Heavier.

Harley tried to turn her head to look at him, but because she was basically tied to him at the shoulders and hips, she couldn't see him. But something was wrong, seriously wrong. She could tell.

Instead of seeing his hands out of her peripheral vision, she couldn't see him at all.

She didn't panic until she reached with one hand to the back of her head to see what the weird sensation was, and it came away covered in blood and feathers.

"Oh my God, oh my God!" she mumbled under her breath, trying more frantically to turn to see if Coach was all right. *She* wasn't hurt, but if she had blood on her, it had to have come from Coach.

"Coach? Coach!" Her words disappeared into the air whooshing around her as they plummeted toward the ground.

Frantically turning, trying to see him, she overcompensated, and suddenly she wasn't facing the ground anymore, she'd flipped them both and they were hurtling ass-first toward the ground now.

Terrified and whimpering, Harley tried to remember what to do. The last thing she wanted to do was go into a flat spin. She'd seen a video online about that, and coming out of it to safely get the parachute launched was almost impossible.

Coach was obviously knocked out. There was no way this was normal. She didn't know the man that well, but she was pretty sure after all his "I'll keep you safe" and "trust me" that he wouldn't do this on purpose. This wasn't a joke. He wasn't playing a prank on her, trying to scare her. He wouldn't do that. She *knew* he wouldn't do that.

Hyperventilating, Harley scissored her legs as if she were in a pool, tucked her arms into her chest and threw herself as hard as she could to the right.

She felt the air move around her as they both rolled, so she was once more facing the ground. Which was looking like it was getting closer and closer every second. Immediately putting her arms out again to try to stabilize them as they fell, Harley tried to think about what to do next.

She wanted to be pissed at Coach. He'd said he'd do all the work. He'd promised he'd keep her safe. Well, big fail on both counts. But honestly, being hit in the head by a bird wasn't something he could've predicted.

He'd said that he'd jumped hundreds of times. It was just a fluke thing. Dammit.

Gulping air that didn't seem to be getting to her lungs, Harley panicked for at least fifteen seconds. Her mind couldn't seem to grasp anything but the thought that she'd soon be smashing face first into the ground. She wondered if it would hurt, but figured it'd be over so quickly that most likely she wouldn't feel a thing.

It was finally the thought of *Coach* dying that made her able to think more clearly.

Coach was a soldier. A hero. There was no way he deserved to die by getting smashed in the face by a bird after jumping out of a plane. It wasn't fair. Not at all. She wasn't anyone special, but Coach was. The thought of disappointing him went a long way toward getting her to pull herself together and think about what she needed to do.

Harley started talking to herself. "The handle! How far are we from the ground? Is it too soon to pull the cord? Too late?"

Keeping her left arm out to balance them as they continued to fall, Harley groped for the handle Coach had pointed out under her arm. She felt it and triumphantly pulled.

But nothing happened.

She jerked on it a couple more times, but it was obvious she didn't have the right angle, or strength, to pull it hard enough to pop out the parachute.

"Shit! Dammit, Coach, you said it'd be easy to pull," she griped. Easy for *him*, probably. His arms were huge and it most likely wasn't a big deal at all for him.

She then tried to reach up to grab his right arm. She wanted to look at the altimeter. But Coach's arm was flopping loosely in the air above his head, and she couldn't get a good grip on it and keep control of their descent. Every time she tried to grab it, she felt them tilting a bit too far to the right.

The sobs were coming out uncontrolled now and even though Harley was trying everything she could think of, she had a suspicion they were both going to die a horrific death.

Suddenly, with no warning, Harley and Coach were jerked to a halt in the air.

She shrieked in terror and couldn't control her legs as they were jerked forward. Coach's legs were right behind hers and his added dead weight made them jerk forward twice. Of course, Harley ended up hitting herself in the face with her knees, just as Coach had warned could happen if she wasn't prepared for it. The googles on her face were knocked askew and she ripped them off impatiently, accidentally throwing off her glasses at the same time.

The automatic chute had apparently gone off, just as it was designed to, and Harley could finally breathe again. In her panic, she'd forgotten all about it. Coach had told her it would deploy automatically if they reached a certain altitude without the main chute being pulled.

Sobbing in relief, and because her face hurt where her knee had bonked it, Harley tried to get her scattered thoughts in order. The harness was digging into her butt and it did feel like she had a wedgie from hell, but they weren't splattered all over the ground, so she'd deal.

Of course, their ordeal still wasn't over, but now that they weren't hurtling to the ground at over a hundred miles an hour, maybe they still had a chance.

The ground was all fuzzy, since Harley couldn't see much without her glasses, but she ignored that small fact for now. She had no idea where they were supposed to be landing, or even what a good landing spot looked like, but she was going to do her best to see what she could do. She and Coach hadn't talked much about where they'd be landing, just what to do once they were there.

Looking around, Harley couldn't see any of the other skydivers. She even tried to look up, figuring they were probably now closer to the ground than all of them, even though they'd left the plane last, but all she could see was their own parachute floating above her head.

The adrenaline in her body was at maximum level

and Harley could feel herself shaking, but she was suddenly in the zone. She could do this. She could save Coach. She could turn just enough now to see him.

He was obviously unconscious. His arms were now loose by his sides, and his head hung backward. His mouth was gaping open and, seeing the blood on his face, she remembered that he'd been hurt. She had no idea if Coach was even breathing, but that position couldn't be conducive to getting oxygen into his lungs. Reaching up and back with one hand, Harley grabbed a fistful of hair on his head and managed to awkwardly tug him forward until his head rested on her shoulder. It seemed like it'd be safer for him to be tucked into her that way, rather than splayed backward when they landed.

His face was a bloody mess, and Harley prayed he was still breathing. She knew resting his head on her shoulder would make more of his blood get on her, but that was the least of both their worries at the moment. For all she knew, the damn bird had killed him when it'd hit.

"No, Harl," she chastised. "Don't think that way. He's fine. Just unconscious. Concentrate on getting down, you can deal with the other stuff after."

Remembering Coach showing her the loops for steering, Harley craned her neck upward. She saw them, but knew she didn't have a prayer of being able to reach them. She was tall, yes, but they were way above her arm span and flapping wildly in the wind.

Glancing down, Harley was alarmed at how quickly the ground seemed to be coming up at them. She needed to get her shit together; she didn't have that much time to come up with a plan.

Remembering Coach telling her that the automatic parachute thing went off fairly close to the ground, she realized that figuring out how to steer was of upmost importance at the moment. More so than the blood she could see oozing down her chest from Coach's face. More so than the wedgie from hell.

Blindly reaching up and behind her, Harley grabbed the lines that went up to the chute. They weren't the fancy loops Coach would've used to steer, but she hoped they'd work, at least a little bit. She mentally thanked Coach for insisting she wear gloves, knowing the lines pulling against her palms would be giving her rope burn right now if he hadn't.

Squinting, Harley could make out a large patch of green in front of her, but they had to get past a big-ass building first. They weren't in Waco city limits, but it did look like there were roads and buildings around them. The last thing she needed was to land on a roof or in the middle of a road and get them both run over after surviving everything else.

"Here goes nothing." Pulling hard on the right cord,

Harley was thrilled when they turned that way a bit. She pulled harder, putting more of her weight behind it, and the wind spun them to the right. Letting go, Harley found that they'd stopped turning and were headed forward in a straight line again.

Feeling more confident, she tugged on the left cord that went up to the parachute, and smiled when they turned left.

"Awesome! It works," Harley told no one as she once again pulled down on the left and right cords. She had to get around the building to that green spot. Hopefully they wouldn't come face-to-face with any angry bulls, but right now, she'd take a pissed-off cow over splatting dead on the ground.

The parachute jerked above their heads as Harley tried to guide it down to where she wanted it. It was definitely harder than it looked. She had no idea if it was because of her and Coach's combined weights, or if it was always like this, but by the time the ground neared, her arms were shaking with the effort it took to pull on the cords.

Harley thought about the landing instructions on the video and on what Coach had told her to expect and what to do if they landed wrong, *Hit the top of your thigh, then hip, then side. Roll into it,* but with him lying heavily on her back, she knew she was going to have to wing it.

She'd missed the building, and there was nothing but a large field under their feet now, but it was coming toward her faster than she would've imagined. She remembered seeing people pulling down on both steering straps when they were landing, but it might've been something she dreamed up. Besides, her arms were noodles and there was no way she could pull on the cords anymore.

Wishing she could close her eyes and have it all be over, Harley watched as the ground got closer and closer. Knowing she'd have to take the brunt of the landing, so as not to break Coach's legs, she tried to gauge when they'd be hitting the prickly looking Texas grass.

The second her feet hit the ground, Harley threw her body to the right. Because Coach's legs were dangling lower than hers they hit a split second before her own. She didn't want his ankles to snap so she tried to take the pressure off of them as soon as she could. She hit the ground on her side and tried not to tumble head over ass. She didn't quite make it. Harley figured they rolled at least three times before she got her arms under her and was able to stop their momentum.

She didn't move for a second, hardly able to believe she was actually still alive. She'd never understood people's desire to kiss the ground when they got off an airplane, but now she got it.

Coach's weight was heavy on her back and she was having a hard time breathing. She tugged the gloves off her hands, giving herself more maneuverability. Fumbling blindly for the clip at her right shoulder, Harley tried to unhook herself from Coach.

It took several tries because her hands were shaking so badly, but she was finally able to get the first clip undone. The other one seemed to be easier, and it gave her the room she needed to push up and ease Coach's upper body off to the side. She reached around and unclipped the two clips at her hips and took a deep breath for the first time in what seemed like forever.

She scrambled all the way out from under Coach and turned to look at him fully for the first time since he'd hooked them together in the plane.

The parachute was wrapped around his legs, but she could clearly see his bloody face.

"Oh my God, Coach," Harley moaned, even as she reached for him. She wiped as much blood away as she could, smearing it more than anything else, to try to see where he was bleeding from. Harley sighed in relief when it looked like the blood was coming from his nose—a very much broken nose, if she had to guess—and not from a gaping hole in his head.

Ignoring the fact that his blood was all over her, Harley concentrated on seeing if she could wake him. He had a pulse and was breathing, so he wasn't dead, thank God. At the very least, other than his broken nose, he probably had a concussion. Whatever the bird was, it had to have been large in order to do the amount of damage it did.

"Coach? Please wake up."

Harley looked around. She had no idea where they were. There weren't any people miraculously running to their rescue. Her phone was back in a locker at the airport, and Coach definitely needed a doctor. She didn't want to leave him, but she was going to have to.

"C-C-Coach?" The tears came in earnest then, rolling down her cheeks as she tried to get the man lying next to her to wake up. "Please w-wake up."

Nothing. He didn't even stir. Shit.

Knowing time was going by, time that Coach didn't have, Harley pushed to her feet and staggered a step. Her legs were wobbly and not too steady. She turned away from the bloodied man at her feet and stepped toward the building in the distance. It was her best chance at finding people, and a phone.

It took her a while to gain the strength to push into a jog, but finally she did it. She wasn't much of a runner, so soon she was huffing and puffing as she made her way toward the building. She wanted to promise herself that she'd start exercising more if Coach was all right, but she knew she wouldn't. Sitting in a chair most of the day working on a computer was what she did.

She'd never be a workout freak. She was already too skinny as it was.

Reaching a barbed-wire fence, Harley dropped down to her hands and knees and shimmied under it, feeling a barb catch on her back, but ignoring it. Hell, a little scratch was nothing after what she'd just lived through.

She ran across a parking lot, thrilled to see the building was a strip mall of sorts. There was a beauty parlor, a pawn shop, a run-down looking café, and one of those quick-loan places. At least that's what she thought they were since she couldn't really see that clearly.

Still sobbing, Harley ran to the closest door, slamming it open as she hit it at a dead run. She burst through the door of the beauty shop and came to a halt, holding on to the doorframe to keep herself upright.

Heart beating out of her chest, Harley blurted, "Please, call an ambulance! I was just in a skydiving accident and my friend needs help."

"Oh lordy!" a voice said in front of her. "Are you all right? Here, sit. You're covered in blood, honey!"

"It's not m-m-mine," Harley sobbed. "Please. Are you calling?"

"Yeah, I'm calling. Where's your friend?"

The lady's voice was hysterical and worried, and she sounded like she was on the verge of freaking out...so not what Harley needed at the moment. She needed firmness, someone to take charge. "He's still back there in the field." Harley gestured behind her. "I have to go back to him. Please, s-send them out there when they get here. Okay? I left h-him alone, b-but I have to get back to him."

"Go back to your man, honey. I'll call the cops."

"Th-th-thank you," Harley stammered before whirling around and heading at a run back to the field.

The barbed-wire fence scraped her on the way back under it again, but Harley barely noticed. All she could see was the lump in the middle of the grass. Breathing hard, she collapsed on her knees next to Coach.

He hadn't moved, but she could see his chest rising and falling with his breaths, so she knew he was still alive.

The blood from his nose had continued to ooze out of his body, and Harley wiped it away again, hating the sight of it.

She unzipped his jumpsuit at the neck, just enough to try to give him some breathing room. The blue of his shirt a striking contrast against the white of the jumpsuit.

Hearing sirens in the distance—thank God for people who kept their promises—Harley leaned down into Coach.

"They're coming, Coach. You're okay. We made it d-down. They'll make you feel better soon. Won't you wake up? Please? You're scaring the s-shit out of me."

The sirens were louder now, obviously pulling into the parking lot behind her. Harley put her head on Coach's chest and cried.

Cried in relief that someone else was there and could take charge.

Cried because she'd been so scared.

Cried because she'd lived through something that she probably shouldn't have.

But most of all, she cried because the most confident, protective, nice man she'd met in her entire life was lying broken and bleeding in front of her.

And it somehow felt like it was her fault.

Chapter Six

H ARLEY WANTED TO go home.
        She was done.

Done.

But she couldn't until she knew Coach was going to be all right.

The medics had arrived at the field and had swung into action. After ascertaining that the blood on her was Coach's, they'd put a C-collar on him and had carried him to the ambulance, Harley following along behind them on shaky legs.

She'd had no idea what to do with the parachute, but hadn't wanted to leave it laying in the field. It was probably expensive, and with her luck she'd be charged for it or something. She'd balled the entire thing up and clutched it to her chest as they'd made their way to the vehicles in the parking lot.

She now sat in the waiting room of the local hospital with the parachute in a ball under her chair, waiting.

Waiting to find out how Coach was doing. She could leave anytime she wanted to simply by calling

Montesa to come get her. But she wasn't anxious to make *that* call anytime soon, especially since her sister wasn't too thrilled about the whole skydiving thing in the first place.

Harley had washed her hands, but was still wearing the harness and her bloody clothes. One of the nurses had offered to give her a pair of scrubs to wear, but Harley just wanted to go home.

She sat curled up in a ball, heels on the chair of the seat, arms around her drawn-up knees. Harley was exhausted, but was also feeling a little shell-shocked after everything that had happened. The adrenaline dump was making her shaky and lightheaded to boot.

The doors whooshed open and Harley looked up to see three men, two women and a little girl come through, looking out of breath and panicked. Well, the women looked panicked. The men looked more concerned than rattled.

Harley didn't move from her spot on the chair in the corner, simply watched as they all went up to the desk together. A small drama ensued when the intake nurse wouldn't tell the group what they wanted to know. She merely pointed to the chairs, obviously telling them to wait.

The group trudged over reluctantly to a cluster of chairs. The women and girl sat, as did two of the men. The third man paced agitatedly in front of the others, running his hand through his perfect-looking hair.

Harley eavesdropped on their conversation. It was better than thinking about what she'd just been through.

"Do you know what happened, Fletch?" the tall, slender woman, obviously the little girl's mother, asked the man sitting to her right.

He shook his head. "Not really. I got a call from the colonel and he said that he'd been in an accident. That's all he said before I called Ghost and Hollywood."

"Can't you call someone else? I mean, someone has to know what happened," the other woman said in a stressed out voice. She was also dark-haired, and had a gorgeous man sitting next to her too.

"I'm not sure anyone has all the details, Princess," the man with his arm around her shoulders said.

"Well, that's just bullcrap," she exclaimed in a huff. "Can that woman really not tell us *anything*? It's stupid and annoying; you guys might as well be brothers."

The man next to her laughed, even though Harley could tell it was strained.

"I'll see if I can get ahold of Tommy," the man who'd been pacing announced, pulling out his phone. "Coach was helping him out at the skydiving club on his leave."

Harley startled so badly at the mention of Coach's name, her foot slipped off the seat of the chair and she threw her arms out to catch herself from pitching to the ground as her body lost its center of gravity. The parachute, which had been under the chair, got jostled and poofed out, unable to be contained by the chair legs anymore.

Harley lowered her other foot to the ground and looked up to the group of friends, who were now all staring at her.

Obviously they were Coach's friends. She should talk to them. Tell them what happened. How Coach had been hurt—but the words stuck in her throat. She wasn't good with people. She always said the wrong thing. And this was important.

The little girl wandered over in the uneasy silence and stood in front of Harley.

"Did you know you're all bloody?"

Harley smiled ruefully. She'd washed her hands, but her shirt and arms still had Coach's blood on them. She opened her mouth to speak, but the little girl went on.

"And what are you wearing? Were you rock climbing? Blade took me the other day. I gotted up really high and he was scared. My daddy, Fletch, wouldn't take me, but that's okay. What's that?" She pointed to the parachute. "It looks like what we use at school at PE. My PE teacher is awesome. She saved the entire school when bad guys tried to shoot up everyone. I wasn't in danger though, we went out the window and got to safety. Can you talk? It's okay if you can't. Mommy says sometimes people have disamilities and they can't hear or see or talk, but that doesn't make them a worser person."

"Annie Grant Fletcher." The woman's voice was dead serious. "Get over here and stop bothering that poor woman. Good Lord."

Harley looked up at the group of people again. They were standing and sitting stock-still, watching her and the little girl. It was easier to talk to the child at that moment, kids were less judgmental. And besides, she liked her outspokenness.

"Annie? Is that your name?"

"Oh, you *can* talk. Cool. Yeah. Annie Fletcher. My new daddy is Fletch. We have the same name, but you can't call me Fletch 'cos that's *his* name."

Harley smiled for the first time in what seemed like forever. "My name is Harley Kelso. I've got blood on me because I was trying to help a friend when he got hurt."

Annie nodded as if she understood perfectly. "Yeah, my daddy's in the Army and sometimes he gets bloody too, but my mommy helps clean him up. Do you have someone to help you clean up?"

Harley cleared her throat at the child's innocent words. No, she didn't have anyone to help her, but that was all right. She'd managed just fine on her own up to now. "I'll be okay. It's my friend who's important right now."

"What happened?" A deep male voice sounded high above her head.

Harley looked up into the blue eyes of the man Annie had said was her father. The bright tattoos on his arms stood out in stark contrast to the white shirt he was wearing. The woman who'd chastised Annie stood at his side, looking worried.

Harley wanted to look away, but the strength and concern in the man's voice prevented it. "Coach got hit in the face by a bird while we were skydiving." She didn't bother telling them all the details, such as the fact that they'd both almost died. If it hadn't been for the automatic thingy shooting off the parachute, they would've splatted on the ground like bugs hitting a windshield.

"Jesus," the man behind the couple said. It was the good-looking one. The one who reminded Harley of a younger Tom Cruise. If he put on a flight suit, like the actor had worn in *Top Gun*, he could pass for him easily. "What else?" he demanded.

Harley shivered, putting both arms around her waist. She wanted to stand up, to face Coach's friends eye-to-eye, but she was fresh out of energy at the moment. "What else, what?"

"He got hit in the face and what else? What's the

rest of the story? It's obvious you aren't telling us everything."

Harley paled. How did he know? The man might look like Tom Cruise, but he was obviously a badass right down to his bones.

"Leave her alone," the other woman said, pushing the man slightly. She came over to Harley and squatted down in front of her. "Sorry about that. Hollywood is a bit high strung. Are you all right? You look pale."

"I'm okay," Harley said automatically, saying what she figured the woman wanted to hear. She didn't know her, so she couldn't really care how she was actually feeling.

"I'm Rayne and that's Emily. These are our boyfriends, Ghost and Fletch. You've already met Annie. And the handsome one is Hollywood. They're Coach's teammates in the Army. They're just worried about him. They've been through a lot together and the fact that Coach got hurt while on leave is unsettling. Coach doesn't have any siblings and his folks aren't from around here, so the hospital won't tell us anything because we aren't related. They have to wait until he wakes up and gives permission. Damn privacy laws. Anyway, we're just trying to figure out how badly he was hurt. Judging by the looks of you, it was pretty bad."

Harley shook her head in denial, trying to make the

woman feel better. "I don't think it's too bad. I think his nose is broken, because it looked funny, but that's what was bleeding. I didn't see any other real wounds. He was unconscious though, so that's probably what's taking so long."

"Unconscious?" the man named Ghost asked impatiently. "I don't understand. How could a bird have hit him hard enough when you were under canopy for it to do that much damage?"

This was it. Harley shouldn't be embarrassed about anything that happened. She should be proud of herself for getting them both down safely, automatic parachute thingy or not, but for some reason she still felt like it was her fault he'd gotten hurt in the first place. "It hit him before the chute opened. We were still in free fall."

"Oh my God," Emily breathed.

"Holy crap," Rayne swore, covering her mouth with her hand.

"Shit," Ghost barked.

"Fuckin' A," Fletch muttered under his breath.

Hollywood just stared at her in disbelief.

"What? I don't understand," little Annie said, tugging on her mom's sleeve.

"Is there a Harley out here?" The question came from a nurse across the room, standing in a doorway.

Saved by the bell, Harley thought as she rose on shaky legs. "Me. I'm Harley."

"Your friend is asking for you," the woman said in a no-nonsense voice.

"Me?" Harley asked in confusion. "Does he know his friends are here?"

"Oh yeah. He knows. Doesn't care. He's demanding to talk to you."

Harley swallowed hard. God. Demanding to talk to her? Was he upset or pissed?

"Go on, Harley," Annie cajoled. "I'm hungry and I can't get anything to eat until Mommy and Fletch make sure Coach is okay."

Harley nodded absently and took a step toward the nurse, then turned back to Annie. "Will you watch my...stuff?" She gestured to the parachute and the now-empty pack Coach had been wearing. "I wouldn't want anyone to steal it."

Annie's head bobbed up and down enthusiastically. "Yeah, I'll guard it for you. No problem. Sergeant Annie's on guard!"

Harley smiled as the girl scrunched up her face in what she obviously thought was a scowl, and looked around as if there were bad guys hiding around the chairs in the waiting room, just waiting to steal the pathetic-looking material on the ground.

"Thanks. I appreciate it." Harley looked up at the others. The men were scrutinizing her as if they could read her mind, and the women smiled at her. "I'll hurry, so you can go in and see your friend," she told them quickly.

"Take your time, Harley," Ghost drawled. "It's obvious where we stand in Coach's eyes. Can't say I blame him. Choosing a pretty woman over us."

"Uh, that's not—"

"Go, Harley. We'll be here when you get out. Stop worrying. If Coach is asking to speak to you, it's obvious he's going to be all right." It was Hollywood who spoke up that time.

She nodded, suddenly reluctant to face Coach. She was so emotionally done, she wanted to lie down and sleep for hours. She'd experienced so many emotions in a short time that day, and it wasn't even noon yet. It was almost hard to believe.

Nervousness, worry, attraction to Coach, embarrassment, nervousness again, terror, relief, terror again, worry when he wouldn't wake up, and now she was just plain tired. Harley trudged toward the nurse and the door to the back hallways of the emergency room, feeling all eyes on her as she went.

Taking a deep breath as she got to the nurse, Harley tried to give herself a pep talk. She could do this. She'd tell Coach what happened, he'd tell her all the things she did wrong, and then she'd call a taxi to take her back to the airport so she could get her stuff and go home. She'd be home by one, tops.

Chapter Seven

"**D**ON'T LOOK SO worried, your boyfriend is going to be fine. We reset his nose, and he's got a concussion, but otherwise he's remarkably lucky."

Harley opened her mouth to contradict the nurse and let her know that she'd just met Coach that day, but decided against it. It was just too much for the moment. Instead, she merely nodded and pushed open the door to the little room.

Coach lay on a bed, the sheet pulled up over his legs. Harley could see the harness he'd been wearing—along with the white jumpsuit, his jeans and blue shirt—lying on a chair next to the bed in a heap. His chest was bare and his eyes were closed. The thought flickered through her brain that if all his clothes were on the chair, that meant he was probably only in his underwear, but she shut it down almost as quickly as it occurred to her. What Coach was or wasn't wearing wasn't any of her business.

He had a bandage over his nose and she could see bruising around both his eyes. He was gonna look like he'd been in a fight, and lost, for a while.

Looking back at the door, Harley saw the nurse closing it softly as she left them alone. Harley stood by the door awkwardly.

Without opening his eyes, Coach said, voice filled with pain, "I know you're there, Harley. Come here. Please." He held out one of his hands, finally opening his eyes to pin her with his dark gaze.

More relieved than she would've guessed, Harley walked toward him, not taking her eyes off his. Hearing his voice after seeing him so still and bloody was such a relief. "You're okay?" she asked softly.

"Thanks to you, yeah." Coach grabbed hold of her hand when she got near him and pulled her closer to the bed.

"I didn't do anything."

"Bull."

"Coach, I didn't," Harley insisted.

"Sit and tell me what happened. I don't remember much. Only being in the plane with you before we jumped."

Harley furrowed her brow. "You don't remember jumping out of the plane?"

Coach growled. "No. Doc says it's because of the concussion. It might come back, or it might not. I only know what you told them…that I got nailed in the face by a bird."

Harley sucked both her lips into her mouth and tried not to cry. Coach was okay. He was fine. He was talking, and even though he didn't remember anything, he was alive.

"Oh, Harl. Don't cry. God. Please."

"I'm not usually such a wuss." The tears were coursing down her face without her even realizing it. Harley tried to pull her hand out of his, but he wouldn't let go.

"You're not a wuss. You've had a tough day. Come on, come here. That's it, sit down right there. You're okay. Let it out." Coach pulled her forward until she sat on the empty chair next to his bed.

She leaned forward and put her head down on her free arm on the mattress next to his hip and sobbed. She wasn't exactly sure why she was crying. She should've been all cried out by now. But sitting next to Coach, seeing him safe and alive, was too much. She'd been so scared, and it'd become impossible to keep her emotions bottled up inside anymore.

As she bawled her eyes out, she was more than aware of his hand caressing her hair and his soft, murmured words of support as she did.

COACH STROKED HARLEY'S hair as she sobbed into her arm at his side. He felt helpless, and that wasn't a feeling he was used to. When he was on a mission, he was in charge, he controlled what happened around him, but not now. He wanted to haul Harley into his arms and comfort her, but this wasn't the time or the place, and he really didn't know her that well.

But *that* was going to change.

He hadn't lied; he didn't remember much after getting up from the benches in the plane, getting ready to jump. Only looking to Harley's eyes as he adjusted the goggles over her glasses. He wanted to know the details about what happened, but one thing was crystal clear in his mind. Harley had done a hell of a job.

She was covered in his blood. That was enough to tell him that whatever had happened had been fairly traumatic. Several scenarios went through his mind, but until he heard the story from Harley, he had no idea when he was knocked unconscious during the jump. But the bottom line was that somehow she'd been able to get them landed and call for help.

The only people he'd ever felt indebted to were his Delta Force teammates. They'd saved his life more than once, as he'd done for them. But this was something different.

Harley was a civilian. And a woman. Oh, he knew that being a woman didn't mean she couldn't save someone's life. But it was *his* life. It made a huge difference. He'd spent his entire life protecting others.

To have a woman protect *him* was a new feeling. A bigger one.

Harley sniffed once, then again, and surreptitiously wiped her nose on her sleeve. Coach smiled, reaching behind her for the box of tissues. Without a word, he held one out to her and he waited patiently as she used it to wipe her face and nose.

"Feel better?" he asked, taking hold of her hand again.

She shook her head. "Not really. I think I'm gonna need a hot bath, a long nap, and some strong drinks to get there."

"I know how you feel. My head is killing me. My face hurts. My nose is never gonna look the same, but I have a feeling after I hear what we went through, I'm gonna need that bath, nap, and drink as much as you do."

At his words, Harley looked up in concern. "Your head hurts? Did they give you something for it? Can I get you anything?"

"No, Harl. I'm okay. Thank you though. Can you tell me what happened? And don't leave anything out. Please?"

Harley nodded and took a deep breath. "We jumped out and it was fine. Good. You were right, it was amazing and exhilarating at the same time. I was scared, but it was something I could never have understood if I hadn't done it for myself."

Coach nodded, rubbing the back of her hand with his thumb. He knew just what she meant. As much as he didn't exactly relish the missions where they had to parachute in, it never failed to get his adrenaline pumping. It was an amazing feeling. "Then I got nailed by a bird."

Harley nodded and sucked her lips into her mouth again before continuing. "Yeah. It's really my fault."

"*Your* fault? Harley, you didn't put that bird at just the right place at the right time. Or is it the wrong place at the wrong time?"

"I ducked."

"What?" Her voice was so sad and quiet, Coach wasn't sure he heard her right.

"I ducked. I saw something out of the corner of my eye, and I ducked. If I hadn't, it would've hit me and not you, and you would've been okay to get us down."

Oh hell no.

"Harley, look at me," Coach ordered sternly. It took a moment, but she finally raised her eyes to his. "This is *not* your fault. If it had hit you rather than me, you might be dead. I'm bigger than you, and as it was, it apparently only glanced off me. If you hadn't ducked, it would've hit you straight on and done a lot more damage than just a broken nose and a headache. Got me?"

She didn't agree, but she didn't disagree either. Coach took that as a win. "What happened after I got hit? I'm assuming it knocked me unconscious? Wait, it hit me before I pulled the chute?"

"Yeah."

"Jesus, Harley. I'm so sorry."

"For what?"

"I said you'd be safe. I said you could trust me to take care of you and get you to the ground, and I didn't."

"It wasn't your fault."

Coach smiled faintly. "Now you sound like me. Go on, tell me the rest." Coach clenched his teeth at the terror he could still see lingering in Harley's eyes. He should've figured it out way before now, but the fact that he'd gotten hit before he pulled the chute was huge. The thought of Harley realizing what had happened and hurtling to the ground made his stomach churn.

She shrugged and hurried through her explanation as to what had happened after he'd been hit. "You were out. I couldn't pull hard enough on the handle to make the chute come out. I panicked, but then the automatic thingie went off and saved us. We hit the ground and I ran to get help."

Coach eyed Harley, knowing there was a lot she was leaving out, but she looked like she was at the end of her rope and he didn't want to push her. Steering a chute wasn't too difficult, but with him being unconscious at her back, that being her first jump, and the experience of not knowing if she was going to live or die...well, that upped the difficulty level quite a bit.

He let go of her hand long enough to lightly palm her cheek. "And the bruise I can see forming here on your cheek?"

She shrugged self-consciously. "I didn't realize I had one. It must be from when I hit myself in the face with my knee when the chute came out."

"I warned you about that," Coach told her with a small smile.

"I know," she whispered.

"Thank you, Harley." The words were completely inadequate for what she'd done. For all that she'd been through, but they were as heartfelt as anything he'd ever told anyone before.

"I didn't do anything. The AAD thing did it all."

"You got us to the ground it one piece. That couldn't have been easy with me being dead weight. You got help. You somehow made it so that we weren't falling head or ass first when the chute went off. There are a ton of other things I can't think of right now because my head is pounding, but there's one thing I *am* sure of."

"What?" Harley asked in a soft voice, her eyes tearing up again at his words.

"That I'm glad it was you strapped to my chest up there."

"Why?"

"Because I don't think Sarah or any of her friends would've reacted the same way as you did. You didn't panic and you did what needed to be done."

"I didn't, not really," Harley told him, not meeting his eyes. "Honestly, I freaked out. And besides, they'd been skydiving before, so they probably would've known better what to do."

"Harley," Coach said sternly, bringing his free hand over to hold the other side of her face. "I would be surprised if you *didn't* freak out. But that's not the point. How people react in emergencies is a crapshoot. I've seen seasoned soldiers run *toward* the enemy rather than away from them when they panicked. It doesn't matter how many times someone has been in combat, or has jumped out of a plane. It's what's inside a person that dictates how they handle themselves when something goes wrong. So, you freaked. Big deal. What matters is that we're both here right now. Dinged up, but alive. Because of that, I know you did everything right. I *know* it. I'm lying here today because you did everything right."

"I was s-scared."

"Oh, honey. Come here."

Coach couldn't have resisted pulling her into his

arms if his life depended on it. He felt a connection to this woman that he'd never felt toward anyone before. She was trying so hard to be strong, but it was obvious how terrified she'd been.

She sat on the side of the bed and lay down against him when Coach engulfed her thin frame into his arms. He simply held Harley to him as she shook. She wasn't sobbing as she'd done earlier, but she was still upset.

When she finally stopped sniffing, he asked quietly, "How many of my teammates are in the waiting room?"

Without lifting her head, Harley said, "Three when I was out there. And two women and a little girl."

"Hmmmm. Not surprised Fletch showed up first. Bet Ghost is out there too. And their women. I'm sure the others are here by now."

"I should go," Harley said, trying to sit up.

Coach's arms tightened before releasing her. He brought a hand up and pushed her hair behind her ear as she wiped her face with her fingers, a thought occurring to him for the first time. "Where are your glasses?"

"Oh, um. I don't know. I knocked my goggles askew at some point and when I took them off, the glasses came too. Some cow is probably wearing them by now."

Coach smiled. Harley was funny. The situation wasn't, but she was. Then he got serious. "Will you let one of my teammates take you home?" He held up a hand when it was obvious she was going to protest. "You can't see, and I'm assuming your car is still back at the airport, right?" When she nodded, he continued, "Please, for my peace of mind. Let Hollywood or Truck or someone take you home. They'll get your car back to your place later."

Harley studied him. "You have a concussion." It wasn't a question.

Coach grimaced. "Yeah."

"Do you have someone at your place who can watch over you?"

He didn't think she was fishing for information, but gave it to her nonetheless. "No wife or girlfriend, Harley. I wouldn't have asked you out if that was the case. One of the guys will stay with me and make sure to wake me up every couple of hours. It's not the first concussion I've had. Unfortunately, the team has had their share of knocks on the head. They'll take care of me."

"Okay."

She sat on the bed looking at him for a long moment before saying, "I'm glad you're okay, Coach."

"Me too. Thank you, Harley."

She stood up and held out her hand. "It was nice meeting you, Beckett Ralston."

Coach looked at the slender hand she held out to him. He wasn't surprised she remembered his name, even after he'd only said it once. He took hold of her hand and squeezed gently. "If you think this is good-bye, you're wrong, Harley. I do remember asking you out before we got in the plane. I would still very much like to."

Her hand jerked in his grasp and Coach grinned, loving that he could surprise her. "Oh, but, I thought—"

"You thought wrong. I'll talk to my teammates. Let one of them take you home. If you're feeling up to it, I'd love to see you in a few days. Make sure you're doing okay. That gives me time to get rid of this monster headache so I can give you the attention you deserve."

"Um, okay, but if you change your mind—"

Coach interrupted her again. "I'm not going to change my mind. The only thing that might change is how much time I let go by before seeing you again."

He loved the blush that blossomed over her cheeks.

Coach tugged on the hand he still held. "I think we're past the handshake stage. I could use a hug." He released her hand and held his arms out.

Harley leaned over him again and wrapped her arms awkwardly around his shoulders. He put his hands flat on her back, one on her spine and the other just above her ass, and held her to him. She squeezed him tightly and sighed, her breath wafting over his ear, making goosebumps break out on his arms. "Thank you for having a hard head and not dying, Coach."

He buried his nose into her neck for a moment. "Thank *you* for getting us out of the sky safely, Harley."

She nodded and pulled back, and Coach let go reluctantly. "Go home, Harley. Take off those clothes stained with my blood and throw them away. Take that bath, sleep. It'll make you feel better. I'll be in touch. Yeah?"

"Yeah, I think I will." She looked down at her dirty clothes for a moment, before bringing her eyes back up to his. "You need my number?"

"Need it? No. But it would make things easier."

Harley was too tired to think about how he might be able to find her phone number without her giving it to him. "Okay, let me see if I can find a piece of paper to write it on."

"Just tell it to me. I'll remember it."

"Oh, but—"

"Harley, I have an eidetic memory. If you say it to me once, I'll remember it. Trust me."

She nodded and recited her number. Coach repeated it in his mind and visualized the numbers. "Got it, thank you. Have a good rest of the day. I'll be in touch soon."

"I'd like that. And you're welcome."

Coach watched the sway of Harley's hips as she left the room. She was an intriguing woman, one he couldn't wait to get to know better.

Chapter Eight

THE NEXT NIGHT, Harley lay on her couch and thought about what a wuss she'd been. Jesus, she'd bawled over the man, and that wasn't like her. She hated women who cried all the time. It was annoying and weak, and yet, there she'd been, snotting up a storm all over him.

She'd been putting it off, but after sleeping for thirteen hours, a long bath, and a pep talk, it was time to call Montesa.

Harley dialed and twisted on the couch until her feet were resting on the back and she was lying backwards, her head almost touching the floor. It was a weird position, but Harley didn't care. It was comfortable.

"Hey, Harl. How was the skydiving thing? I didn't hear from you afterwards. You were supposed to call so I didn't think you'd landed on your head or something."

Harley swallowed hard. Best to get it over with, like a Band-Aid. "So, you were right, sis. I should've just looked it up online. There was an accident. My jumpmaster got hit in the face with a bird and was knocked unconscious. But the emergency chute opened and we landed without too many issues. He was taken to the hospital, but he's okay. Just had a broken nose and a concussion. I'm fine." Harley's words were rushed and to the point. It was never good to beat around the bush with her sister.

"Are you freaking kidding me?"

Harley winced and held the phone away from the ear as Montesa continued to screech. Finally, hearing her wind down, Harley brought the phone back to her ear in time to hear her sister say, "—listen to me next time!"

"You're right. I should've listened to you," Harley soothed. "You were right and I was wrong. But, before you claim big sister bragging rights for being correct, can I say something?"

"What?"

"I have to say, as much as the experience sucked, I did get what I needed for my code."

"For Christ's sake," Montesa snapped. "Figures you'd think that way. Davidson is home tomorrow. I'm moving our dinner up. Saturday night. My house. Be there."

"Yes, ma'am," Harley said meekly, although she was smiling inside. Montesa sounded tough, but Harley knew it was just because she was worried about her.

They exchanged a few more platitudes and hung up. Harley put both arms over her head and touched the floor, stretching out her back. She had bruises on her hips where the harness had bit into her skin, and every muscle was sore. The scratches on her back from crawling under the barbed wire itched and were slightly bruised as well. She'd been tense for the entire jump, not surprising, and it would take a few days to work out all the kinks.

The bruise on her face from where she'd smacked herself with her knees was still there, but it hadn't turned an ugly purple, so Harley could live with it. Besides, it wasn't as if she got out much anyway.

Taking a deep breath, Harley did a crunch and pulled herself up into a sitting position on the couch, spinning so her feet were once more on the ground. She had a deadline for the game, it was time she got to it.

COACH TURNED TO Hollywood and said, "Thanks for staying last night. I appreciate it."

"No problem. You've done the same for me."

"And probably will again."

The two men shared a smile before Hollywood asked, "So what are you going to do about Harley?"

Coach didn't even pretend to misunderstand. "I'm

calling her later today."

"Good." Hollywood nodded approvingly. "She seemed a bit freaked out about the whole thing, but I can't blame her. You gotta tread lightly though. She didn't seem that comfortable with all of us in the waiting room. She did loosen up a bit with Annie, not surprisingly. That kid could make even a serial killer melt. But seriously, she's not like Rayne, or even Emily."

"I wouldn't want her to be," Coach responded immediately. "Look. I don't know how Ghost or Fletch felt when they met their women, but something with Harley resonates with me. She's smart as hell, but shy. She writes code for video games for a living. That's why she was jumping in the first place...wanted to get it right for the game or something. But the little I got to know her before we went up was..." Coach's voice trailed off, not knowing how to explain it to his teammate.

"Right?" Hollywood suggested.

"Yeah. Right. It's as good a word as any. I'm not an idiot, I see how women sometimes look at me. I'm not hard on the eyes, but it was as if Harley saw *me*, not my body."

Hollywood nodded. "If anyone understands that, it's me. You deserve it, man. Anything you need from me, you know you got it."

"Thanks, I appreciate it. Did the guys get her car back to her place?"

"Yeah. That thing's a piece of shit," Hollywood observed with a smile.

Coach looked concerned. "Really? Damn, I didn't even ask what kind of car she drove."

"It's a Ford Focus. Mid-two thousands model. Tires have definitely seen better days. They're almost bald."

"Shit. That thing's a death trap," Coach grumbled.

"I'm not sure I'd go that far. She's taken good care of it, obviously, but it still has some weird rattling noise and the tires need rotating at the very least. Fletch said he'd take a look at it."

"Appreciate it. He's the best at tinkering with machines."

"Yeah. You talk to your friend at the skydiving place yet?"

"Tommy? Yeah, he called this morning."

"Was he freaked?"

Coach nodded. "Oh yeah. But, the AAD did just what it was supposed to do. Went off as calibrated. He's a little pissed that his safety record of no accidents has been blasted all to hell though."

Hollywood rolled his eyes. "It's not like anyone could've predicted that damn goose being in your trajectory or anything."

"True. But he's not pissed at me, just at the situation. When we didn't land at the drop zone as planned, and no one could find us, he panicked. It wasn't until an hour after we were supposed to land that he found out I'd been admitted at the hospital." Coach shrugged. "At least I have another five days off before having to check back in on base."

Hollywood stood up and held out his hand to Coach. "Glad you're okay, man. Seriously. Freak accident or not, we couldn't do without you on the team."

Coach shook his friend's hand. "Thanks, Hollywood. Means a lot."

"Call her," Hollywood advised. "I don't know when you said you'd be in touch, but if I were you, I wouldn't let it sit too long. You went through some shit, but you don't remember it. She's probably replaying it over and over."

"I will."

"Good. Later. Call if you need anything. Oh, and I'm supposed to pass along a message from Rayne."

"Shoot."

Hollywood raised his voice as though mimicking Rayne's higher-pitched tone. "Tell Coach that Emily and I want to have lunch with Harley to thank her for saving Coach's life."

They both chuckled.

"I think I'll wait just a bit before I spring those two

on her."

"Good call. Especially if Mary comes too."

"I'll get ahold of Fletch, though, about her car," Coach mused.

"Do that. Talk to you later," Hollywood said as he headed toward Coach's front door.

"Later. Thanks again for everything."

Hollywood didn't respond, merely waved his hand and disappeared out the front door of the apartment.

HARLEY ALMOST IGNORED the ring of her cell phone later that day. She was deep inside the code for the new *This is War* game, trying to get the opening parachute scene just right. She'd added what she thought was some realism to the actual jump, and was working on the scenery shots for when the soldiers were floating through the air. As much as the experience had sucked, it *had* helped her with what she needed for the game.

Glancing at the screen of her phone, and expecting to see Davidson's name, Harley was surprised instead to see the word "unknown."

Biting her hip, Harley hesitated. On the one hand, it could be a telemarketer. But what if it wasn't? She'd given her number to Coach, but hadn't gotten his in return.

Deciding she could just hang up if it wasn't anyone she wanted to talk to, Harley swiped the phone and said, "Hello?"

"Hi, is Harley there?"

"This is she."

"Hey. It's Coach."

Harley's heart stopped for a moment, then resumed beating at a pace twice what it had been. He'd called.

"Hi, Coach. How are you?"

"I'm good. Nose is a bit tender, but the headache is mostly gone."

"I'm glad."

There was silence for a beat. Harley didn't really know what to say, and she'd never been that good at the whole phone thing. She was bad enough at the social thing, but not being able to see nonverbal clues of the person she was talking to had gotten her in trouble more than once when she'd been in high school. Her siblings didn't mind her brusque phone manner, they'd known her too long.

"Whatcha doing?" Coach asked.

"Working."

There was a chuckle on the other end of the line. "Need a break?"

"Need? No."

"Let me rephrase that then. Want to take a break?"

"With you?" Harley mentally smacked herself on the

forehead. God, she might as well just blurt out "I like you!" and be done with it.

But Coach didn't laugh at her. He merely said, "Yeah. With me."

"Sure."

"You mind if I come over there? I'm not sure my head is ready for a loud restaurant or anything yet."

He wanted to come over to her place? Harley couldn't remember the last time she'd had someone over. Well, someone who wasn't related to her that is. "Oh, yeah, okay. But," she looked around, grimacing at the mess that was her space, "my place is a mess. When I get in the groove, I kinda forget to clean."

"I'm not coming over to inspect the place, Harl."

"Why *are* you coming over?" The words popped out before Harley could stop them. She closed her eyes and sighed before quickly saying, "Sorry. Don't answer that. I'm not good on the phone."

As if she hadn't said that last part, Coach responded, "I'm coming over because I like you, Harley. I'm tired of my own company and I wouldn't mind spending some time with you. Getting to know you better, making sure you're really all right after what happened."

Harley didn't have any comeback for that. She still didn't quite believe a man like Coach would want to date *her*, but she certainly wasn't going to dissuade him.

"You still there?"

"Yeah, sorry. So, what time?"

"Maybe in an hour or so? Want me to bring something to eat?"

"Only if it's Chinese from that new place on Main Street. Not the fast food place, that stuff sucks. And I like anything chicken. Oh and spicy. But not the cashew chicken, they always skimp on the nuts and it irritates me."

Coach laughed on the other end. "Got it. Spicy chicken, no cashews."

"Do you know where I live?"

"I do. I talked to the guys. Oh, and in case you hadn't noticed, your car is outside. They brought it over last night."

"I saw that. Thanks."

"Key is under the mat on the passenger side backseat."

"Great. I'll get it later."

"Thanks for letting me come over, Harl. I'll see you soon."

"Okay, Coach. Later."

"'Bye."

Harley hung up the phone and sat back in her seat, staring unseeingly at the computer screen in front of her. What a weird two days it had been. She looked at her watch. Eleven-thirty. She'd woken up early after a nightmare. Of course she'd been falling in the dream.

Figured. At least she'd woken up before she'd splatted on the ground.

It had been a couple of hours since she'd spoken with her sister and she had forgotten to eat once she'd gotten in the zone with her work.

Focusing on the lines of code in front of her, an idea struck, and Harley leaned forward eagerly. She'd just finish this one small tweak, then she'd get up and clean a bit before Coach got there.

Chapter Nine

COACH WIPED HIS hands down his pants before reaching out and knocking on Harley's door. He was nervous. It was ridiculous, but he couldn't help it. It was different being the one chasing rather than being chased. He liked it. A lot.

Harley lived in a nicer part of Temple, in a small subdivision of townhouses. They all looked the same, although they were painted different colors. Harley's place was in the middle of a row of six. Which was in the middle of a triangle of other buildings. The parking was in the center of the group of buildings. It looked well-maintained, and the older lady who'd peered out her curtains at him while he'd walked up to Harley's door had smiled at him in a friendly way.

After waiting for what seemed like forever, Coach smiled when the door opened. But instead of seeing Harley's smiling face, she merely cracked the door and peered through it.

"Hey, Coach. I, uh...I lost track of time, and I'm not ready."

"Not ready? Are you all right?"

"Yeah. I'm good. It's just that—"

"If you've changed your mind, it's okay. I know I'm probably coming on too strong, but I'm going stir crazy with nothing to do, and I really *do* want to get to know you better," Coach hurried to reassure her. The last thing he wanted was to make Harley uneasy.

"No! It's not that. I mean, I want to find out more about you too. But…I'll be honest with you. I look like crap. I took a shower yesterday when I got home, but didn't bother this morning. I'm wearing," Coach saw her look down at herself before continuing, "a ratty old T-shirt and my fat pants. I haven't even put on underwear today."

Coach almost choked at hearing that, but luckily she didn't notice and kept on rambling.

"I wanted to change. To look better for you. I'm not the prettiest woman around, even when I'm dressed up, but I at least wanted to put some effort into it tonight. I mean, you're hot, so it seemed the prudent thing to do, but then I started working on my game, and I didn't realize—"

"Let me in, Harley," Coach demanded firmly.

"I'm not sure—"

"Let me in," he repeated.

"Oh. Okay, but don't say I didn't warn you."

Harley opened her door and stood in front of him,

shifting uncomfortably. Without looking away from her face, Coach stepped into the small foyer of her apartment and closed the door when she backed up, giving him some space.

Once the door was shut, Coach checked Harley out from head to toe. She was wearing a gray T-shirt that depicted the evolution of man, from a stooped-over ape to a man playing an arcade game. It looked huge on her thin frame, but only hung a bit past her hips. Her pants were black and made out of a soft-looking cotton. He didn't know what "fat pants" were, but they looked like regular cotton pajama bottoms to him. They were tied at her waist with a large bow and had wide legs, hiding most of her sock-covered feet. Harley's brown hair was piled on top of her head in a messy knot.

She pushed a pair of glasses up on her nose and put her hands on her hips, and said belligerently, "See? I told you."

"What would you have put on if you'd had the time?"

"What? Oh, well…" Harley shrugged a little self-consciously. "I don't know. Probably a pair of jeans and maybe a sweater or something. I would've at least taken a shower so I didn't smell like butt."

Coach couldn't help himself. He shuffled forward two steps and leaned into her, burying his nose into her neck by her ear, and inhaled. He heard her take a quick breath, but she didn't back away from him, merely tilted her head a fraction of an inch, giving him more room. He felt one of her hands rest tentatively on his side.

"You don't smell like butt. I'd say laundry detergent and cinnamon."

"Oh, well. Yeah, I had cinnamon toast this morning for breakfast. Probably spilled it on my shirt and didn't notice."

Coach smiled at her and eased back. He looked down her body again, noticing that her nipples were once more peeking through the cotton of her T-shirt. He wasn't an expert, but the fact that she couldn't control her body's reaction around him was a good sign. At least for him. Of course, thinking about her nipples got him thinking about what she wasn't wearing underneath her clothes and about how, if he knew her better, he would've loved to take hold of the end of the bow at her waist and pull.

"So, you brought the Chinese?"

Her words jerked Coach out of his sexual daze. God. He hadn't even been around her for more than a couple of hours and already he was fantasizing about stripping her naked. He was an asshole.

"Yeah, I got you Hunan spicy chicken with jalapeno poppers on the side."

Coach flinched when Harley reached out and grabbed him by the front of his shirt, towing him into her apartment. "Why didn't you say so when you first got here? That's my favorite! The spicier the better! And the poppers are the icing on the cake," she exclaimed.

Coach smiled and let her manhandle him into her kitchen. She reached out a hand, demanding he hand over the paper bag he'd been holding since he'd arrived. "Gimmie."

"Yes, ma'am. Far be it from me to get between a woman and her food."

Harley glared at him for a moment. "Are you making fun of me?"

"No," Coach told her immediately with a smile. "I'm actually being serious. You have no idea how much of a turn on it is to be with a woman who knows what she wants. Not to mention the whole eating thing."

"The eating thing?"

Coach nodded and watched as she turned her attention to unloading the food onto the counter. "Yeah, you know, how most of the time women on a date only want to eat salads and maybe a plain chicken breast when they're out with a guy."

His words stopped her in her tracks for the second time. "A date?"

He grinned. "Yeah. A date. I'm considering this our first date. It involves food, conversation, and hopefully a kiss at the end of the night. A date."

Coach knew he'd thrown Harley for a loop when

she merely stared at him in bewilderment. Didn't she go on dates? She had to; she was funny, pretty, and interesting. A home run in his book. Too many times Coach met women who only wanted to get him into bed. Who had no desire to find out who he was as a person…to see past his uniform to the man beneath. For some reason, he knew Harley was different. Not only had she had the gumption to get them out of the life-or-death situation she'd found herself in the day before, but she'd stayed at the hospital until he'd come to, and had been considerate to Emily's daughter. Yeah, he so wanted to date her.

"Oh, well. Okay then. I just thought you were…you know."

"I *don't* know, Harley. What?" Coach put his hand over hers on the counter, halting her jerky motions in removing the white takeout containers from the bag.

She shrugged. "Thanking me for yesterday or something."

"I am," Coach agreed easily. "But it's more than that. Remember, I wanted to take you out to eat before the accident. But I'll tell you, you've intrigued me even more now."

Harley took a deep breath. "Okay, but this," she spread her arms out, "is me. I sometimes forget to eat and shower for days when I get in the zone with my work. I'm a nerd. I have nerd friends, most of them people I met online. I'd rather stay home and play video games with those online friends than go out. I'm an introvert. I like people, but if I had a choice, I'd choose to be by myself at home. I like to read, and I can eat…a lot. I'm skinny and no matter what I eat, I can't seem to gain weight. I have a high tolerance for alcohol and could probably drink you under the table." She stopped and bit her lip as she let her arms fall to her sides.

Coach, grabbed one of her hands and put his other one on her face, running his thumb over her lips once. "I'm in the Army. There are times when my friends and I go days without showering either. We eat packaged meals when we're on a mission, when we have the time. I don't care about you being a nerd. If you must know, it intrigues me. I have no problem with you playing video games, I only hope you'll let me join you. Believe it or not, I'm somewhat of an introvert myself. Even though I can, and will, defend myself, I learned long ago that people are mean. So to avoid that, I avoid putting myself in situations where I have to watch it. That being said, I have no problem stepping in when people are being assholes, and inserting myself into a situation."

Coach moved the hand that had been cupping her cheek to her waist, then continued, "I have no complaints about your body, Harley. None. In fact, from what I've seen so far, it's perfect for me." His eyes moved down her body as he spoke. "Long legs, slender fingers, small chest, but oh so responsive." His eyes sparkled and he saw her shift where she stood when he tightened his fingers at her side.

Finally, he met her eyes again. "As far as food goes? Eat what you want. I would rather have a girlfriend who eats real food than one who's trying to impress those around her. There's nothing less sexy than listening to a woman's stomach growl when we're out. The only thing I have to disagree with you about is your drinking me under the table. First, I'd never make that a contest, I wouldn't risk your health. But, if you want to drink, knock yourself out. All I ask is that you do it somewhere safe. And maybe let me pick you up to make sure you get home safely."

Harley's mouth dropped open, but no words came out. Eventually she brought her free hand up to his chest and poked. Hard.

"Ow." Coach grabbed her fingers, encircling them with his palm to keep her from doing it again. "What was that for?"

"I was just checking to see if you're real or not. I figure you have to be a robot or something. Maybe a cyborg who has been programmed to say exactly the right thing to women."

Coach grinned. "One hundred percent flesh and blood, Harl. Now, we gonna eat or what?"

"Give me back my hands, and yeah, we're gonna eat."

Coach didn't stop smiling, but he let go of her.

She turned her attention back to the food. "Is eating on the couch all right?"

"Sure."

"Cool. I couldn't remember the last time I actually ate at my table."

Harley turned to the cabinet and pulled out two large bowls and then grabbed two spoons and forks from the drawer underneath it. She brought them over to where he was standing at the counter and handed him a spoon. "For your rice."

Coach dutifully scooped out a blob of rice and put it in his bowl. He then added his own beef and broccoli to the rice and mixed it together with the fork she'd also handed him. "No chopsticks?" he inquired with a grin.

"Pbfft," Harley scoffed without looking up as she fixed her own meal. "I can use chopsticks with the best of them, but I'm hungry. It's much more efficient to use a fork."

"Can't argue with that," Coach told her, thinking to himself how freaking adorable she was. He liked her frank talk. It was refreshing. It was almost like being around his teammates...almost.

They finished getting their meals prepared, topping them off with a few jalapeño poppers, and headed to the couch. Harley sat and tucked one leg under her and got to work on her chicken, not talking to him and not looking up.

Instead of feeling slighted, Coach felt…comfortable. Even though it was the first time he'd been to her house or hung out with her, he didn't feel awkward or scared he'd say the wrong thing. Harley was down-to-earth and comfortable in her own skin.

He tucked into his own food, not bothering to try to talk to her as they were eating. Harley hadn't lied. She could eat. She polished off her bowl of food faster than he would've believed. He was only moments behind her when he put the late bite of his own food in his mouth.

Harley wiped her mouth with a paper towel she'd grabbed from the kitchen before sitting back and wrinkling her nose at him. "No comments about how fast I eat?"

"Nope. We're well matched." Coach held up his own empty bowl.

She held out her hand for his dish. "I'm done, but you want more?"

Coach shook his head. "No, I'm good. But I got it, give me yours."

Harley didn't argue, merely handed over her own now-empty bowl. As he walked the short distance to the kitchen to put the dishes into the sink, she commented, "People are always giving me crap about eating too fast."

Coach looked over at her. Harley had turned so one

elbow was resting on the back of the black leather couch and was looking his way.

He ran water over the dirty dishes and admitted, "Yeah, me too. My mom gives me shit every time I go home."

"My sister says I eat like I'm a starving kid from Africa."

They smiled at each other.

"But, I'm hungry. I don't see any reason to pause between bites, or put my fork down while I chew. It's just more economical to get it done and move on to something more interesting," Harley tried to explain.

If it was any other woman, Coach might've made a sexual innuendo, but it was obvious Harley wasn't trying to come on to him in any way. "You'll feel right at home around my friends then. Emily and Rayne always complain we're like a pack of jackals." He shrugged unselfconsciously as he folded up the Chinese food boxes with the leftovers and put them into the fridge. "When we're in the field, sometimes there's just no time to sit and enjoy a meal. We stuff in what we can, when we can."

"Can you tell me more about what you do?"

Coach came back around the couch and sat next to Harley again. All of her attention was on him. She wasn't fiddling with her cell phone. Wasn't reaching for the remote to the television. She was focused on *him*.

She was proving with each minute that went by that she was different from every other woman he'd dated in the past. In a good way. A very good way.

He wanted to answer her question, but also knew he had to be careful. "You know I'm in the Army," he began carefully.

She nodded and encouraged him to continue.

"I'm a thirty-five foxtrot."

Harley eyed him, then admitted, "Okay, I have no idea what that means. I know some of the basic ones. Like eleven bravo is infantry, twelve bravo is a combat engineer, the one fifty-threes are pilots, and twenty-seven bravo is a judge, but I don't know any others."

"I'm impressed you know that much."

Harley shrugged. "My sister is a lawyer, and I've learned some stuff over the years from playing video games." She grinned sheepishly.

"A thirty-five foxtrot is a part of the military intelligence branch." When Harley opened her mouth to say something, Coach cut her off with a laugh. "And no, that's not an oxymoron." They both laughed.

"How'd you know that's what I was going to say?" She finally got out between giggles. When she'd gotten herself under control, she asked, "What do you do?"

"Officially my job is intelligence analyst." Coach didn't tell her that, on paper—paper that was top secret—he was actually coded as an eighteen foxtrot...a part of the Special Forces branch. "Basically I use information to try to determine what the enemy is capable of, what their vulnerabilities might be, and what should be done about both."

Harley nodded. "That makes sense. Bet your eidetic memory comes in handy."

"Yeah, it certainly does."

"So you work with a team?"

"What do you mean?"

"The guys at the hospital yesterday. You called them teammates. Are they all thirty-five foxtrots too?"

Coach bit back a snort. Ghost and the others would get a kick out of that. Harley might call herself a nerd, but the guys called *him* the nerd of their group. He liked numbers and figuring stuff out. Logic puzzles were like his crack.

"No, they each have their own specialty. We work together a lot. So much that we're more like brothers than coworkers."

Coach didn't even flinch as Harley eyed him. He'd have to keep reminding himself that she was a lot smarter than most women he'd dated. His explanation had sufficed with everyone else. He continued on, "We do get sent on missions together a lot, so we *are* like teammates."

"Missions. Not deployed together?"

Shit, shit, and triple shit. Coach didn't say anything,

but kept eye contact with Harley until she broke it.

"Okay. I get it. I can see you're uncomfortable and I won't ask about it anymore. But can I say one thing?"

"Of course."

"I think it's cool. I mean, they were at the hospital like fifteen minutes after we got there. I don't know any of the people I know, besides my family, who would do that for me. They were extremely worried about you, even the two women. I like that for you."

"I like it for me too, Harl. But you know what?"

"What?"

"If I knew you were in the hospital, I'd be there in less than fifteen minutes."

"You don't even know me," Harley whispered in confusion while shaking her head. "Why would you say that?"

"I might not know the small stuff, but I know enough of the important stuff to know that I would care if you got hurt. That I would worry about you. That I'd want to be there when you woke up."

Coach could see the confusion still swirling in her brown eyes, and decided to change the subject. "Tell me more about your job. You design video games. Apparently ones involving war stuff."

It was the right thing to ask. Coach nodded and um-hmmmed through fifteen minutes of Harley talking excitedly about her job and what she did on the computer. She worked for a large, famous graphics company and she was one of many people who worked behind the scenes to make games kids played today more realistic and intense.

"Do you get any credit for it?"

"Credit?"

"Yeah, like is your name listed in the credits or anything of the games? Or are you totally behind the scenes?"

Her eyes lit up, and Coach loved the sight.

"You wanna see?"

"Your name on the game? Hell yeah."

Harley scrambled off the couch and over to her TV and the game console. She didn't say anything, but looked through the shelf of games and pulled one out. She popped it in the player and grabbed a remote, turning on the television as she sat back down.

"Okay, don't get too excited, it's just my name among about twenty others, but we're listed in the opening credits when the game is first turned on. I know most people just go right by it, but it's still pretty cool."

Coach watched Harley instead of the screen. When she was excited, her entire face lit up. It was a side of her he hadn't seen yet. And he liked it. A lot.

"Okay, ready?" Harley asked, turning to him, obviously expecting to see him looking at the screen instead of at her. "Coach?"

"Sorry, yeah, I'm ready."

"Okay, I'll try to pause the screen, but you gotta look fast." She pushed her glasses up on her nose and leaned forward, as if that was helping her concentrate. "There!" she exclaimed, pointing at the screen. "I got it!"

Coach looked at the fifty-four-inch screen and saw a list of names, and in the middle was Harley Kelso, designer. He beamed over at her. "That's neat."

"Wanna play?"

"Yes." Coach's answer was immediate. "Although I must admit that *Bejeweled* is my specialty. I saw you have it."

"Forget it," Harley told him without pause. "I only have it because my sister can't play any of my first-person games to save her life. That game's for sissies."

"So you suck at it," Coach teased.

She turned and glared at him. "You wanna play or not?"

Holding up his hands in a surrender gesture, Coach placated, "Yeah, sorry. Whatever you want is fine."

Luckily she forgave him for his apparently subpar choice of game. "We can either play against each other, or on the same team."

"Same team."

"That's probably smart. I'd wipe the floor with

you," Harley told him, grinning.

"I have no doubt." And he didn't. Coach might be a big bad Delta Force soldier, but if Harley helped design the game, she would be much better at it than he was…and he considered himself a pretty good gamer.

"Here." Harley handed him a controller. "Have you played this version of *This is War* before?"

"Not this one, but the one with the soldiers that were aliens, yes."

"Okay, this one is so much better than that one. And before you ask, yes, I helped design the other one, but this one is newer and we did some cool stuff with it. I'll put it on medium level and let you take point."

"Try not to shoot me in the ass, would ya, Kelso?"

She giggled, and Coach's insides tightened at the sound. She sounded happy and unconcerned with anything. It almost erased his memory of her sobbing into his chest from the day before. Almost.

"Okay, Ralston, let's do this."

Chapter Ten

"LOOK OUT! BEHIND you! Shit, he's got a grenade! Run, Coach! Get out of there!"

"Fuck, where'd he come from? Get him, Harl! Shoot his ass!"

"I don't have a good angle! Dammit!"

"No, no, no, no! Damn!" Coach sagged back against the couch cushions in defeat as he watched his character die for what seemed like the twentieth time that night. He looked over at Harley with a rueful grimace. "The designers of this game are sadistic."

She full-out laughed. Literally threw back her head and laughed until she was clutching her stomach. When Harley finally had herself somewhat under control, she gasped, "We're only playing on the medium difficulty, you big baby. You should see it on expert."

Coach threw up his hands in defeat. "Lord. I'm done. Damn good job, Harley. Seriously." He looked down at his watch and his brows rose in surprise. "Is it really nine o'clock?"

Harley looked surprised and whipped her head

around to look at the clock on the wall by the kitchen. "Holy shit. I guess so." She turned back to Coach and shrugged. "It's not a good game unless eight hours of your life are sucked away while playing."

"It's a good game. But honestly? The company is what made it worth losing an entire day."

Harley blushed, but smiled back at him. "I haven't had this much fun in a really long time. Thanks, Coach."

"The pleasure was mine, believe me."

Harley stood up and stretched, putting her hands in the small of her back and leaning into them, much as she'd done before they'd jumped.

Coach nearly swallowed his tongue. She obviously had no clue about her appeal. He could tell she wasn't being coy, or trying to come on to him. But when she leaned back, her breasts were thrust forward, and while her nipples weren't as tight as when they'd been standing together at the airport getting fitted to jump, he had a better view of how she was shaped.

She was slender, yes, but her tits were perfect for her frame. If he had to guess, Coach would say she was probably a B cup, a nice handful. But it was the thought of getting his lips around her nipples that made his mouth water. He remembered how they'd peaked with her growing interest in him.

Coach felt himself stir in his jeans. Jesus, he hadn't

seen an inch of Harley's bare skin, but he'd already undressed her and sucked her tits until she orgasmed under him in his head.

She looked over at him and froze, obviously seeing the look of lust on his face. Coach tried to wipe his face clear of any emotion, and knew he'd failed when she brought her arms down and crossed them over her waist self-consciously.

"How's your head? Do you need any more ibuprofen?"

Coach shook his head. "No, I'm good. The last couple I took when we stopped for a break and to eat the rest of the Chinese is still doing its thing. Thanks though."

"Okay. Good."

Coach stood. "I should go. I took way too much of your time today."

"No, it's fine. I needed the break. Honestly, playing one of the older games with you was not only fun, but it gave me some good ideas for the new game."

Taking a step closer to Harley, wanting to make his point, Coach said in a low voice, "I'm glad. I had fun. Thank you for sharing this part of your life with me. I find it, and you, fascinating. Even though we got to eat together, I'd still like to take you out sometime."

"Really?" Harley winced, then quickly tried to cover her skeptical answer. "I mean, sure. I'd like that."

Coach smiled. "Walk me to the door?"

They walked side by side to the front of the town-house. Harley unlocked the deadbolt and opened the door, standing to the side.

Coach stood there next to her for a moment, drinking her in. He hadn't lied. He'd had a wonderful time. Playing the video game, seeing how riled and excited Harley got while she was playing, was refreshing. It would've been like competing with the guys on the team, except that there was no way Coach could forget for even a second that Harley was all woman. She might've been wearing huge cotton pants and a T-shirt that swallowed her frame, but he'd never been as aware of a woman as he was her.

Leaning into Harley, but not touching her, Coach kept his eyes on hers as he said, "I'd like to kiss you."

His heart skipped a beat when she didn't immediately answer, but finally started up again when she nodded.

"I'd like that."

Taking his time, knowing he'd never get another first kiss with her, Coach put one hand on her shoulder, and putting the knuckle of his other hand under her chin, tilted her so she was at the perfect angle. Her height was ideal. He still needed to lean over, but he didn't have to worry about throwing his back out.

Harley licked her lips nervously and he felt her hesitantly put her hands on his waist as he stepped closer. Coach licked his own lips in preparation and watched as Harley closed her eyes.

Not wanting to miss a second of the moment, Coach kept his eyes open as he closed the distance between them. His lips touched hers once in a fleeting caress, then twice. The third time, he lingered, and she reacted as she did to everything else, she threw herself wholeheartedly into the experience.

Coach felt her hands clench at his side and she opened under him. Wanting to taste her more than he wanted his next breath, Coach slid his tongue into her mouth, meeting and dancing with her own as she reciprocated.

She tasted slightly of the spicy chicken she'd eaten for dinner, but more than that, she tasted like…Harley. Coach inhaled as he slanted his head and moved his hand to the back of her head to hold her to him. He could smell…her. Not soap, not shampoo, but the slightly musky, dewy smell of woman.

He groaned into her mouth and took control of the kiss. Holding her still, he devoured her as if it was the last time he'd ever get to kiss her. He sucked on her tongue, then nipped at her lips. Coach wanted to drink from her lips all night, but when she shivered under him, he pulled back. The last thing he wanted to do was scare her, or push her to a place she didn't want to go.

Coach felt like a Neanderthal. He wanted to drag her back into her apartment and into her bedroom, throw her on the bed, and rip off her clothes, see what she'd been hiding under them. But he had time. He didn't want to rush into sex. Playing the video game with her tonight was fun. And something he'd never done with any other woman. Something he'd never *wanted* to do with any other woman.

He pulled back, but rested his forehead on hers, loving the way her breaths came in short pants. "Thank you, Harley. That was a gift."

She leaned back and looked up at him in confusion.

He couldn't help it. He'd been curious since he'd first laid his lips on hers. His eyes wandered down to her chest, and he smiled.

Harley's nipples were peaked and pressing against the gray T-shirt toward him. He could clearly see how excited his kiss had made her. Shifting a hand from her head to her side, Coach brushed his thumb over the bottom curve of her breast. Not being a perv, but definitely touching her more intimately than a friend would, and probably way out of bounds for how long they'd known each other, but he couldn't've stopped himself if he'd had a gun to his head. He *needed* to touch her.

"Thank you for the best first kiss I've ever had. It exceeded all of my expectations." He met her eyes, but his thumb never stopped its gentle caress. "I want you, Harley Kelso. But more than I want your body at the moment, I want you to trust me. I broke that trust when we jumped, through no fault of my own, but still. I want to spend more days lounging on your couch by your side. I want to know more about your job, what you do and how it works. I want to meet your siblings. I want you to get to know my teammates and Emily and Rayne. The bottom line is that I want you in my life. I've never felt like this about anyone before, and I'm not blowing smoke up your ass to get you into bed. As much as I want to see, and touch, your beautiful body, I want to get acquainted with who Harley is. Your fears, your dreams, and your fantasies."

"You feel grateful toward me."

Coach shook his head in denial at her shaky words. "No. It's not that. I'm as proud as I can be of you for what you did yesterday, don't get me wrong. But honestly, the AAD would've gone off no matter who was strapped to my chest. Yeah, if someone else was with me and didn't do half what you did, I might've been hurt worse when we landed. But I'm grateful it was *you*. I'm thankful for all you did. But this isn't that, Harley. I don't know what it is about you, but I'm attracted to you. Obsessed."

"It must be my nerdy glasses and runway-perfect outfit," Harley commented sarcastically.

It seemed that he needed to teach her how to accept a compliment. "It *is* your glasses. And your clothes. You're *you*. You don't give a shit what others say or think about you. You're comfortable in your skin. And that's a total turn on. There aren't many women in the world today who are like that. It's attractive as hell, and, Harl, I gotta warn you, I'm into you. I hope like hell you might feel the same about me, but I'm gonna give this my best shot."

"You go, young man."

The voice sounded like it came from next door. Both he and Harley stuck their heads out the door and he saw the same older woman standing in her doorway in the townhouse next to them, smiling.

"It's rude to eavesdrop, Gretel," Harley scolded with a blush.

"Ha. It's only rude if you mean to do harm with what you hear."

"She's mostly right," Coach agreed, not letting go of Harley.

"Whatever," she mumbled under her breath. "Good night, Gretel," she called, pulling back into the doorway of her place.

When Coach raised his eyebrows at her, Harley quickly explained, "That's Gretel Owens. She's in her eighties and has a crush on my other neighbor. She stalks him, popping out whenever he comes or goes.

She's basically the neighborhood watch lady. She's harmless."

"Does the neighbor want her back?"

"Henry? I have no idea. I think he does, but he's leading her on a merry chase, that's for sure."

"I hope you aren't planning on leading me on a merry chase, but I'll tell ya now, if you are, I'll gladly play along."

Coach smiled as it looked like he'd finally rendered Harley speechless. He leaned into her once more, brushing his mouth over hers in a way-too-brief kiss, before pulling back. "I'll call you tomorrow. I've still got a few days of leave left. I'd like to see you again."

"I have dinner with my brother and sister on Saturday."

"Okay, no problem. Sunday then? I think Fletch is going to have a barbeque at his house. Would you come with me?"

Harley looked at her feet before meeting his gaze. "I'm not good in social situations, Coach. Seriously. I always say the wrong thing, and the last thing I want to do is make you uncomfortable around your friends."

"You'll be fine."

"What if they don't like me?"

"They already do. Harley, you met them at the hospital. Fletch told me that Annie has talked about you nonstop. How calm and collected you were, even though you were covered in my blood. It's the coolest thing that has happened to her in at least a week." Coach smiled, letting her know he was joking.

When she didn't look convinced, he quickly said, "We don't have to stay long if you're uncomfortable. I'll pick you up, and we can stop in, say hi, and then we can come back here if you want. Or we can go to my place and hang out. Whatever you want."

"Okay. Fine. I'd like to get to know your friends better."

"Thank fuck," Coach breathed in relief. "I swear you've made me work harder for a date than anyone I've ever met."

"I'm sorry. I'm not trying to play hard to get," Harley told him with a worried frown on her face.

"I know," Coach soothed. "That makes it all the more satisfying that you said yes. I'll call you tomorrow and we can talk, learn more about each other."

"Okay."

"Lock up after me," Coach ordered, reluctantly letting go of Harley and stepping back.

"Of course," Harley told him. "I do every night anyway."

"Good night, Harley. Thanks for the fun day."

"Night."

Coach smiled all the way home. His head hurt, and his nose was beyond sore, but he couldn't care less at the moment. Harley was going to be his—she just didn't realize it yet.

Chapter Eleven

HARLEY SMILED AT her brother and sister. They'd eaten dinner and were sitting on Montesa's couch. Coach had texted her a few times and he'd called last night. They stayed up late debating the merits of puzzle games, like *Bejeweled*, over first-person shooter games, like *This is War*. Harley's stomach had hurt from laughing by the time she'd hung up.

"So tell me more about this Coach guy," Davidson demanded in a harsh yet concerned voice only a big brother could have.

"He's in the Army. A sergeant. His MOS is intelligence and he works with a group of other guys."

"Don't they all work with other guys?" Montesa asked, sipping her third glass of wine.

"He with Special Forces?" Davidson questioned out of the blue.

Harley eyed her brother before answering slowly, "I think so, but he was uncomfortable talking about it, so I didn't press."

"Hmmm, probably not a Ranger then. Those guys

love to talk about their Ranger tab."

"That's not nice, Davidson," Harley scolded. "You shouldn't be so cynical."

"Sorry, can't help it. So, you think he's Delta Force then? He's Army, so he can't be a SEAL."

"How should I know?" Harley asked, exasperated. "Aren't they like, top secret? It's not like he'd tell me if he was."

"That's true."

"So you like him?" Montesa asked, getting to the meat of the issue.

"Yeah, I do," Harley admitted without a qualm. These were her siblings. They were closer than most brother and sisters were. She knew she could tell them anything and they'd never judge her. Well, maybe she wouldn't talk with her brother about sex she might be having, but with Montesa, yes. "He's different from most of the military guys I've met. He's funny, and he eats as fast as I do."

"I'm not sure that's a selling point, Harley," her brother told her with his lip curled.

Laughing, Harley disagreed. "Actually, it is. He didn't care that I ate the entire takeout by myself. You know how I feel about guys commenting on how much or how fast I eat. The fact that he eats just as fast as me means that I don't have to worry about the snide comments."

"True," Davidson agreed reluctantly. "But I'm not sure you should build an entire relationship on the fact that he can eat fast. Besides, until I've met him, I'm going to withhold judgement, one way or another."

"Fair enough," Harley agreed. She valued Davidson's judgement, and couldn't wait to see what he thought of Coach.

"What's with his nickname?" Montesa asked.

Harley shrugged. "Not sure. I haven't asked him about it yet."

"Oh, please let me know. I find it fascinating how those military guys get their nicknames. Most of the time it's hilarious."

"I know. They make one wrong move and they're branded with some silly name for the rest of their lives. Although, his friend Fletch has that name because his last name is Fletcher, so it might be something innocuous."

"How in the world do you know that about his friend, but don't know the meaning behind the name of the guy you're crushing on?"

"Fletch's daughter told me."

Montesa shook her head in exasperation and drained her glass. "I don't want to know. Seriously. Your life is a soap opera."

"No it's not," Harley disagreed. "It's usually extremely boring. You tell me all the time I need to get out more."

"True. Okay then, don't *make* your life a soap opera, yeah?"

Harley smiled at her sister. "Gotcha. No *General Hospital* in my life. Deal."

"It's time we got out of your hair, sis," Davidson told Montesa. "I have a conference call in the morning."

"On Sunday?"

He grimaced. "Yeah."

"That sucks."

"Yeah," Davidson repeated. "You okay to get home, Harley? You get your car looked over yet?"

"No. There's nothing wrong with my car."

"The tires are almost bald," Davidson disagreed. "It's making a weird noise, and don't try to deny it. I pulled in behind you tonight and almost went deaf until you shut off the engine."

Harley threw a balled-up napkin at her brother. "Whatever."

He caught it before it hit his head, and smiled at her. "Get it looked at, Harley."

"Okay, okay. I will."

"Same time next week?"

"Can't. Sorry," Montesa told her brother. "John and I are going to a conference in San Francisco. We won't be home until Sunday night."

Harley could tell that Davidson wanted to comment

on the odd relationship between their sister and her law partner, but he didn't. They'd both learned to leave it alone. Montesa was sensitive about it, and neither wanted to hurt her feelings.

"Okay, maybe the next week then."

"Sounds good."

"It's a plan."

Harley waved at Montesa as she and her brother walked to their cars. She gave him a hug and kiss—and promptly forgot about her siblings as soon as she got into her car and checked her texts.

Hope you had a good time at your sister's house.

It was sweet that Coach remembered she was having dinner at Montesa's that night. They hadn't talked about it last night on the phone. His eidetic memory must extend to conversations as well. Harley made a mental note to remember that about him. Checking her watch, and seeing it wasn't too late, she sent a short text back.

I did, thanks. It's always good to spend time with them.

His response was immediate. *You're lucky.*

Harley knew it. Not many people had such close relationships with their siblings. But for some reason she got the feeling there was more to Coach's text than simple politeness. Before she could comment about it, he sent another message.

We still on for the barbeque tomorrow?
Yeah. What time?

I can pick you up around twelve-thirty. That work?

Sure. Casual, right?

Definitely. We'll all be in jeans.

Harley sighed in relief. She could do jeans.

Okay, see you then.

Can't wait.

Her smile didn't wane even after she'd crawled in bed an hour later. She'd forgotten the feeling of euphoria when dating someone new. It was nice. More than nice.

Chapter Twelve

COACH WAS RIGHT on time the next day. At twelve-thirty on the dot, Harley looked outside and saw him talking with Henry. They were obviously having a lively conversation because Coach was laughing and gesturing with his hands. They both turned to Gretel's place and waved, catching her in the act of spying on them.

Finally, Coach shook Henry's hand and then came up to her door. He raised his hand to knock, but Harley opened it before his knuckles could connect with the wood.

"Hey."

"Hey, yourself. You look great."

Harley blushed. She'd tried extra hard today to make up for the last time he'd been at her house. She was wearing a pair of skinny jeans that hugged her ass. Montesa had told her once that they were sexy as hell on her. She'd paired them with one of her favorite T-shirts. It was a V-neck and said Harvard in big letters, but underneath it, in smaller font, it said, "just kidding."

"Nice shirt."

"Thanks. Decided to forgo the fat pants today." It wasn't anything fancy, but then again, Harley wasn't fancy.

Coach brought a hand up to her head and brushed a lock of hair behind her ear. "I like your hair too."

She smiled self-consciously. "Thought I would put a bit more effort into it than just pulling it up in a ponytail for once. Oh, and I even showered this morning. Just for you," she teased.

He grinned widely at her and put a hand on his chest. "Be still my heart."

Harley relaxed, glad he wasn't going to make a big deal out of it. She'd spent a lot of time that morning trying to get her hair to cooperate. It was somewhere between straight and curly and wouldn't really do much either way. When she curled it, it only held the curl for about an hour, and when she tried to straighten it, inevitably it'd frizz up. So today she'd chosen to leave it natural, with help from a little gel. She blew it dry upside down to give it some volume, and then prayed for the best. So far, so good.

"You ready to go?"

Harley nodded. "As I'll ever be."

Coach waited patiently as she locked the door behind her, and then held out his hand, as if to point out the way to his car.

Harley studied his vehicle, as it was the first time she'd seen it, and turned to him with a smile. "A Toyota Highlander? Isn't that…uh…how do I put this…a bit soccer-momish?"

He laughed, unashamed of his ride, and unlocked the doors with the key fob as they got close to it. "Maybe. But I don't care. I love this baby." He stroked his hand down the hood as he walked past. "Just wait until you sit in her. The ride is smooth, the safety features are out of this world, and besides, it's just fun to drive."

"Not a truck? I thought all Texas badass soldiers had a truck."

Coach held out a hand and helped her in. Once she was seated, he leaned into her. "The back of this is much more comfortable than a truck bed." Then he winked and shut the door, grinning.

Harley rolled her eyes. She wouldn't admit it to him, but she was impressed. The inside of the SUV was leather and obviously had all the bells and whistles. There were captain's chairs in the back and a panoramic roof. It was gorgeous. Her car definitely seemed like a piece of crap compared to his.

She had herself under control by the time he got to his side of the vehicle. He pushed the button to start the car, and Harley didn't even give him shit about having a car that didn't need a key to be put in the ignition to start it.

"I asked Fletch if he would look over your car for you," Coach said nonchalantly when they were on the road.

"What? Why?"

"Because Hollywood said it was making a weird noise and that your tires were on their last leg, and because Fletch loves tinkering with cars. He's got a Charger that he's been working on for a while." Looking over at Harley and seeing the unsure look on her face, he went on quickly. "It's not a big deal. He's not going to overhaul the whole thing, but he can change your oil, rotate your tires, change them for you if you want, and check the filters and stuff. He can tell you what he thinks might need to be done, so the mechanics don't take advantage of you."

"Oh, okay. I'd like that. But please don't say anything to him today about it. If he meets me and can't stand me, I'd feel weird if you made him look at my car."

"First," Coach told her easily, "he already likes you. Second, he'd love to do it. Tinkering under the hood relaxes him. It'll be fine. We'll figure out a time later that'll work."

They made more small talk for a while as they headed for Coach's teammate's house. Harley was glad to see Coach was a safe driver. Constantly checking the mirrors and keeping his eyes on the road. "So, dinner was all right last night?" he inquired as they headed to Fletch's place.

"Yeah. It's always good to catch up with Montesa and Davidson."

"Wait, your siblings are also named after motorcycles?"

"Good catch. And yes. I told you before that my parents had a thing for bikes."

"So you did," he agreed with a smile. "Do they go by nicknames?"

"Like David or Tesa? No. My parents refused to shorten their names, and then when they died, we all wanted to keep our names just as they were, for them."

Coach put his hand over hers on the center console. "I'm sorry about your parents. I didn't know. How did they die, if you don't mind me asking?"

"I don't mind. It was a long time ago. They were on their way to Sturgis, you know, that big motorcycle thing out in South Dakota? Anyway, they were minding their own business, when a pickup didn't see them in his blind spot and switched lanes. Dad's motorcycle collided with Mom's and they both ended up over the side of the mountain they were on."

"Jesus, Harley, I'm sorry."

"Thanks. It sucked, but it also made me, Montesa, and Davidson a lot closer. I've learned to try to see the good things that come out of the bad. It helps."

"I admire that about you."

Harley blushed. She liked the fact that he was still holding her hand and squeezed it in answer. "What about your folks?"

"They're still alive and well. They got divorced when I was in high school, but they're on friendly terms. Neither is remarried, but they recently retired from their day jobs."

"Where do they live?"

"Mom's in Maine, and my dad's in Florida." He shrugged when she laughed. "Mom always loved the snow, and Dad couldn't stand it. Now they're both happy."

"That's great."

"We're here."

Harley looked up in surprise. She hadn't been paying attention to where they were going. She'd been too enamored of Coach and his really slick car. They were pulling down a long driveway toward a really cute house. It had a big porch as well as a separate garage that looked like it had an apartment over it.

"It's nice."

"You sound surprised."

"I am a little. I didn't mean to be rude about it though. It's a lot nicer than I thought an Army guy would have. I mean, most military guys I know have apartments because they move so much."

"Like me."

"Yeah, I guess."

"Fletch moved in a while ago. He was renting out the garage to help pay for the mortgage."

"Ah."

"I know you met them briefly, but the short version is that Emily rented the place with her daughter, Annie. There was this asshole at work who was blackmailing her. There was a misunderstanding and Fletch thought the guy was her boyfriend."

"Shit. Really? But she's okay now?"

"Yeah. The guy grabbed both Em and Annie and wanted to get revenge on my team. But all's well that ends well."

"I think you're leaving a whole lot of that story out," Harley accused.

"Yeah, I am. But it's too nice of a day to get into it now. I'm sure if you get to know Emily, she'll tell you the entire story."

"Okay. And Rayne?"

"They have a story too."

Harley laughed. "How did I guess?"

"Well, we have one too now."

Harley was stunned into silence for a moment. "I guess we do."

Coach smiled at her and shut off the engine with a

press of a button. "Come on, let's go meet the gang. Remember, whenever you've had enough, just say the word. We can always go back to your place and play *Bejeweled*."

Harley had started to get nervous again, but at his words she smiled and relaxed. "What is it with you and that game?"

"I'm a pro. I have to beat you at something. I sure as hell will never come close with any of your games. Come on, let's go."

Harley jumped out of the SUV and met Coach at the front of the car.

"I was gonna come around," he pouted.

Harley rolled her eyes. "Do I look like I need help getting out of a car?"

"No. But it's the gentlemanly thing to do."

"Coach, its fine. I appreciate the gesture, but I'm not exactly the kind of woman who needs to be treated as if she's a delicate flower."

"Believe me, I know firsthand that you're entirely competent at everything you do. If you weren't, you wouldn't have handled that skydive the way you did. And you might not think you deserve it, but that's all the more reason why I *want* to do it."

Harley put her hand on his biceps. She felt them flex under her fingertips. His button-down shirt tightening around his arm with his movements. She wanted to wrap both hands around it, simply to measure how large he was, but refrained. "Thanks. But you'd make me feel even more awkward if you treated me as if I was a superstar or something."

"Humph."

It wasn't exactly a word, or an agreement, but Harley let it slide for the moment.

Coach grabbed her hand and headed around the side of the house, obviously feeling right at home at his friend's place. He turned the corner and waved at the group of people standing around.

Freezing for a moment at the number of people who were there, Harley took a deep breath. She could do this. She was an adult who could shoot the shit with Coach's friends for a few hours. Even if it was outside her comfort zone.

"Coaaaaaaach," Annie yelled out, obviously overjoyed to see him.

Coach dropped Harley's hand and held out his arms, catching the little girl as she threw herself at him. "How you doing, pipsqueak?"

"I'm not a pipsqueak," she protested, laughing when Coach tipped her backwards and held her upside down.

He brought her upright and sat her on his hip. "You remember Harley, right?"

Annie looked at Harley and smiled. "Yeah! She was covered in your blood!" She brought her hand up to poke Coach's nose, but he caught it before she could touch him. "Your nose is a funny blue and green color. Are you okay now, Coach?"

"I'm great, Annie. I appreciate you asking. You save us any food?"

The little girl giggled. "Of course. Daddy made enough for an army!"

"Good thing there are lots of soldiers here to help him eat it all."

"Yeah! And I'm a soldier too!" Annie squirmed until Coach let her down and she went running back to the group of people smiling and waiting patiently for Coach to get to them.

"She's a little obsessed with the military," Coach explained, holding out his hand to Harley again.

She grabbed on, telling herself she'd only hold it for a while, until she felt more comfortable, and smiled. "There are worse things to be obsessed with."

"Exactly. Come on, let's go meet everyone."

Taking a deep breath, Harley let herself be led over to his friends. Coach didn't waste any time.

"Everyone, this is Harley Kelso. She helped save my ugly hide when that damn bird took a detour into my face."

The men and women all said hello, and Harley tried to relax. She'd never been comfortable meeting new people.

"This is Ghost. He's the leader of us, I guess you'd say. Beside him is Rayne. You met them both in the hospital, I think."

Harley nodded and held her hand out to the pair, shaking both their hands in greeting.

"You also met Emily and Fletch and their daughter, Annie."

Harley grinned and waved at the gorgeous family. Seriously, they were like a Hallmark Channel movie come to life or something.

"Then there's Hollywood, he's the good-looking one. Then Beatle, Blade, and Truck."

Each of the men came up to her and shook her hand.

"Thank you for keeping your cool while up there with our man," Hollywood told her earnestly.

"Yeah, it would've been embarrassing for him to have landed on top of a cow or something," Blade joked.

Harley smiled, feeling more comfortable. "Yeah well, I tried to hit the cow I saw in the field, but missed."

The guys all laughed and Harley relaxed even more. She liked his friends so far. They didn't mind joking around with her, and it was obvious they were all close.

"By the way, I like your shirt," Beatle told her, gesturing to her chest.

"Thanks. I cracked up when I saw it online and knew I had to have it," Harley explained.

"So you didn't graduate from Harvard?" Rayne asked.

"Hardly."

Everyone grinned.

"The only one I think missing is Mary," Coach noted.

"Mary?"

"Mary is my best friend," Rayne told her. "She had a doctor's appointment today that she couldn't miss."

"On Sunday?" Harley asked. Then immediately decided that was rude. "Sorry, it's none of my business."

"No, it's okay," Rayne insisted. "Her doctor is up in Fort Worth and he knows she moved down here. He's on call at the hospital today, so it worked out that she could go today and get it done."

"And she wouldn't let anyone go with her," Truck grumbled.

"It was just a recheck," Rayne told the giant man gently.

"Still. She shouldn't have gone alone."

"Try telling *her* that," Rayne groused.

"I did," Truck immediately responded.

Everyone laughed. Harley didn't understand the undercurrents between Truck and Rayne's friend, but it wasn't any of her business.

"You hungry?" Fletch asked, grabbing a plate from the table. "There's a ton of food. Annie already ate, but the rest of us were waiting for you guys."

"Starved," Coach told his friend. "Lead on."

As the group started toward the table to fill their plates, Harley turned to Coach. "Thanks for bringing me. I like them."

"They're likable people." He grabbed Harley's hand and brought it up to his lips and kissed the back. "Come on, if we don't get in there, the guys'll eat it all."

"It smells way too good for them to get it all," Harley said with a smile, her stomach jumping at the feel of his lips on the back of her hand.

As she filled up her plate, Harley thought that she might, just might, have found a group of people she could be herself with. Everyone was dressed much as she was, and they were acting totally relaxed and casual around her. It was a good start.

Chapter Thirteen

"SO HOW DID you get your name?" Harley asked Coach. They'd just had a rip-roaring conversation about the other nicknames of the men in the group.

"Oh, it's a good story, but the more important question is, what's his *first* name," Rayne said with a smile.

"Your name isn't Beckett?" Harley asked, turning to Coach. She froze, however, at the look on his face. Whatever the story was behind his first name, it wasn't a pleasant one for him. She regretted even asking.

"No. Beckett is my middle name. I don't go by my first name."

Harley put her hand over his on the arm of the chair, trying to tell him without words that it was okay if he didn't talk about it. They were sitting next to each other, everyone in a circle having finished eating. Luckily, everyone did seem to eat as fast as she and Coach, except for Rayne and Emily, but Harley wasn't surprised the women were much more ladylike.

Changing the subject from Coach's first name, Harley tried to steer the conversation to his nickname. "So,

Coach?"

He smiled at her in thanks at the diversion, and explained. "Yeah, so in basic training, there was this guy who was an absolute disaster in everything he did. He just couldn't get the hang of anything. Making his bed, cleaning the latrine, PT, marching…you name it, he fucked it up. I got sick of our drill sergeant making us redo everything when he screwed up. You know, the whole teamwork thing. I started coaching him. Showing him how he was supposed to do everything. I wasn't doing it for his sake; I didn't give a shit about him. I did it for my own sanity. I was sick of being woken up at oh-three hundred and having to do suicides out in the yard.

"It took a week or so, but the drill sergeant finally figured out that Smith hadn't all of a sudden learned how to be a soldier. He started calling me Coach, and it stuck." He shrugged. "It could've been worse. At least my nickname's not Hollywood."

"Hey," the man in question complained, and threw a balled-up napkin at Coach. "Not cool. It's not my fault I'm the pretty one in the group."

Everyone laughed and Harley was glad the tension had been broken. Although she was curious as to what Coach's first name was, she didn't want him to be uncomfortable or bring back bad memories. She was suddenly sure Coach had a really good reason not to want to use his first name.

"Are you planning on re-renting out the apartment, Fletch?" Truck asked.

He shook his head. "No. When it was just me, I didn't mind having a stranger living there. But now that Emily and Annie are here too, I don't want a random person living so close. Especially when we might be sent off on a moment's notice."

Truck nodded in agreement. "Don't blame you. What are your plans for the place?"

"Not sure yet."

"If you haven't completely ruled out renting it, I might have someone who needs it," Hollywood said. It was obvious he was trying to be nonchalant about it, but wasn't quite pulling it off.

"Yeah?" Fletch asked.

Hollywood nodded.

Harley could see the nonverbal communication flying back and forth between Fletch and his friend. She didn't exactly understand it, but they were obviously talking without saying a word. It was weird and cool at the same time.

"We'll talk later," Fletch finally said.

"Cool."

"So, Coach tells us you design video games," Beatle said during the lull in conversation.

"I do."

"How'd you get into that?" Rayne asked, sipping a glass of iced tea.

Harley wasn't entirely comfortable talking about herself, but she couldn't exactly clam up when everyone had been so nice. She shrugged. "I'm not exactly sure. It just kinda happened. I played a lot of games when I was in high school, and got irritated at how unrealistic some of them were. I was bitching about it in my computer science class, and Mr. Wardham, my teacher, overheard me, and told me to do something about it. To design them myself. The idea had merit. I took some classes in college and found out I loved it. The rest is history."

"That's so cool," Emily said a bit wistfully. "I'd love to do something other than work at the PX for the rest of my life."

"Why don't you?" The words came out before Harley could call them back, and she immediately felt bad when Fletch's eyebrows drew down over his eyes. She tried to backpedal. "I didn't mean that the way it sounded, I just—"

Emily cut her off. "No, you're right. If I want to do something different, I should do it. It's just that I was barely keeping my head above water, trying to keep me and Annie clothed and fed." She gestured to her daughter, who was happily playing with some Army figures off to their left. "I couldn't afford to go to school or anything. But, now that we have Fletch, I need to decide what it is I want to do with my life."

"You don't have to do anything, Em. I can take care of you both."

Emily patted Fletch's hand and smiled up at him. "I know, but I'd get bored. And besides, I've been taking care of myself for a long time, there's no way I could sit around on my butt and let you 'take care of me.'"

"You know, you're really good at designing stuff. You're always finding stuff in thrift stores and garage sales that you fix up and make pretty. I bet you could do something like that. Especially for some of the Army spouses on base. The housing is so plain." Rayne had sat forward on her chair and leaned into the group, excited. "I saw that table that you refinished the other day. You know, the one that's in the front hall? It's beautiful! I couldn't believe that you did it yourself. I couldn't decoupage my way out of a paper bag!"

Everyone laughed.

"Well, if you need any help, I've learned a lot about financial aid forms, and applying to college. I'm happy to help you out, if you want," Harley told Emily.

"Thanks. I appreciate it. I'll think on it. You might just be the kick in the pants I need to get started on my degree," Emily told the other woman.

Harley opened her mouth to respond when Truck's cell phone rang. The theme to the TV show *The Big Bang Theory* blasting loud around the group. When

everyone laughed, the large man merely smiled lopsided-
ly and brought the phone up to his ear.

"Truck."

The smile immediately left his face, to be replaced
by a hard, intense scowl.

"Where are you? No, stay put. Do. Not. Move.
Woman. It's not an imposition. I'll be there in about
thirty minutes. Go inside…shit…then stay in your car.
Take a deep breath. That's it. Another. I'm coming to
you, everything's gonna be fine. I'll call you back in ten.
Make sure you answer." His voice dropped. "I
know…me too. I'll be there soon…I won't. 'Bye."

Truck stood up and motioned to Hollywood with
his head. The other man stood up and Harley saw them
talking intently with each other before Truck abruptly
turned and headed to the front of the house without a
word to the rest of the group.

When Hollywood came back to the group, Ghost
questioned, "Everything all right?"

Harley felt uncomfortable. It seemed as though
something was wrong and she didn't really know this
group of friends well enough to be in the middle of it.
Obviously sensing her unease, Coach took her hand in
his and squeezed.

"Yeah."

They all heard Truck's vehicle headed down the
road at a high rate of speed.

Hollywood continued, looking at Ghost. "It was Mary. She—"

"Mary?" Rayne exclaimed, standing up. She looked down at Ghost, panic in her gaze. "I should—"

"Truck's on it, Rayne. Sit." Ghost's tone was firm, but loving. He drew Rayne down until she was sitting in his lap and motioned for Hollywood to continue.

"Truck didn't say much. Just that Mary was on her way back from her appointment and needed some assistance. She didn't want to bother you, Rayne, so she called Truck."

"Oh. Okay, yeah. Her car has been having issues. Truck'll take care of it for her. I'm sure it really galled her to have to call him." Rayne half-laughed, not sounding as convincing as she probably thought she did.

Harley caught the glances between the men sitting around the table. It seemed to her that something was up, more than just Mary having car problems, but it wasn't her place to pry. Maybe later when she knew everyone better.

"He will," Ghost reassured his girlfriend easily. Changing the subject, and not being subtle about it, Ghost turned to Harley. "Thank you for saving Coach up there," he gestured upwards with his eyes. "We've gotten pretty fond of the guy and it would've sucked to have found another intelligence expert if he'd bit it."

Harley laughed weakly, not liking the fact that the

other man was joking around about Coach being dead, but understanding it was a part of the male badass psyche. "I'm not sure I really did much, as I've already told him, but you're welcome."

"So what happened up there after he was hit?" Beatle asked, leaning his elbows on the table in front of him.

Harley stiffened. She hadn't even really talked about everything with Coach, and wasn't sure she wanted to discuss it with all of his friends. She still remembered the feeling of panic she'd felt when they'd been flipped on their backs as they fell. Her mouth watered as the food she had just eaten sat in a ball in her throat, ready to come back up.

Everyone was looking at her expectedly.

"Excuse me, I need to use the restroom."

It was the only thing she could think to say to get herself out of the situation halfway politely. She stood, ignoring Beatle's, "Oh shit, I didn't mean to upset her," and fled the patio, letting herself into the house. She had no idea which way the bathroom was, but it couldn't be too hard to find.

After quickly wandering around, she found the small powder room off the front hall and shut herself in, sliding down the wall until she landed on her butt and resting her head on her knees. Her breaths came in quick pants, remembering the feeling of helplessness she'd felt as they'd been falling to the ground.

It wasn't a minute later when Harley heard a soft knock on the door.

"Harley? It's Coach. Can I come in?"

"I'll be out in a m-minute," she said back, not moving from her spot on the floor. She needed more than a minute to get herself put back together, especially if she was going to go back out and pretend that all was okay with Coach's friends. More so if she was going to have to talk about what had happened.

Harley looked up in shock as the door opened and Coach stepped in, closing the door behind him, engaging the lock…which was something she should've done in the first place.

"What are—"

She cut off her own words when Coach didn't speak, but merely sat down on the floor in front of her and pulled her into his embrace. It was awkward, they were both too tall to really be sitting on the floor of a small bathroom, but it still felt comforting to Harley.

Neither said anything for a long moment.

"We never really talked in-depth about what happened, did we, Harl?" Coach's words were low and gentle.

She shook her head, but didn't speak.

"I'm sorry. I should've asked. It helps to talk about it. The Army has gotten a lot better over the years in having their soldiers talk about shit with a psychiatrist when they get back from deployments. I've had my share of sessions, and as much as I hated it at first, I've found that it really does help me work through things in my head."

"I walked out on your friends," Harley told him without lifting her head from Coach's shoulder.

"They're fine. I'm sure Rayne is grilling Hollywood on her friend Mary, and why she called Truck instead of her. Hell, I'd like to know that myself, since it's always seemed as if Mary can't stand Truck, but I have more important things on my mind at the moment. Tell me, Harl. All of it."

Without moving her head, Harley did just that. If nothing else, she supposed Coach had a right to know, as it happened to him too…even if he wasn't conscious. She didn't leave anything out. From her thoughts about how beautiful the jump had been at first, how fast they seemed to be falling when she'd seen the plane above their heads, to the moment she flinched away from the shape coming at her head.

She told him when she realized for the first time that he was unconscious and how, when she'd tried to turn to look at him, she'd flipped them over and had almost put them into a flat spin. Harley even described her despair when she couldn't reach his hand or the steering loops to help them get to the ground.

It wasn't until she told him how she was afraid that

he'd break his ankles when he landed that Coach moved.

He pulled back and took hold of her head in his hands. He leaned in close, and whispered, "I'm amazed by you Harley. You did everything right. Everything."

"No, I—"

"Harley, listen to me," Coach insisted, not letting her continue. "Yes, you were scared. I would worry about you if you hadn't been. But you didn't panic. Even when we were on our backs. You used your head and got us back in the right position. When the AAD fired, you figured out what needed to be done, steered us away from a building, and then even got us landed. I could've been hurt more in so many ways, but you did everything right. I'm so sorry that this happened. So fucking sorry. But at the same time, I'm glad. If nothing else, it showed you how tough you are."

"I don't think I want to go skydiving again anytime soon."

Coach chuckled softly. "I don't blame you. And don't worry, this isn't like riding a horse. There's no need to get back on just to prove you can."

Harley nodded and looked up at Coach with dry eyes. "I'm okay now. Thanks for making me talk about it. You're right, I do feel better."

"You're welcome."

"I'm ready to go back outside."

"We're leaving." Coach shifted to the side and stood up, holding his hand down to Harley.

Without thought, she allowed him to help her to her feet. "But, that's rude. I need to go back out there and—"

"I already told them we'd be leaving."

"Seriously, Coach. I don't want them to—"

"It's fine. They understand."

"Would you quit interrupting me?" Harley groused, putting her free hand on her hip in agitation.

Coach smiled. "If you quit trying to say things that aren't true, then I'd quit interrupting you."

Harley rolled her eyes. "Please. I'm trying really hard to get better at this social thing. I'd like to say good-bye to your friends."

Coach eyed her for a moment, then put his hands on either side of her neck.

Harley liked the feel of his warm hands on her. She didn't feel confined or pressured. He was just resting his hands on her body. She closed her eyes and sighed, bringing her own hands up to rest on his forearms.

"Okay. Not that they would, but I won't let them, or anyone else, bully you into talking about what happened if you don't want to."

"Thanks. I don't want to talk about it," Harley admitted immediately. "At least not to them. I'll let you tell your friends whatever you want to…later. I'm just going to go out there and thank Fletch and Emily for their hospitality, maybe give Annie a hug if she can tear herself away from her Army men long enough, and tell everyone else it was nice to meet them."

"Sounds like a plan." Coach didn't pull back or otherwise move.

"Coach?"

He sighed. "I'm thinking about when I can see you again."

"After today, you still want to?" Harley joked.

He didn't even smile. "Oh yeah. Even more than when I picked you up."

"You're strange. Did you know that?" Harley teased, moving her hands up to grasp his wrists. They stood like that for a moment.

"We all go back on duty next week. We generally get up early and do PT, physical training, then we have time to go home and shower. We work pretty much all day, most days, with some flexibility. There's a chance we could get deployed at any moment. Sometimes we have a week or so notice, but more often than not we might only get an hour or so."

"Okay."

"I want to spend time with you. Meet your brother and sister. I'd love to watch you work, and help answer any questions you might have while you're doing it. I loved playing the video game with you the other night,

I'd like to do more of that too. I think with time you'll get more comfortable with my friends and their girlfriends as well. Bottom line, Harley, is that the thought of dropping you off at your place and not seeing you again for who knows how long, isn't that appealing to me. I like you. You're fun to be around. Relaxing. I don't feel like I have to put on a show with you. You have no idea how refreshing that is."

"I do know. I feel it too."

Coach leaned down and pressed his lips against hers, lightly, teasing her lips with his tongue, but not deepening the kiss when she opened to him. He pulled back. "Okay, so we'll talk on the phone. We'll do dinners together, your place or mine. We'll text and maybe chat online. If I can figure it out, I'll hook up my game player to the Internet and we can play together that way. I'm not rushing this."

"I can help figure out your game system thing."

"Good. But make no mistake, Harley."

He paused long enough, that Harley felt the need to ask, "No mistake about what?"

"I want you. I want to feel you writhing under me as I take you. I can't wait to see what you're hiding, not so successfully, under those T-shirts of yours. But this isn't just a sex thing. I like everything that I've seen so far."

"I'm not perfect, Coach. Far from it."

"I know. Neither am I. I wouldn't want to be

around you so much if you were. Don't you get it, Harl? The fact that your house is a mess, you eat too fast, tend to leave dishes in the sink, and forget to shower because you're so into your work…they're just a few reasons I'm into you. You're real."

"Oh."

"Yeah. Oh. After a while, when we're more comfortable with each other, and we've made out a few times, and when we can't keep our hands off each other for one more minute, we'll move our relationship to the next level."

"I'm a virgin," Harley blurted out, then immediately closed her eyes in embarrassment and hurried on. "Well, not exactly. There was this guy in college, he was trying to get me off and shoved his fingers inside me, thinking what he was doing was sexy, but it hurt. I accidently kneed him in the balls and that was that. Anyway, he didn't call me again, and I haven't exactly been feeling the need to jump into bed with anyone else. So I hope you don't build up what you think is gonna happen in your mind. It's probably gonna be awkward and I'm gonna suck at it."

Coach chuckled and Harley opened her eyes, only to see him even closer than he was before. "It might be awkward. Sex with someone the first time usually is, Harl. But I can promise you, I won't hurt you. I'm gonna make you feel so good, you won't feel uncomfortable at all."

"I'm so embarrassed I told you all that."

"I'm not. I'm glad. I was already going to go slow with you, now I know I just need to make sure you're really ready for me before I take you."

Harley couldn't look away from Coach's hazel eyes. She felt as if she was in someone else's body. This sort of thing didn't happen to her.

"Come on, Harley. Enough heavy talk for the bathroom. Let's go say 'bye to my friends and get you home."

"Yeah, I do need to work some more on my game."

Coach smiled and leaned down and kissed her one more time, before enveloping her in a hug. Without a word, he let go, and took hold of her hand. They left the bathroom together and went back onto the porch.

Harley said her good-byes, got a hug from Annie, just as she wanted to, and she and Coach left, promising to come back again soon.

After arriving at her townhouse, Coach walked her to her door, smiling as the curtains fluttered in the window next door. Good ol' Gretel, keeping watch on the neighborhood.

"Don't stay up too late. I'll call you later. Okay?"

"I'd like that. I'm sorry if I made you leave before you were ready."

"It's fine. I was ready to go. I have a slight headache

and I'm gonna go home and take a nap." He held up a hand to forestall any comments from her. "And before you say anything. It's not bad. I'll take a Tylenol or two and sleep for an hour, and be fine."

"Call me when you get up."

He smiled. "I will. Will you answer?"

"Of course. I might be engrossed in my code, but I always have my phone nearby just in case Davidson or Montesa calls."

"Or me."

Harley blushed, but agreed. "Or you now."

Coach kissed her one more time, and brushed the back of his hand down her cheek. "We'll talk soon. Later."

"Thanks for taking me to meet your friends, Coach. Even if I was a weirdo."

He merely smiled as he stepped away from her. "My pleasure. 'Bye, Harley."

"'Bye, Coach."

She watched as he climbed back into his Highlander and pulled out of the parking lot. Harley closed the door and smiled. It'd been a weird day, but she was pretty sure she and Coach were now dating. She hugged herself. It felt good. Damn good.

Chapter Fourteen

"**H**EY, COACH."

"Harl. Are you about ready?"

Harley looked up at the clock over her computer. Shit. She meant to get up about thirty minutes ago and change, but as usual, got engrossed in what she was doing.

"No." She didn't try to lie.

Coach merely laughed. "Yeah, I didn't think so. It's okay, our reservations aren't for another hour. Go get ready. I'll be there in thirty."

Harley smiled. He hadn't told her he was doing it, but it was obvious he'd started telling her he'd be there thirty minutes before he actually would. He'd call before he came over as his thirty-minute warning. She appreciated it. She'd never be ready if he didn't prod her to get going before he came over.

"Okay. I'll leave the door open for you."

"No," Coach said. "Don't. It's not safe. I'll just knock when I get there. No big deal."

"I should give you a key," Harley mused, more to

herself than Coach as she walked toward her bedroom so she could change.

"As much as I'd love to have unfettered access to you and your place whenever I wanted, I would rather you wait and give me a key once you're one hundred percent sure of our relationship."

Harley sat heavily on the side of her bed. The unmade state not fazing her in the least. "What do you mean?"

"I mean that I have a feeling you're waiting for the other shoe to fall," Coach said matter-of-factly. "There's a part of you that still believes I'm going to 'wise up' and realize I don't know what I'm doing with you. That I'll be there one day and gone the next."

Harley didn't say anything. She couldn't. He was right.

"Right. So until you're sure of my feelings for you, I'll wait. You can give me a key to your place when you completely trust that I'm not fucking around with you. Okay?"

"I don't mean to—"

"I know you don't. And it's fine. To tell you the truth, I like it."

"You like the fact that there's a part of me that doubts you really like me as much as you seem to?" Harley was confused.

He chuckled. "Yeah. It means that when you *do* finally realize it, I'll have you heart and soul. You'll be mine forever."

"Um…"

"I've had a key made for you since the barbeque at Fletch's house a month ago."

"What?"

"Yup. I'll bring it over tonight. I probably should've waited and talked about this face-to-face rather than over the phone, but when you said you'd leave your door unlocked, I couldn't. So…go get changed. I'll be there in half an hour and we'll go meet Davidson and Montesa at the restaurant. We'll come back to my place and hang out for a while. Yeah?"

Harley swallowed hard. "Okay."

"And don't worry. I'm not going to do anything crazy in front of your siblings. They'll like me."

"I'm not worried about that."

"What are you worried about then?"

"Gah. You are too perceptive, Coach."

He laughed. "What are you worried about, Harl?"

"That they'll think you're too good for me."

Coach burst out laughing on the other end of the line. He laughed so hard and so long, Harley got mad. "Coach! It's not funny."

"Oh man, it's hilarious. Harley, your brother and sister are gonna like me, but there's no way they're going to think I'm too good for you. You have it all backwards. They're gonna start out the night thinking you, their baby sister, is way too good for *me*. I'm an Army soldier. They'll probably think I'm out only to get in your pants. Eventually, hopefully by the end of the night, they'll see that I'm crazy about you. That as much as I want in those delectable pants of yours, that's not why I'm with you. I'm nowhere in your league, but I'm hoping that my sincerity and genuine interest in you will shine through and they'll give me their blessing anyway."

"I don't know what to say to that."

"That's because I'm right. Go get dressed. Time's a ticking. I'll be there in twenty-five minutes now."

"Okay. See you soon."

"'Bye, Harl."

Harley clicked off her phone and fell backward on her messy covers.

Was Coach right? She'd always thought *he* was too good for *her*, but now that she thought about it, she could see his point. She'd earned her master's degree and had a great job that she loved. She had a great family and was happy with her life. Army life wasn't exactly the most stable, with all the moving around the soldiers had to do. Not to mention the fact of Coach's mysterious "missions." He'd been gone once since they'd been seeing each other, and it was only for three days, but it was enough for her to really question what it was he did for the Army. Before she slept with him, she needed to know.

She sat up and ran her fingers through her hair. Yeah, Montesa and Davidson would be more concerned about Coach and if he was good enough for her. The thought made her grin. She was sure Coach could hold his own against Montesa's courtroom tactics, but it'd be fun to watch.

Her brother and sister had been pushing her to let them meet Coach for a couple of weeks, ever since they'd figured out that she'd been spending every extra minute with the man. Between their schedules, and hers, this was the first time everyone had been free.

They were meeting at Bella Sera. It was a high-end Italian restaurant, but not so much so that her siblings would feel uncomfortable. It was a local favorite and Coach figured Montesa and Davidson had most likely been there before. Montesa had wanted to bring John along, but Harley refused. She didn't want anyone else ganging up against her, or Coach, in their quest to make their relationship work. It was bad enough he had to go head-to-head with her siblings, adding in extra people wasn't fair right off the bat.

Standing up, Harley wandered to her closet, knowing just what she wanted to wear. Montesa had bought it for her a while ago, and it wasn't normally something Harley felt comfortable wearing. But tonight seemed right. It would make a statement to Montesa that she was wearing the dress for the first time…but also to Coach. Hopefully he'd read her message to him loud and clear.

Harley got dressed and studied herself in the mirror in her bathroom. She felt good. Pretty. She had no desire to dress like this on a regular basis, but she understood a bit more now why women got all dolled up when going out with their boyfriends or husbands. She just hoped Coach would appreciate the effort she'd gone to for him. And make no mistake, it was most definitely for him, and not herself.

Hearing a knock on her door downstairs, Harley shoved her feet into the two-inch black heels that she'd only worn once. Again, Montesa had urged her to buy them one day, and in a moment of weakness, Harley had given in. They had straps that wound around her ankles, and her freshly painted red toenails peeked out the toes. They weren't Jimmy Choos or Manolo Blahniks, but for her, they might as well have been.

She made her way carefully down the stairs, so she didn't fall flat on her face in the unfamiliar heels, and to the door. Looking through the peephole, Harley saw that it was indeed Coach and opened the door, anticipation at his reaction coursing through her veins.

"Hey, Coach. For once I'm ready when you get here."

Coach stood on the step that led into Harley's townhome and stared in disbelief. He ran his eyes from her head down to her toes, then back up again. He couldn't even believe it was the same woman he'd gotten to know over the last month or so. The Harley he knew eschewed dresses and skirts, and usually wore oversize T-shirts when they were hanging around together. He'd seen her in a tank top once, but that was only because he'd stopped by to see her one evening when she wasn't expecting him. She'd quickly gone to change into something less revealing.

Knowing his mouth was hanging open, but not able to close it, Coach looked his fill at the woman who had begun to mean the world to him.

She was wearing a black dress that would've been modest on most women, but because it was Harley, and she wasn't secure in her femininity, it was even more sexy. The dress had a halter top that tied around the back of her neck and dipped low in front, showcasing her shoulders. Coach could see a hint of cleavage where the V ended between her breasts. It clung tightly to her ribcage, outlining her body and delectable curves. Instead of flaring out at her hips, it went straight down to right above her knees. There was a slit in one side, and when she turned to grab a small black purse sitting on a table near the door, Coach could see nothing but bare back.

Rounding out her outfit was a pair of black heels. The straps looked complicated, and sexy as hell, as they wrapped around her ankles. The only splash of color on her body was the red paint on her toes.

He wanted to tug on the small bow at the nape of her neck to bare her to his gaze. He wanted to put his hands on her and learn every curve, up close and personal. Over the last month, they'd made out on her couch, or his, but Coach had tried to keep his hands on top of her clothes. He could literally feel his mouth watering with the need to taste her…all over.

"Is it…do I look okay?" Harley asked in a trembling voice, pushing her glasses up on her nose. "I know my glasses don't exactly go with the outfit."

"Shit. Yes. You look amazing. The glasses are perfect. They give you that naughty librarian look or something, I…" Coach couldn't think straight. A thought suddenly came to him. "Are you wearing anything under that?"

"Underwear, yes. A bra, no. Why? Should I be? It's backless…Shit, are my nipples showing?" Harley looked down at herself, trying to see if she was indecent. When she turned to head toward the bathroom off the hallway to check her outfit, Coach caught her arm and pulled her back to face him.

He couldn't keep his hands off her if his life depended on it. Not having the ability to look her in the eyes at the moment, he ran one fingertip across her collarbone and into the V of the dress, skimming her warm skin as he went. He felt her inhale as his finger brushed against the side of one breast, then the other.

"Your nipples aren't showing at all. More's the pity." He finally looked up into her eyes. "You are beautiful. And it's not the dress. You've always been beautiful. But tonight…" His finger veered farther under the dress, entering territory he hadn't explored skin-on-skin yet. "You wore this for me, didn't you?"

Harley nodded, speechless.

Coach moved his finger just a bit more to the right and encountered his target. Her nipple beaded even further as he ran his fingernail over it. "You know tonight will be torture for me, don't you?" He didn't seem to expect a response, because he kept talking. "I'll be thinking about what you don't have on under this."

"Coach," Harley warned, bringing one hand up to grab his wrist. She didn't pull it away from herself though, she just held on, as if she wasn't sure if she wanted to stop or urge him to keep going.

He moved his finger away from her erect nipple and meandered it over to her other breast, circling the beaded nub there, giving it the same attention he gave the opposite one as he spoke. "You're beautiful, Harley. I can't wait to get my lips around these beauties. But to ease your worries for tonight, the dress has enough material that I can't tell you're excited under it…I only know because of this…" He flicked the tip of her nipple and smiled at her indrawn breath.

"I wouldn't embarrass you in front of your family. I'd tell you if I thought the dress was inappropriate. It's anything but. It's beautiful, and so are you. But damn, I might embarrass *myself* with this hard-on if I'm not careful." He smiled, not embarrassed in the least at the erection prodding against her stomach.

Keeping one hand on her breast, Coach brought the other one up to her face and held her gently. "Thank you for getting dressed up for me, Harley."

"You're welcome. Um, Coach?"

"Yeah?"

She shifted in front of him, and he smiled at her obvious arousal.

"When we go back to your apartment tonight…I'd like to stay, if that's all right."

Coach closed his eyes and fought to bring his libido under control. He opened them again and gazed into her anxious brown eyes. "That's more than all right. But, Harley, I'm repeating this, just so you understand it…"

He waited for her to acknowledge his serious tone. When she raised her eyebrows at him, he continued.

"I've wanted you for a month. You wearing this sexy-as-all-get-out dress isn't why I want you. Okay?"

She smiled and nodded. "It's a good thing. Because I think it's the only dress I own and don't be surprised if I spill half my dinner all over myself when we eat."

Coach removed his hand from the front of her dress, reluctantly, and kissed her on the lips gently. "I'll help clean you up if you spill. You'll never know what it means to me, however, that you went all out for me tonight. You have a bag packed?"

Harley nodded shyly. "It's around the corner. I wasn't going to bring it up if you weren't receptive to the idea."

"I'm receptive. Extremely receptive."

"Good."

"Tell me where it is, I'll grab it and we'll get going. I don't want to be late the first time I meet Montesa and Davidson. But Harley?"

"Yeah?"

"If we weren't meeting them, we wouldn't leave the house."

Harley giggled, loving that she could turn him on so much that he didn't really even want to leave her place. "My bag is sitting in the kitchen, around the counter."

Coach leaned down and kissed her briefly before taking a step back. He adjusted his obvious erection as he walked, which made Harley smile even wider. She'd never been the kind of woman to make men get hard-ons…and it felt good.

He came back around the corner, her bag in his hand, and smiled. "Jesus. Seriously. You look great."

Coach held out his elbow, and Harley grabbed hold, handing her keys to him so he could lock her door. "I don't know about that, but I appreciate the sentiment."

"I don't care if you believe it or not, honestly," Coach told her as he locked her door, keeping her by his side. "But every man who sees you tonight is gonna be jealous as hell of me. As much as I want to take you to my apartment and unwrap you, I'm looking forward to having you by my side, meeting your siblings, and generally showing everyone we meet tonight how beautiful you are."

They walked toward his Highlander. "But don't mistake me, Harley," he cautioned.

She looked up at him in confusion. "About what?"

"Every time I go somewhere with you, I feel the same way. No matter what you're wearing. I'm a lucky man, and I know it."

Harley rolled her eyes. "Coach, I don't mind if you compliment me while I'm wearing this. I did make a conscious decision to put it on tonight, hoping to surprise you. Just as I don't expect you to put on your dress-blue uniform every time we go out, you shouldn't expect me to always make this much effort. I'm sure I'll love you in your uniform, just as you love me in this dress, but most of the time we'll be in our normal clothes. I'm happy being around you no matter what you wear."

"There's an Army Ball later this year. Will you go with me?"

"Will you be wearing your uniform?"

"Yes. And all the guys will be there in theirs too."

"Yes. If we're still together, I'd love to go with you."

Coach helped Harley step up into the vehicle, making sure she didn't lose her balance as she scooted in. When she was seated, he held out her seat belt and leaned in as she buckled it. "We're still going to be together."

Harley smiled up at him. "Okay."

"We are," he insisted.

"I said okay, Coach."

"You said it, but I'm not sure you believe it."

Harley rolled her eyes. "You aren't a fortune teller. You can't know for sure. You might get annoyed with all the time I spend on my computer. Or I might decide that you're too much of a neat freak for me. You can't know what will happen in the future. I'd love to go to the ball with you, but we'll cross that bridge when we come to it."

"I'm not going to get annoyed with you, and if it will make you feel better, I'll leave my dishes in the sink overnight. I might not be able to tell the future, but I have no doubt whatsoever that, after tonight, taking your sweet body for the first time, I'll want to get in there again. And again. Making love with you is going to be unbelievably awesome, and it's going to be the icing on the cake that is Harley Kelso. Because I'm already so addicted to you it's not even funny. So yeah, a few months is nothing. I'm tempted to ask you to go to my retirement ceremony as well. I'm *that* sure I'll still want to be with you in the future."

"Coach," Harley protested in a weak voice. She hadn't heard such heartfelt words...ever. Certainly not aimed at herself.

"Watch your arm, I'm closing your door," he warned, grinning warmly at her as he stepped back.

She held her arm out of the way and waited as Coach walked around the car, opened the back door to put her bag on the floor of the backseat, then got into the driver's seat. He started the SUV as if he hadn't just rocked her world.

"Are you planning on retiring soon?" Harley asked as they started toward the restaurant.

"Nope. I've got at least ten more years to go."

Harley was silent when he didn't elaborate. Deciding to let it go and bring up one more heavy subject before dinner, she ventured, "I have a question, but I'm not sure you're gonna want to answer it. And I'm not asking because I'm being nosey, I just need to know what to tell Montesa and Davidson. They've already asked, and I didn't know how to answer them."

"Shoot."

"Are you Delta Force?"

If she hadn't been watching him so carefully, she would've missed the flinch that he immediately controlled. Harley went on quickly. "Again, I don't care. But it's just that Davidson brought it up right after the accident. I didn't know, and he said that you probably were since you have missions that don't last for long periods of time. He mentioned something about Rangers and Special Forces, but I don't remember what he said. I won't say anything about it to anyone, I just—"

"You're too smart for your own good." Coach said as he put his hand over hers on the console between them. "I can't talk about my job. Not to you or your family. Delta Force is one of the most secretive Special Forces groups in the military. You might hear on the news that SEAL Team Six was on a mission to kill Osama Bin Laden, or you might see a movie about them being dropped into Mogadishu, but you'll never see or hear anything like that about Delta Force teams. Deltas never talk about what they do. They're sent into situations knowing no one will ever know they were there.

"The divorce rates of Delta Force soldiers are high, higher than the rest of the Army, simply because of the secrecy involved. They can't tell their spouses where they're going or when they'll be back. It's too much for a lot of couples. I never thought about it in the past. Never thought about how tough it would be to keep that kind of secret from someone I was with, it hasn't ever been an issue in my past relationships because I knew they weren't the forever kind. But, I find myself understanding now how hard that would be on a SF soldier."

Coach paused, but his thumb ran back and forth over the back of her hand as they waited for the light to turn green. Finally, he turned to Harley and looked her straight in the eye. "I won't ever lie to you, Harl. Being with me won't always be a walk in the park, but I don't lie."

Harley nodded, understanding what he was saying. He hadn't said he *was* a Delta Force soldier, but he also hadn't denied it. Lying was one thing, leaving details out was another thing altogether.

"I appreciate that, Coach," she told him earnestly, not looking away from his eyes.

It wasn't until a honk behind them sounded that they looked away from each other. As he started driving, he said casually, "The good thing about me having such good work friends, and some of them having girlfriends, is that you can now go to them to talk when you're worried about something. They'll be feeling the same thing as you. It gives you a support system of sorts."

"It does," Harley agreed, smiling. "Thank you. I'll

try not to ask too many questions about what you do."

"You can ask," he quickly countered. "Just understand when I can't answer."

"I will. I appreciate your help the other night when I was stuck on my code."

Smiling wider now that she'd changed the subject, Coach said, "No problem. I had thought maybe you were calling to continue where we left off at your doorstep, but quickly realized that it wasn't phone sex you were after, just for me to describe, in detail, what happens when a sniper sets up on top of a building."

"Oh, did you want to have phone sex?" Harley asked innocently with a gleam in her eye.

Coach laughed. The tension in the car was gone. "I wouldn't turn it down, just so you know, but I think the real thing is gonna ruin me for any kind of phone sex we might have in the future."

Harley squirmed in her seat. She shouldn't even have brought it up. She knew Coach wouldn't let it go. But she was glad that she'd lightened the mood. "I don't know; we'll just need to get creative."

"Shit, Harl. I know I walked right into that one, but have a little mercy on me, would ya? I already got rid of one hard-on tonight. Please don't give me another right before we get to the restaurant. I'm not sure I've got it in me to will another one away."

Harley patted Coach's hand. "You'll be fine. Oh,

and I did tell you that Montesa is one of the most successful trial lawyers in the area, right?"

"Okay, that worked," Coach griped good-naturedly. "Yeah, you told me. I'm a little afraid of her, if you want to know."

"As you should be," she returned immediately, teasing Coach further.

They grinned at each other and Coach turned into the parking lot of the restaurant. He parked and turned to face Harley.

"I'm excited to meet your brother and sister, but the bottom line is, even if they don't like me, we're still going back to my apartment tonight. I'll just have to work harder to gain their approval. I'm not letting you slip out of my fingers, Harley."

"They're gonna like you," Harley told him. "Don't worry. But yeah, I've waited long enough. I want you. I'm ready."

"Fuuuuck," Coach groaned. "Come on, we're five minutes late, I'm sure they're waiting for us."

Harley didn't take offense at Coach abruptly ending their conversation and jumping out of the car. It was kind of fun to tease him. But she hadn't lied. She couldn't wait until tonight. She wasn't even nervous. Much. She wanted to see Coach without a stitch of clothing on more than she wanted to preserve her own modesty. She was that into him.

For once, Harley waited for Coach to come around and give her his arm before she got out. She wouldn't put it past herself to fall flat on her face trying to get out of the Highlander in the small heels on her own.

As they walked to the front door of the restaurant, Harley turned to Coach and whispered, "Thank you for tonight."

"For what?"

"For wanting to meet Davidson and Montesa. For making me feel beautiful. For recognizing the effort I went to for you. For it all."

"You're welcome. Although the pleasure was all mine. And *will* be all mine later." He opened the door and they entered the dim and intimate restaurant.

Harley opened her mouth to respond to Coach when she heard, "Harley!" She turned and saw Montesa and Davidson standing by the hostess's station, grinning from ear to ear, as if they'd been able to hear Coach's last words.

She blushed. Harley knew they hadn't overheard him, but it looked as though this was going to be a long dinner.

As she went forward to give her siblings a hug, for the first time ever, she wished that she was an only child and she and Coach could go straight back to his place.

Chapter Fifteen

"SO YOU REALLY like this guy, huh?" Montesa remarked when she and Harley were in the restroom later that evening.

"Yeah. I do."

"For what it's worth, I do too."

"Whew!" Harley pantomimed, wiping her brow. Then got serious. "Thanks, Montesa. I appreciate you going easy on him tonight and not pulling out the whole lawyer persona."

Her sister laughed. "I have to admit that I *had* planned on grilling him."

"What changed your mind?" Harley asked, wiping her hands dry on a paper towel before throwing it away.

"You did. Specifically, your outfit."

"What? Really?" She tried to sound surprised, but wasn't sure she pulled it off.

"Uh huh. Harley, in the two years since we bought that dress together, you haven't worn it once. Not once. When I asked why, you told me—"

Harley interrupted her sister, knowing what she was

going to say. "That I would wear it when I had someone I wanted to impress." She remembered that conversation clearly. At the time she hadn't thought it'd ever happen.

"Exactly. So you wearing it, tonight of all nights, when you're introducing Coach to us, told me that he wasn't just another guy."

Harley hugged her sister tightly. "I like him," she whispered, as if she were spilling state secrets. "And I think he likes me too."

Montesa pulled back. "Oh he likes you all right."

"Really?"

"Really. He can't take his eyes off of you."

Harley smiled in delight. "What awful things do you think Davidson is telling him about me?"

"There's no telling with him. We'd better get back out there before he spills the beans about that time when you were five and sleepwalked naked through his slumber party."

"Oh shit," Harley exclaimed, horrified. "You're right, he'd totally tell Coach that story. Come on, let's go!"

"I DON'T KNOW why she's embarrassed by it, she was asleep. *I* was mortified…all my friends had seen my sister naked!"

Coach chuckled at Davidson's story about Harley surprising him and his friends during a sleepover when he was nine when she'd suddenly appeared, naked as the day she was born, and walked through the group, oblivious as to what she was doing since she was asleep.

The night had been good. He genuinely liked both Montesa and Davidson. They were down-to-earth people who obviously cared a great deal about their sister. It made him feel good that Harley had that.

Montesa had only grilled him a little bit, and seemed to rein herself in when she realized she was doing it. Davidson had given him a few side glances, obviously trying to get a good feel for him and what his thoughts were for his little sister.

"So, you like Harley," Davidson said, bringing it out in the open for the first time.

Finished with their meals and hanging out in the lounge area waiting for Harley and her sister to return from the bathroom, Coach didn't mind addressing it, but only until they got back. He didn't want to embarrass Harley in any way.

"Yeah. She's great. I like everything about her."

"She looks nice tonight," Davidson noted.

"She does."

"She doesn't always look like that—"

"Seriously?" Coach ground out. "You think I don't know that? You think I care?" Not giving Harley's brother a chance to respond, he went on, agitated, "If you must know, I actually prefer her everyday look. She's too nervous tonight. Part of it is you and your sister and the fact I'm meeting you guys for the first time, I know, but the other part is that she's just not comfortable in the dress. I love that she wore it for me, but she's much more…Harley…when she's wearing her sweats and T-shirt and swearing at her TV or computer screen as she tries to figure out the game she's working on."

Coach took a breath to continue berating the other man, but paused when he saw Davidson was smiling. "What?"

"You. I was just making a comment. I was *going* to say, that she doesn't always look like that, but it's obvious you don't care."

"Oh."

Davidson chuckled. "Yeah, oh. And I'm pleased as all get out that you think so and would jump to her defense so quickly. Harley hasn't had an easy life, but she's an amazing person, through and through. All I ask is that if there comes a time when you find you don't care for her as much as a man who wants her in his life forever would, please let her down easy."

"I will. Although you should know, I have no intention of letting her go. I'm not an idiot. I've been around the block a few times and have seen way more than my share of shit. I know a good thing when I see it. And when I find something I like, I stick. Like glue."

"I have one other thing I'd like to discuss, but I know that it's a tricky subject."

"My job," Coach responded accurately.

"Yeah." Davidson held up a hand to forestall the denial that Coach obviously was ready to give. "I'm not asking for you to tell me any details. I just wanted to say that I've worked a few government contracts in my time, living near Killeen makes that almost inevitable, but now that I've met you, I can see my suspicions about you and your friends are most likely correct."

Davidson took a breath, obviously considering his next words, then continued. "Thank you for what you do. Seriously. I know the world will never know the half of it, but thank you anyway. With that said, you need to do whatever you can to keep your work from affecting Harley as much as possible. Whether it's a damn terrorist who wants to get back at you and your team for something, or if she can't deal with long absences from you, or even if the secrecy starts to get to her…take care of my sister. Don't let her stew on anything, because she will, if only to try to keep you from knowing something is going on in her head. She acts tough, but she's not nearly as hardy as she might portray to the world."

Coach leaned forward on the bar-height table, resting on his elbows. He met Davidson's gaze directly. "I hear you, and I have every intention of making sure I'm always communicating with Harley. I'm sure in time she'll learn more about what it is I do, but you have nothing to worry about when it comes to your sister. I'll protect her with my life, and my teammates will do the same. I have no intention of doing anything to make her worry more than I know she already will. And if there's anything I don't think I can handle myself, I'll call you."

"Then welcome to the family, Coach." Davidson stuck out his hand.

Coach grasped it and shook hands firmly with Harley's brother. "Thanks. I appreciate it. More than you know."

"What do you appreciate?" Harley asked, arriving at the table with her sister. Coach reached out and put an arm around her waist as she stood next to the table. She settled into his half embrace, enjoying the feeling of his arm around her.

"Nothing. Guy talk, sis," Davidson told her with a teasing grin.

"Shit, we don't want to know," Montesa griped. "I hate to be the one to bring this little party to a close, but I need to get going. John and I have a case we're trying in the morning."

"Thank you for coming," Harley told her earnestly. "We missed our dinner last week, so it was good to catch up."

"Definitely." Montesa pulled back and turned her gaze to Coach. "Take care of her."

"Always," Coach returned easily, shaking her hand as well. "It was great meeting you. Maybe sometime we can do this again, and I can meet your friend, John."

"Sure. That'd be great."

"On that note, I need to be going too," Davidson said. "You guys stay as long as you want. I've already paid the bill."

"What? No! It was my turn this week!" Harley protested.

"Nope. You got pizza the other week," her brother told her definitively.

"That didn't count! Jesus, you guys never let me pay," Harley sulked.

Coach smirked, liking Harley's siblings even more. He wouldn't let her pay either if she was his little sister.

"Deal," Montesa told her unsympathetically.

"Whatever." Then as if she hadn't been pouting, Harley smiled. "Drive safe, you guys. Let me know when you get home."

"Of course."

"Always do."

Both Montesa and Davidson waved as they headed toward the front of the restaurant.

Harley turned to Coach. She was still standing next to the table and she felt Coach's fingers stroking her hip over the material of the dress. "You want anything else?"

"No."

"You sure?" Harley pressed. "We could get another glass of wine or something."

Coach leaned into Harley and brushed a lock of hair back over her ear. His lips brushed her lobe as he said, "What I want, I can't get here in the middle of a public place."

"Oh."

Harley's breaths sped up, and Coach inwardly smiled, glad he could affect her the same way she affected him. "You ready to go?"

"Yeah." Harley turned to him fully. "They liked you."

"And I liked them. They're great, Harley."

She smiled, seemingly relieved that her siblings liked her boyfriend, and the feeling had been mutual. "I'm ready to go."

"Just to be clear about what's going to happen to-night." Coach kept his voice low so the people at the surrounding tables couldn't hear him. "We're gonna go back to my place and I'm gonna strip this dress, which has been driving me crazy all night, off your body. Then I'm going to take my time, learning what you like and what makes you squirm under me. You're going to orgasm at least once before I ease myself inside your hot, wet body. I'll go slowly so you can adjust to me. Once you're comfortable, I'm going to move, slowly at first, then faster, until you can feel nothing but me. You okay with all that?"

"Yes and no."

Coach didn't even tense up. Harley was practically panting. She shifted from foot to foot as she stood next to him. She was aroused by his blunt talk. "What's the no part?"

"I want to touch you too."

"Jesus," Coach breathed. "Okay, amended plan then. I'll learn what you like, you learn what I like. Then I'll make you come, then I'll make love to you. Better?"

"Uh huh."

Coach put one hand under Harley's chin and turned her head until she had no choice but to look at him. "If at any time you want to stop, just say so. I'll stop. Got it?"

"Stop? Coach, there's no way I'll want you to stop. I can't wait for you to put your hands and mouth on me. Your finger on my...nipple tonight almost made me explode as I stood there. I can only imagine what your mouth on me will do. So no, I'm not going to want you to stop. No way, no how."

Coach couldn't stop the silly smile from curving over his lips. "Okay, sweetheart. No stopping. Come on, let's get this show on the road."

Chapter Sixteen

HARLEY SUPPOSED SHE should've been nervous about finally being naked with Coach, but she wasn't. Over the last month or so, she'd spent almost every waking hour with him. When they weren't together, and weren't working, they'd talked on the phone. He'd come over and they'd play a quick game of *This is War*, or he'd sit in her office and they'd both work until it was time for him to go home.

She'd been over to his apartment a couple of times, but it seemed they both usually preferred her townhouse. But it was important to her, for some reason, that they made love the first time in his bed. Harley wasn't sure why, except that it seemed right.

The ride to his apartment was quiet, but not uncomfortably so. Harley could barely sit still; she was more than ready to take this next step with Coach. They'd spent so much time together, she felt as if she truly knew the man. She knew his favorite things to eat, how he tended to always look to the right first when he cleared a scene in one of her video games, that he preferred to sleep on his back than in any other position, that the men he worked with were like brothers to him, and that he had a soft spot for little Annie.

All in all, Harley liked everything about him. The fact that her sister and brother also seemed to like him was simply a home run.

Coach pulled up into his parking space at his apartment complex and shut off the engine. Without a word, he climbed out. Harley followed suit and managed to get out without tripping over her feet. Before she could take a step, Coach was there. He didn't comment on the fact that she hadn't waited for him to open her door, as usual, merely put one arm around her waist and pulled her into his side.

Harley snuck her own arm around his waist and tucked her hand into one of his back pockets. As they walked toward his apartment, she could feel his butt flexing as they walked. Smirking, and feeling bold, she squeezed it tightly and smiled up at him. His stride faltered, but he didn't stop.

"You're playing with fire, Harl," he commented dryly as they approached his door.

"Good."

Coach unlocked the door and held it open for her. Harley walked into his space and before she could turn around to face him again, felt both of Coach's arms engulf her from behind. The door snicked closed, but all

Harley could concentrate on was the man standing behind her.

One arm wrapped around her waist and rested on her opposite hip. He'd swung the other one over her shoulder and his palm snaked inside the V of her dress to cup her naked breast. Harley moaned and rested her head back on his shoulder.

"God, Coach."

"You have no idea how much this dress has been driving me crazy all night. How *you* have been driving me crazy. Every time you moved, I swore I could see a hint of your nipple. When you leaned over the table to smack your brother, your dress dipped just enough that I *know* I could see your nipple. Your scent, your sideways glances…all of it has been a precursor to this moment. To me having you in my arms."

Harley moaned as Coach's fingers lightly pinched her nipple, making it even harder than it'd been all night. She tried to turn in his arms, but he wouldn't let her.

"No, let me play, Harley. Please."

She squirmed where she stood, but didn't try to get away.

"You're perfect," Coach murmured in her ear, his warm breath tickling and making goosebumps break out on her arms. "Spread your legs farther apart."

She did as Coach asked, widening her stance. She

felt the hand at her waist slowly pulling up the skirt of the dress.

"I imagined doing this from the moment I saw you tonight. Putting my hands on you. Listening to you moan as I touched you. You're beautiful, Harley. Wearing a sexy-as-sin black dress, or wearing what you call your fat pants. It doesn't matter. I can't tell you how many times I've fantasized about pulling the drawstring to your sweats and stripping them down your legs. Or pushing up whatever huge T-shirt you're wearing and sucking on your nipples."

Harley reached behind her and palmed the back of Coach's head. "If you don't stop talking, I'm gonna lose it right here."

"That's the goal, Harl. I can see, and feel, how turned on you are by my dirty words."

He tightened his hold on her breast and squeezed. His thumb stroked her nipple as he did it, and Harley could swear she felt herself swell in his hand. She arched her back and pushed into his grip. "Yes. God, Coach. Harder."

Coach took her earlobe between his lips and sucked, running his tongue over the small diamond stud in her ear. Harley shivered again.

"Just feel, Harley. I've got this. I've got you. Let's see if I can get you off this way."

Coach's hand had gathered up the skirt of her dress

far enough to expose her panties. They were black lace, to match her outfit. "Later, I want to see these more clearly, but man, from this angle, they are sexy as hell."

Harley looked down and saw Coach's dark hand against the white of her thigh. It was erotic as anything she'd ever seen and she couldn't look away.

"Hold this, Harley. Hold your skirt up and out of the way so I can see what I'm doing to you."

Without thinking, Harley's free hand moved to grab hold of the material of her dress, freeing Coach's fingers to trace the front panel of her panties. She shivered, and couldn't stop her natural reaction of pushing her hips into his touch.

"Shhhh, I've got you, Harl. No worries. Close your eyes."

She tipped her head back, resting it again on Coach's shoulder and doing as he suggested, closing her eyes. She couldn't think straight, from his fingers on her nipple, rolling and tugging, to his other hand getting closer and closer to her soaked folds. All she could think about was Coach.

"So pretty. I can feel how wet you are already, and I haven't even touched you yet." Coach ran a finger down her panties, tracing her folds through the cotton.

Harley moaned again. "Please, Coach. Touch me."

"I am touching you."

"You know what I mean."

"Tell me," he ordered in a gruff voice.

"My clit. Please. I want to come."

"Oh yeah, I love that. Tell me what you want."

Harley squirmed in Coach's tight grip, wanting his fingers inside her, stroking her...wanting all of it.

His touch went back up to the front of her panties and instead of pushing them off, his hand pushed under the elastic and down, brushing against her tight curls. He didn't tease this time, and she felt two fingers glide over her clit, down through her folds, and push just inside her.

"Yes, Coach!" She tipped her hips forward, trying to give him more room, a better angle, something.

"Soaked," Coach breathed. His fingers continued their sweep of her sex, spreading her juices up to her clit, then pushing back down and teasing her entrance before gliding back up. He kept a running commentary as he teased her.

"I can't wait to bury my face down there. You'll taste so good, I won't be able to get enough of you. You're gonna be so tight around my dick, you'll squeeze me so hard I have a feeling I'm gonna lose it before I even get started. It's been a while for me, hon, and I can't wait to feel your hot sheath sucking me in. Are you always this wet? It's amazing."

Harley couldn't answer him if her life depended on it. She was so close to the edge and needed to be pushed over. But Coach's fingers never stayed in one place long enough to get her there.

When his fingers brushed over her clit once more, she jolted in his embrace and couldn't stop the plea. "There. More. Coach, please."

"Here, Harley?" he teased, rubbing against her clit with two fingers.

She moaned. "Yesssss. Harder."

His hand tightened on her breast and Harley arched her back, pushing against both his hand at her chest and the one down her panties at the same time.

"Hang on to me, Harley," Coach ordered in a voice that was no longer teasing. "I can't wait to see you come."

Harley opened her mouth to respond, but gasped instead. Coach had stopped messing around. His index finger started rubbing against her clit as if he knew exactly what kind of touch she needed to get off. At the same time, he pinched her turgid nipple with two fingers, alternating rolling it between his fingers and flicking it with his thumb.

The combined assault on her sensitive body parts did exactly what he intended. Harley felt the orgasm surging up from the depths of her soul and moved both hands to the forearm around her chest. Her skirt dropped, but Coach's fingers didn't stop their frantic movements.

Harley tried to pull backwards, away from his fingers on her clit, but she had nowhere to go. She vaguely felt Coach's erection against her back, but it didn't fully register in the midst of her pleasure.

"Let go, Harley. I've got you."

Coach's protective words did the trick, throwing her over the edge. She bucked in his grasp as the first wave hit. Harley could feel her heart beating overtime and knew her breaths came in pants, but she was lost in the ecstasy of having an orgasm at the hands of a man for the first time.

Jerking as the orgasm continued, Harley tried once more to pull away from Coach's touch.

"No, don't pull away. One more, Harl. One more."

His fingers didn't let up on her clit, but instead increased their pace, rubbing and flicking over her engorged bud, trying to coax one more orgasm out of her body.

"Uhhhhh," Harley moaned as the second orgasm tore through her. This one was bigger, more intense than the first. "Coach!" Her fingernails dug into his forearms as she convulsed, lost in the pleasure of his touch.

It could've been seconds, or minutes, before Harley realized that Coach was no longer stroking her clit, but was instead running all four of his fingers soothingly up and down her soaked folds under her panties. It was almost a caress, but every time they swiped over her clit she jerked in pleasurable reaction.

"Beautiful," Coach breathed into her ear. "That was the most beautiful thing I've ever seen in my life. Thank you."

Harley opened her eyes and cleared her throat. She swallowed twice before she was finally able to speak. "I think I should be the one thanking you."

Coach didn't respond, but he finally pulled his hand out of her panties and brought it up to his mouth.

Harley could smell her arousal on his fingers and blushed. "What are you…" Her voice trailed off as Coach licked each finger clean.

"I don't think—"

She screeched in surprise as Coach abruptly turned her in his arms and held her against him. The look in his eyes was intense, much more intense than anything she'd seen from him in the past.

"Don't think, Harley. Feel. That was seriously one of the hottest things I've ever done or seen in my life. You were so uninhibited. I loved it. I wanted to wait until you were in my bed, but I couldn't. The whole way home, all I could think of was getting my hands under that dress. The second you were in my space, I couldn't control myself. Thank you for not freaking out. Thank you for trusting me."

He took one of her hands in his and brought it

down to the front of his dress slacks. "I'm so hard and ready for you. I swear I've been this way all night."

Harley stroked his length through the material of his pants. She could feel the heat and how hard he was…for her.

"Take me to bed?" It came out as more of a question than a request, but Coach merely nodded. He shifted his grip so he was holding her hand and led the way to his bedroom.

Chapter Seventeen

HARLEY HAD BEEN in Coach's apartment a couple of times before tonight, and it had been neat as a pin every time. His room was no exception.

There was a dresser against one wall, with absolutely nothing sitting on top of it. There were no clothes strewn about the room. A tall, skinny bookshelf stood beside the bed, filled with books. They were all lined up in alphabetical order.

The bed covers had been pulled back precisely, as if he'd done it before he'd left the house. The sheets were white, and looked extremely inviting. Coach stopped her before the bed and turned her so her back was to him.

Taking hold of the tie at her nape, he slowly tugged it, loosening the dress until the bodice threatened to fall to her waist. Harley put up one hand to hold it in place, feeling self-conscious for the first time. It was ridiculous, the man had both hands on her body just moments before, but she'd still been mostly covered.

Coach turned her again until she faced him. He

took her head in his hands and leaned in to kiss her. One of his hands moved to the back of her neck and held her to him as he devoured her mouth. Finally, he pulled back, but kept his eyes on hers.

"I've said it before, and I'll say it again. I'll keep saying it until you believe me. You're beautiful, Harley. Inside and out. I am so lucky you're giving yourself to me."

His words did the trick, and Harley let her hand drop to her side, the dress losing its battle with gravity, and fluttering to her feet. She held her breath.

Coach inhaled as he took in Harley's almost naked form for the first time. He'd felt it with his hands, but seeing it was a whole different thing.

She was tall and her tits were exactly as he'd imagined them. They sat like little apples on her chest, but it was her nipples that made his mouth water. They were erect and pointing right at him. They were large—it was no wonder he'd been able to see them through her clothes that first day at the skydiving hangar. Even as he ogled her, they grew tighter under his gaze.

Harley shifted nervously, so Coach put his hands on her shoulders to calm her. He wasn't nearly done with his first glimpse of her. She settled under his touch and his eyes continued down her body.

She was slender, he could almost see her ribs. He smiled, bringing one of his hands down to touch her little outtie belly button. She giggled and tried to wrench away from him. Coach wrapped one of his large hands around her waist to keep her where he wanted her.

"An outtie," he breathed. "I love it."

"It's weird," Harley countered.

"No. It's you," Coach reassured her. Then, looking up to her eyes, he asked as he fingered her panties. "May I?"

Harley nodded and Coach breathed out a sigh of relief. He brought his hands to her sides, putting his fingers under the thin strips at her hips and pushing slowly down, taking her panties with him.

He went down on his knees in front of her as he lowered her underwear and sucked in a deep breath, inhaling her scent as he came face-to-face with her pussy. He didn't even notice her kicking away her dress or undies; his entire focus was on the small patch of curls and her glistening folds.

His hands spanned her waist and he rested his thumbs on the creases where her thighs met her torso. Coach couldn't take his eyes off her. He'd seen pussies before. But he couldn't remember ever being as enamored of any of them as he was Harley's.

She kept her hair trimmed, so he could see her pouty lips glistening with the juices from her earlier orgasm. But it was her clit that fascinated him. He'd felt it earlier, but he could see it peeking out from its protective hood as he kneeled in front of her. It was as though she was still just as aroused as she'd been when in the midst of her orgasm in his hallway.

Not able to help himself, Coach leaned forward an inch and blew lightly on the bundle of nerves and felt himself leak precome as she sighed and shifted in his grasp. She was so sensitive and reactive to his touch. He could hardly wait to get inside her.

Knowing if he spent any more time smelling her and watching her react to his touch, he wouldn't be able to keep his promise to go slow and let her explore his own body, Coach stood up in front of her.

"Sit, Harl. Let me help you get those shoes off."

She did as he asked, and lowered herself gently to his bed. He'd changed the sheets that morning, hoping against hope that he'd have Harley right where she was now. He'd folded back the comforter, trying to make his space look inviting and comfortable for her, realizing now that it didn't matter what the bed looked like.

Coach removed Harley's shoes, placing them off to the side so they wouldn't trip over them if they had to get up in the middle of the night. He stood and removed his shirt, not bothering with undoing the buttons down the front, simply peeling it over his head. He next stripped off the undershirt and threw it to the side as well.

Feeling vulnerable, and realizing how Harley must've felt, Coach hurried to remove the rest of his clothes. He knew he was in shape, but there was just something about standing naked for the first time in front of someone who was important to you that was disconcerting.

Straightening up in front of Harley, Coach let her take him in. He was fully erect, his cock bobbing with his movements in front of her. Her hands came out to touch him, and Coach took a step closer, making his body more accessible.

She ran her slender fingers up his defined abs to his nipples, where she stopped and tweaked them playfully, smiling when he inhaled in pleasure. Moving on to his biceps, Harley circled each one with her hands, her fingers not even coming close to meeting. She moved her exploration back to his chest and down. She fingered the V muscles along his sides that pointed down to his cock.

Finally, bracing herself with one hand on his thigh, she took his length into her other hand and stroked up to the tip, then back down to his base.

"Ah, God, Harley," Coach ground out, the feeling of her soft, warm hand on his dick for the first time almost bringing him to his knees. She felt so good. He could tell she was tentative in her exploration, but at the same time, she wasn't shy either.

Her other hand moved until she touched one of his balls, and at his small moan, she gained confidence, and tested their weight in her hand.

"I can feel you pulsing in my hand," she told him in awe, not looking away from what she was doing. "It's soft, but hard at the same time."

Coach groaned, and put one hand on her shoulder to keep his balance. He widened his stance, trying to give her time to explore him. It was more intimate than anything any other woman had done. Maybe it was her inexperience, or her natural curiosity, but whatever it was, it made him want to push her backward and fuck her harder than he'd ever taken anyone before.

"Oh," Harley exclaimed as his cock jumped in her hand at his thought of pushing inside her hot body. "It moved!"

She looked up at him, as if wanting reassurance his reaction was normal.

"Yeah, it does that," Coach said, not knowing exactly what he was saying.

Harley licked her lips, and all he could think about was her leaning forward and taking him into her mouth. He swallowed hard. There'd be time for that later. If she so much as touched his cock with her lips, he'd lose it.

Coach stood as still as he could as Harley continued to caress and stroke him, learning the size and shape of him. She squeezed his balls, marveling at their weight and feel. Coach had been doing great, until she swiped the mushroomed head of his dick with one finger and brought a bead of precome up to her lips. Harley sucked her finger into her mouth and looked up into his eyes, the lust clear to see.

"Fuck," Coach groaned, and then moved.

He grabbed both her hands and pushed her backward onto the mattress. "Scoot up, Harley." Without a word, she did as he asked, pushing backward until she was lying fully on the bed.

Coach crouched over her, looking down at her splayed out on his sheets. He held her wrists in his hands, pressing them over her head. She smiled up at him, not concerned at all that he outweighed her and could do whatever he wanted to her right now.

"I need you, Harley."

"Yes. Please."

"I don't want to hurt you."

"You won't. I promise not to knee you in the balls."

Coach loved that she still had her sense of humor in bed. She looked a bit uncertain, but not scared. He sighed in relief.

"Reach up to the drawer over your head, grab the box of condoms for me."

She did as he asked, stretching under him, brushing against his hard cock, smearing his precome on her belly as she did.

She settled back where she'd been with the brand-new box in her hand. Kneeling up over her, Coach asked as he fought to open the box, "Have you ever seen this before?"

"A guy putting on a condom? Only in videos," Harley told him with a twinkle in her eye.

"Not the same."

"Can I do it?"

"No," Coach answered immediately. "I'll lose it, and the first time you make me come, I want to be inside you."

"Oh."

"Yeah, oh. Now watch."

Having her eyes on him was arousing as hell. Coach didn't think any part of putting on a rubber could be sexy, but explaining, and showing Harley the proper way to hold a condom and roll it down his cock was almost too much.

"Does it hurt?" she asked.

"No."

"Can I touch you?"

"Yeah," Coach ground out between gritted teeth, wanting to give this to her. Her natural curiosity was killing him, but he'd give her the world if she asked.

She ran a finger down the length of the condom, then questioned, "Does it feel the same, you know, inside, whether you wear one or not?"

"I don't know."

"What?"

"I don't know. I've never had sex without one before."

She opened her mouth to respond, but Coach stopped her. "And tonight's not the time to change that." At the slight look of hurt on Harley's face, Coach scooted back until their hips were aligned. His hard cock rested at the top of her pussy, her short curls caressing his length with every breath they took.

"Believe me, there's nothing more I want than to be bare inside you. But I'm going to protect you. We should've had this talk already, but now's not the time. Later we'll talk about birth control and I'll tell you about my sexual history and how I'm clean. We can make the adult decision when and if to ditch the condoms, but now isn't the time to make that choice."

"Okay. You're right. I just wanted…" She paused, before getting the gumption to say what was on her mind. "I just wanted to make sure it was good for you."

"Oh, Harl. It's already good for me." He rested on his elbows and brought his hands up to frame her face. "I could stop right now and it'd still be perfect for me. Having you naked under me. Giving you those orgasms earlier, feeling you jerk in my arms…your hands on me, exploring me…it's never been so good before. Being inside you will simply be the crowning stroke. Pun intended."

"Are you even real?"

Coach laughed at the disbelief and tenderness in her voice.

"Yeah. This is how you should always be treated, Harley." He braced himself up on a hand, and moved the other one down between them. He shifted until he could reach her folds again, running his fingers over her, much as he had earlier.

"You're so wet."

"It's a permanent condition around you, I think," Harley groaned out, arching into his touch.

"Do you trust me?" Coach asked, looking into her eyes as his fingers continued to tease and arouse her further.

"Yes."

Feeling his chest swell at her immediate response, Coach leaned down and kissed her briefly. "Good. Later, I'm gonna play with your tits. I love your nipples. I can't wait to spend hours with them. But I'm too close right now. I won't hurt you. Promise."

"Fuck me, Coach. Please."

"Not fucking. We're making love."

Coach put a hand on his cock and lifted, aligning himself. "Spread your legs, that's it. Oh yeah, beautiful."

He pushed in a fraction, feeling Harley clench her muscles, trying to keep him out. "Easy, Harley. Relax."

Coach used both hands to gently knead her breasts, taking her attention away from what was happening down below. "That's it. Let me in. I'm not going to hurt you."

Harley gasped as Coach pushed slowly inside her tight sheath. He felt her fingernails dig into his forearms once again as he entered her for the first time.

Coach gritted his teeth as Harley's muscles closed around his length. He felt himself about to blow, and quickly reached down and grasped the base of his cock with one hand, squeezing tightly until the urge to orgasm passed.

He chuckled. "Whew, that was close."

"What?" Harley asked in a daze.

"You felt so good I almost lost it."

"Isn't that the point?" she asked.

"Yeah, but not the second I get inside you. I want this to last as long as possible. I want to remember it forever. Also, I'd be a bastard if the first time you did this I didn't at least try to make you orgasm."

"I've heard women don't usually get off their first time," she said in a dreamy voice.

"That's true," Coach told her, loving that Harley was so practical, even in the midst of discussing losing her virginity. "But since your hymen was broken long ago, I'm hoping I'm not causing you pain, and that you'll be an exception."

"Me too," she told him, looking him in the eye. "It doesn't hurt, Coach. I feel full, and it's a bit uncomfortable, but you feel good too. I need...I want...I don't know. Is that weird?"

"No. It's not weird. I'm big, and this is your first time." He pulled back a fraction, then pushed in again, gaining ground. "Okay?"

"Ummmm. Are you in yet?"

"Not all the way."

"Well, get in then."

Coach laughed and pushed a bit more into her. "I'm trying not to hurt you."

"You're not. And I can feel you moving inside me when you laugh."

Coach smiled again. Making love to Harley was like nothing he'd ever felt in the past. He'd never had a casual conversation about what the woman was feeling before. Never had anyone ask him if he was in yet. But experiencing sex for the first time with Harley was something he'd never forget.

"Okay, Harley. I'm going to push all the way in. Are you ready?"

In response, Harley opened her legs wider and put her feet flat on the mattress. She even tilted her hips up to him. "I'm ready."

Coach pulled back a fraction, not able to help himself, and pushed forward until he felt her hip bones against his own. He held his breath, willing himself not to come. She felt amazing. Hot. Wet. Perfect.

Harley squirmed against him and Coach felt himself slip inside her another millimeter. He held still for several beats, trying to memorize the moment.

"Is that it?" she asked in a strained voice.

"Is what it?"

"Sex. I thought there was thrusting involved."

Coach barked out a laugh. "I'm waiting until you've adjusted."

She squirmed under him again. "I've adjusted. Please. I need you to move or something."

Coach did as Harley asked. He pulled out until only the tip of his cock was still inside her, waiting until her hips tilted up a fraction of an inch, then he pushed all the way back inside. Seeing her flinch as he bottomed out made Coach rethink his approach. Earlier he'd told her he would start slow, then end up with fast thrusts, but she was too tight, not ready for making love that intensely this time.

He sat up, keeping them connected and pulling her onto his lap. She ended up with her upper back lying on the mattress and her lower half propped up on his bent knees. The position didn't give him much room, if any, to thrust into her, but it gave her better access to her own body.

"Give me your hand."

"Why?"

"Just do it."

She did as he asked, and laid her hand trustingly in his. Coach brought it down to where they were joined. "Feel us."

She didn't hesitate. As soon as Coach let go, Harley's fingers roamed over their bodies, feeling where his cock was buried inside her, and brushing against her clit as she explored. She inhaled. "You can't move in this position," she semi-complained.

"I know. But you can reach yourself better," he countered, meeting her wide eyes. "I will not hurt you, and you're too new to this for me to take you like we both need. So this time, you'll have to do all the work. Rub yourself. Show me what you like."

"But…"

Reading the concern in her eyes, Coach reassured her. "Trust me. I like this. You are so tight, and you're squeezing me so hard. Every time you flex, it's like a thousand fingers are caressing my cock. I really want us both to come with me inside you. But me banging in and out isn't going to work this first time for you, it'll only cause you pain. I guarantee though, if you come like this, I will too. Come on, Harley. Don't be shy. Get yourself there."

She didn't respond verbally, but Coach saw her pupils dilate and felt her fingers tentatively caress the small bundle of nerves. He put one of his large hands over her belly, feeling her little outtie belly button on his palm. The other hand he put next to their hips to prop himself up. He had a feeling that he was going to have one of the most intense orgasms he'd ever had...even without moving an inch in and out of her body.

The first time her channel clenched around his, Coach bucked, then ruthlessly held himself still again. "Fuck, yeah. Do that again, Harley."

She did. The more aroused she got, the less inhibited she got. She went from using one finger to tentatively flick against her clit, to using three, rubbing roughly as she shifted and bucked in his lap.

It was the most beautiful thing Coach had ever seen. Harley was lost in her own world, and he could feel every twitch of her muscles, each time she bucked up against him, trying to take him deeper. It was amazing, and something he'd never experienced with any other woman. Trying to make sure Harley was satisfied had, in return, given him the most erotic experience in bed he'd ever had.

Sensing she was close, Coach moved the hand on her belly up to one of her tits. He pinched her nipple, just this side of painful, and ordered, "Come, Harley. Let go."

She did.

She thrashed in his lap, her head arching backward,

her fingers falling away from her body. Coach moved the hand that had been propping himself up to her clit and mimicked her own actions, rubbing roughly over her clit, prolonging her orgasm.

Feeling her channel loosen around his cock, Coach finally allowed himself his own release. He groaned, keeping his hand over Harley's clit, feeling his come surge up from his balls and exploding out of the tip of his dick deep inside her. The warmth of his seed filling the condom, as little aftershocks continued to caress him, made Coach tremble as he came down.

Not realizing he'd closed his eyes, he opened them several moments later and looked down at Harley. She was lying still under him, a small smile on her face. She didn't try to pull away or avoid his eyes.

"Wow. I had no idea it was that intense for guys."

Coach smiled at her. "With the right person, it is."

"What now?"

"What now what?"

"Well, you came. I came, what now?"

Coach shifted until he was hovering over Harley once more, careful to keep her pelvis up tight against his so he didn't slip out of her. "I have to get rid of the condom. Then we'll both nap for a bit. I'll wake up with a hard-on and want to get inside you again."

"Okay."

"Okay?"

"Yeah. Sounds like a good plan to me. Although this time, I want you to move inside me."

Coach closed his eyes and rested his forehead against Harley's. "I've created a monster."

"Hey, it's all for the sake of education, right? I'm thinking I need to add some sex to my next video game."

"You are not putting our sex life into a video game." His voice was harsher than he intended it to be. But the thought of her putting what they'd just shared on a game for everyone to see was appalling.

"I was kidding, Coach. There's no way I'd want to share one second of what we just did with anyone else, even if they do rate the games for adults only."

"Good. I don't share well."

"Me neither."

They smiled at each other for a moment.

"Okay, go on, remove the condom then we'll sleep. The sooner we nap, the sooner we can do that again."

Coach pulled out slowly, earning a groan from Harley. "Sore?"

"No. That felt good. I'm so sensitive down there."

Coach kissed her again. "I'll be right back. Don't move."

"Don't worry. I'm not going anywhere."

He was back in seconds with a warm washcloth. "Here, I thought you might like this."

Harley took it from him and he watched as she rested it on herself for a moment. "God, that feels so good. Thank you."

"You're welcome. Need any help?"

She smiled up at him, blushing. "No, but thank you." After a second, she observed, "You're staring."

"Can't help it," Coach returned.

Harley wiped herself once with the fast-cooling cloth, and handed it to him. "I'm not sure I'll ever get used to you staring at me."

"I'll give you lots of practice." Coach put the wet washcloth on the table next to the bed and turned back to her. "Thank you, Harley. That was amazing. I feel honored to have been your first."

"I'm too old to have been a virgin," she complained.

"Nope. You're perfect."

"Stop saying that. I'm not perfect."

"Perfect for me then."

She rolled her eyes. "Whatever."

Coach pulled Harley into his arms and tugged the comforter up and over them both.

"Is it normal to feel this tired after sex?" she inquired sleepily.

"Yup."

"Okay. Coach?"

"Yeah?"

"That was awesome. I can't wait to do it again."

"Me neither. Good night."

"Night."

Harley fell asleep almost immediately, but Coach didn't sleep a wink. He was too wired. Too happy. He wanted Harley in his life forever. There were things they hadn't talked about, things about his past, but there'd be time for that later. It was enough, for now, that she slept peacefully and safely in his arms.

Chapter Eighteen

COACH LAY IN bed next to Harley, listening to her breathing, and thanked God that he and all his teammates had made it back from another mission in one piece.

This one had been a doozy. They were sent to the Middle East to gather intel and hopefully rescue a service member who'd been taken captive by the Taliban. Most of the time incidents like this one didn't even make the news anymore, not when ISIS was blowing up malls and nightclubs around the world.

They'd joined up with another Delta squad, one they'd worked with before. The men on the other team were funny as hell and damn good soldiers. But something had gone wrong. They'd all been caught with their pants down and five of the six men on the other team had been wiped off the face of the earth in the blink of an eye.

One minute they'd been driving down the road and the next, their Humvees were nothing but burning hunks of metal. Thank God they'd been able to rescue one of the Deltas. Dane "Fish" Munroe had been missing part of his arm, but Truck had been able to clamp off the artery and they'd hotfooted it out of the volatile area.

Coach closed his eyes and shook his head in despair. The men Fish had worked with had been good men. Brothers, sons, and in two cases, husbands. It could've easily been him and his friends who'd been blown up.

Fish was struggling with what had happened. Not only losing part of his arm, but his teammates as well. Truck was keeping an ear to the ground to find out when he was out of the hospital and where he would end up. Word was that he had several months of physical therapy to go through and that he'd most likely be chaptered out of the Army.

It wasn't the way any of the Deltas would choose to go out. Fish might not know it yet, but wherever he ended up, Coach, Truck, and the rest of the team would have his back. He was now an unofficial member of their close-knit group…whether he wanted to be or not.

Coach ran his hand up and down Harley's back and smiled as she arched into him, snuggling into his side at his touch. He closed his eyes and sighed, happy to be home, happy to have Harley by his side, and happy to be back in Texas. He slept.

HARLEY GOT OUT of the car and smiled as Coach scowled at her. She always refused to wait for him to come over to her side and open the door. She'd told him over and over that she was a competent woman who could open her own door, but he never stopped trying. It was the fact that he wanted to pamper her, treat her like a lady, that made her smile. He should know by now, especially after last night, that she was no lady.

Coach growled under his breath as he shut the door behind her. "Seriously, Harl, I wish you'd let me be a gentleman at least once."

Harley leaned against her man and whispered into his ear, "I let you pull my chair out for me and open doors into buildings, but my favorite is how you always let me come first. Every time. *That* is all the gentleman I need."

"Jesus, Harl," Coach grumbled, looking around the parking lot to see if anyone was nearby. "That was a low blow. Now I'm replaying last night in my mind and remembering how hot and wet you were when I pushed into your tight body."

"It's your own fault," Harley teased. "You made me come twice this morning before you got inside me."

"Fuck, woman. Whose idea was it to meet the gang for lunch today?"

"Yours."

"Well, next time, talk me out of it, okay?"

The last couple of months had been like a dream for her. Coach was an attentive boyfriend, but not smothering. When she got into her weird moods when her code wasn't working, Coach hadn't pushed her. He'd left her alone and waited for her to text to let him know it was safe to come back to her place.

They hadn't talked much about his job, it was enough for Harley to know that what he did was top secret, and that he had the rest of his teammates at his back. She knew his missions weren't safe, and that point had been driven home when he'd told her the last time he'd come home from being deployed about his friend, Fish, who had been wounded, and how Truck had saved his life. It made Harley appreciate every minute she got to be with Coach. She knew the next time it could be *him* who was wounded.

And while they didn't spend every night together, they were moving toward that more and more. Coach would come over after work and hang out with her, until they couldn't keep their hands off each other anymore. They'd had shower sex, bathtub sex, living room sofa sex, wall sex, table sex, and even hallway floor sex. They'd not only done it doggy, cowgirl, and spooning styles, but he'd introduced her to some kinkier positions, such as the waterfall, the hot seat, reverse cowgirl, pole position, the pretzel, and the spider. He'd taught her how to give him a blowjob, and she'd gotten a thorough education on the difference between having sex and making love…loving both.

All in all, things were going great. Harley knew she'd fallen hard and fast for Coach, and it seemed as if he felt the same, even if neither of them had said the words yet. There was no rush though; they had plenty of time to get there.

Harley smiled up at Coach when he tucked his hand into the back pocket of her jeans as they walked. She snaked her arm around his waist and grabbed hold of the belt loop on his cargo pants as they headed toward the entrance to the fast food burrito restaurant. It was a popular place to eat, especially this time of day.

The high school, a block away, allowed its seniors to have lunch off campus and the place was filled with teenagers when they walked in. Coach gave a chin lift to Rayne and Ghost who were standing off to the side, obviously waiting for them to arrive. Truck was there, as was Blade and Hollywood. Rayne's friend, Mary, had also tagged along, making it a lively group.

Something was still up with Truck and Mary, but Harley didn't really know either of them well enough to comment on it. She saw Rayne giving her friend a side-eyed, what-the-hell-is-going-on glance, but Mary turned her back on the group and studied the menu as if her life depended on it.

Truck didn't look happy, but got in line behind everyone else, and in front of Harley and Coach. He crossed his arms in front of him and glared at the back of Mary's head.

Harley looked up at Coach and raised her eyebrows in question, but Coach merely shook his head. It was a weird situation, but at the moment Harley was too happy with her own life to butt into anyone else's. Looking one more time at Truck, she was glad *she* wasn't on the other end of the scowl on his face. Truck was a large, intimidating man, and if he looked at her like that, she'd be spilling her pin number for her ATM card, her bank account info, and anything else the man wanted to know.

Harley snuggled into Coach's side and sighed in contentment as she felt his hand move from the back pocket of her pants to rest at the small of her back, under her shirt. His long fingers covered most of her back, but his pinky was pushed down into the top of her undies, teasing her with a back and forth movement along her bare butt.

"I can't believe the nerds decided to tear themselves away from their computers long enough to eat."

"They should've known better than to have come *here* though. They know this is our hangout."

"Dumb bitches won't know what's coming when they leave."

Harley felt Coach stiffen next to her. It was as if every muscle in his body had readied itself for attack. She wondered if this was how he was in battle.

Harley turned her head casually to the side, just enough to see a group of three teenagers standing behind them. They were obviously in high school, and reminded her a lot of herself when she was that age.

Two wore glasses, not unlike her own, and the other was overweight. All three wore jeans and oversize T-shirts, one with the Army logo on it, one with a picture of Pokémon, and the third was red with the Star Trek logo on the upper left chest. They were carrying backpacks, which looked like they were full of books or other school paraphernalia. They wouldn't meet anyone's eyes, but kept their gazes focused forward on the menu board, as if that would make the other girls standing behind them disappear.

The girls who had spoken were in line behind the awkward trio. There were four of them, and they were young and beautiful. Two had blonde hair, one was Asian and had long, straight black hair, and the fourth was African-American with very short, curly hair. They were wearing short skirts and heels. They were dressed as if they were going out to a club on Saturday night and carried nothing but small purses. All four had condescending sneers on their faces, aimed at the three teenagers who now looked panicked.

"Look, how cute, they think if they ignore us, we

won't know they're here. You're gonna regret coming to our lunch spot," one of the blondes threatened.

Her words made Coach stiffen even further, if that was possible. Harley wasn't any happier with the situation than Coach was, but confronting the mean girls was a sure way to make the situation worse. She knew. She'd been right where the trio had been. The taunting and threats brought back way too many bad memories of high school for Harley.

"What do you want to eat, Harl?" Coach asked, nudging her to the counter. Harley hadn't even realized they'd shuffled forward and were now at the front of the line. She turned and ordered her extra-large chicken burrito—she'd burned a lot of calories the night before—and waited for Coach by the cash register.

He paid, and indicated the large table that Ghost and the others had commandeered. "Will you get me a water?" When she nodded, he thanked her. "Appreciate it. Don't wait for me, go and sit, I'll be there in a sec."

Harley nodded and grabbed the cups from the cashier and headed to the soda fountain to get their drinks. She turned when she heard Coach talking to someone.

"Hey, ladies, there aren't too many seats...we've got some extras at our table, want to sit with us?"

Harley saw Coach talking to the three girls who'd been picked on while in the line. They were standing at the cash register with their mouths open, obviously confused about why Coach was asking *them* to sit with him.

Seeing their hesitation and realizing he needed a wingman, Harley quickly joined him.

"Hey, baby. Oh, you asked them. Good. You guys will sit with us, right? There's lots of room. My boyfriend saw your Army T-shirt and decided right then and there you have great taste." She laughed and gestured toward the long table, trying to put them at ease. Hollywood, Blade, and Truck were sitting on the far side of the table. Ghost, Rayne, and Mary had their backs to the food line. There were still two tables next to theirs that were empty. Plenty of room for five more people.

"Uh, sure, okay," one of the girls stammered out for the group.

Harley smiled at them, trying to look as friendly as possible. Being social wasn't really her thing, but it was obvious what Coach was trying to do. She was one hundred percent down with it. Damn mean girls.

They all sauntered over to the table and Coach held out a chair for one of the teenagers, and Truck stood up and did the same for the other two on his side of the table. They all sat down, and Coach took Harley's hand and led her to the end of the table, making sure there weren't any other seats around the teenagers, protecting them from the other girls.

As Harley could've guessed would've happened, the popular girls sat at a table nearby, close enough to hear what was being said at their own table.

Bless Rayne and Mary, even without being told what was going on, they jumped right in and made the teenagers feel at ease. They started out making small talk about the fact that the guys were all in the Army and wasn't it a coincidence that one of them was wearing an Army T-shirt, and the conversation flowed easily from there.

It was an interesting lunch, with Ghost and Coach giving each other nonverbal signals with their eyes, Rayne and Mary carrying the conversation with the high schoolers, and Blade and Hollywood smiling and flirting in a nonthreatening way. Harley had blushed when Coach had bragged about how she was a hotshot video game developer and the girls had gushed over her, asking all sorts of questions about how she'd gotten into the business and what games she'd worked on.

After thirty minutes or so, the girls said they had to get back to class. Everyone was about done and started gathering their stuff. Garbage was thrown away and everyone exited the small restaurant. Harley watched as the three girls waved and walked away, back toward the high school.

She was startled when she heard Coach say, "Just a second, ladies."

Turning to see who he was talking to, she saw the quartet of girls who'd been in line behind them standing near Coach. Her stomach churning, because she had no idea what Coach was doing, Harley quickly went to his side, noticing that the other guys did the same.

"I know you girls think you've got the world eating out of your hands, but that's not the case." Coach's words were quiet…and lethal. Goosebumps rose on Harley's arms. She'd seen Coach upset, but not like this. He was pissed. Extremely pissed, and he wasn't hiding it in the least. It was as if he was holding himself back from tearing these girls new assholes, and it scared her. This wasn't like the tender lover she'd had the night before, not even close.

He went on, without looking away from them. "You're bullies. You think nothing can touch you and that you'll skate by in this world with your looks. But you know what? You're rotten inside. To the core. I'd like to say there's still time for you to change, but I'm not sure there is. Those girls that you were threatening and making fun of are worth ten of you. Did you know that Brittany has a full ride to A&M next year? She got accepted into their pre-vet program. Who do you think is gonna take care of your yappy Chihuahua when it gets sick years from now? And Lexie is going into the Army. She's smart enough to go to college, but wants to spare her family the expense. She's going to be a doctor and thought that the Army would be a good place to start on that education. And she's right. I wouldn't be surprised if she ends up being a general someday. And Donna? She's going to Yale. *Yale*."

Harley put her hand on Coach's back. He didn't act like he even felt her standing there behind him. His back was ramrod straight and she could almost feel the energy coursing through his body. Every muscle was tight and his fists were clenched at his sides.

Coach's words were bit out in a cutting tone. It wasn't as if the girls didn't deserve his ire, to some extent, but they were kids. They were engrossed in their own little worlds, with no clue as to how their actions today might affect others years from now.

Coach went on with no mercy. "I'd say *they* are well on their way to being productive, important members of society. And yet you stand there and judge them because they're not wearing high heels or skanky skirts. Get over yourselves."

The last words were said with such scorn, all four of the teenagers in front of them flinched.

But Coach wasn't done. He continued his harangue. "Live your pathetically narrow lives, only worrying about who you're going to prom with and which football player you're going to fuck next, but leave them alone. Leave *all* of the, quote, unpopular, kids alone. You know what? Someday you're gonna need those 'nerds.' Your kids might be sick and need a specialized doctor. Your computer might get a virus, or you might just find that the boys you used to pick on are four times better in the sack than the jocks because they *care* about the women they're with."

"Coach," Ghost warned in a low voice. "Enough."

Coach gestured to his teammate with a hand movement Harley didn't understand, but Ghost took a step back, obviously reading the nonverbal signal and trusting his friend.

"You see this woman next to me?" Harley jolted when Coach snaked his hand around her waist and pulled her into him.

"She's the best thing that ever happened to me. I love her and would lay down my life for hers, no questions asked. Look at her. She's a nerd. Glasses, jeans, sneakers, no makeup, her hair up in a messy bun. But she's the most beautiful person I've ever met in my life because of who she is inside. If I was a teenager again, I'd pick one of those girls you were just making fun of back there over any of you, any day of the week, and twice on Sunday."

The teenagers hadn't said anything, had only gaped at the gorgeous man ripping them to shreds with his harsh words.

Without another word to the teenagers who were standing stock still, eyes wide, watching them, Coach gave a chin lift to his friends and headed for his High-lander, his arm around Harley's shoulders in a tight grip.

Harley didn't even look back to see what the fallout would be for Coach's harangue. As turned on as she was, she was more worried for him. His jaw was tight and he was breathing heavily through his nose. She didn't say a word as he held open the passenger door for her. Without making her usual fuss, she climbed in and kept her eyes on him as he stalked around the front of the vehicle to the driver's side.

She still didn't say a word as he drove her home to her apartment, and neither did he. They'd spent a carnal night with each other, learning everything there was to know about each other, inside and out, and now it was as if a brick wall was standing between them. Harley had no idea how to get to the other side to get to Coach.

He pulled up outside her apartment and turned to her. "I'll call you later."

"Why don't you come in? I—"

"I wouldn't be good company right now, Harley. I'll call you later."

Harley sucked her lips together. She didn't want to leave him like this. He wasn't acting like himself and it was scaring her. The man *she* knew would never have said what he had to those teenagers. She was missing something. A big something.

"Coach—"

He leaned across in front of her and, with his long arm, pushed open her door. "Later, Harley."

That was certainly definitive enough. Without a choice, Harley unbuckled her seat belt and swung her legs out of the door. She reluctantly climbed out and stood next to the door frame, clutching it with one hand. She tried one more time to reach him. "I love you, Coach. Please come inside. We can talk about what just happened."

His fingers grasped the steering wheel tightly, his knuckles turning white. But he didn't say a word. Didn't acknowledge her in any way.

Wanting to beg him to talk to her, to tell her what was wrong, to make him come inside until he calmed down, Harley stared at him for one more second. She opened her mouth to say something, but closed it again.

Coach was an adult. He didn't have to talk to her, although it hurt her heart that he was obviously struggling with some deep emotion that he didn't want to share.

Without another word, Harley closed the door and took a step backward. For the first time ever, Coach didn't wait for her to go up to her door; he pulled away, leaving her standing on the pavement outside her townhouse. She stood still, watching as the SUV pulled out of the parking lot and turned right onto the road outside her complex. The lights disappearing from sight.

A tear rolled down Harley's face. Coach was hurting, and therefore she was too.

Chapter Nineteen

HARLEY FRETTED AND worried about Coach. After she'd sent at least five texts, wanting to make sure he was all right, he'd texted back once, saying only, *I'm fine.*

The two words had freaked her out even more, because he obviously *wasn't* fine. She'd resorted to calling Hollywood. He and Coach seemed close, and he seemed like a good choice to try to find out what in the world was going on.

Unfortunately, he hadn't told her much. Only that Coach was working through some shit, and he'd be in touch soon.

Harley had even called Montesa. Her sister had told her simply that he needed to blow off steam and he'd be back when he was ready. Not satisfied with that response, and really wanting to get a guy's perspective of the entire incident, she'd called her brother.

"It was as if he was a different person, Davidson. I don't understand why he's not talking to me."

"Sis, I love you, but I don't think you're looking at this the right way."

"How should I be looking at it?"

"Look, Coach is a guy. He's in the military. He's a soldier. He's used to taking care of others. You told me that he recently got back from some mission where one of his friends got hurt and others killed. He's obviously dealing with a lot. On top of that, something with those girls flipped a switch inside of him. I don't know what happened in his life to make him abhor bullies, but whatever it is, he has to work through it by himself. He's not gonna want to look weak in front of you."

"But I know he's not weak."

"Harley, this isn't about *you*. It's about *him*."

It was that sentence that made Harley understand, finally. Coach was a strong man. He hadn't earned his nickname by being someone who stood on the sidelines and watched the world passing him by. He was a take-charge man. Someone who Harley knew firsthand, from the first day they'd met, wouldn't stand back when a person was being treated unfairly. From the way he always left a twenty-percent tip to his defense of his country and always supporting his friends. It was just his way.

He wasn't purposely shutting her out. He was dealing with something heavy, and it had absolutely nothing to do with her. She'd be worse than a teenager if she flew off the handle and got pissed at Coach. Too many relationships went bad because one person internalized what the other was doing and assumed they were purposely being excluded.

Whatever had happened today, was more. It was more than she knew. Coach wouldn't have gone off on those girls...*girls*...if it had been only a simple case of bullying. He was too honorable. Too protective. No, it was something bigger. Something she didn't understand.

Harley just had to wait for him to come to her. Whatever Coach needed, whenever he needed it, she'd be there for him.

When she lay down to try to get some sleep, hours later, she still hadn't heard from Coach, or from any of his teammates. She'd made the decision earlier that night to wait for him to come to her, but it was one of the toughest things she'd ever done.

After tossing and turning, a noise woke her out of a light sleep. Harley looked at the clock. Two forty-two in the morning. Her phone pinged again. A text.

You up? I'm outside.

Harley didn't bother with a return text, simply leaped out of bed and shoved her feet into a pair of flip flops lying on the floor. She ran through her place to the front door and swung it open, looking out into the parking lot eagerly.

Coach was leaning against the front bumper of his car. He was wearing the same cargo pants and shirt from earlier that day. He was looking down at his phone, brows drawn down into a frown, as if waiting for her return text. He looked tired. Exhausted.

Harley didn't wait for him to notice or come to her, she hurried across the lot. Coach saw her out of the corner of his eye before she was halfway there. He pocketed his phone and strode toward her.

Without a word, in the dark of the parking lot, Coach engulfed her in his arms and held on tight. Harley didn't need the words; the desperation of his grip told her everything she needed to know. He was hurting and her man needed her. Davidson had been right. This wasn't about her. It was all about Coach.

She squeezed him tight, allowing the relief of him being safe to course through her. The worst memory of her life was when the cops had come to her childhood home to tell her and her siblings that their parents had been killed. A part of her had dreaded waking up to a knock on the door and being told that Coach had been in an accident and was hurt, or God forbid, had been killed.

She finally pulled back, just enough to turn and put her arm around Coach's back and lead him toward her open door. They shuffled inside and Harley kicked off her shoes. She shut and locked the door and walked with Coach straight to her bedroom. He didn't resist in any way, telling her without words that he was still mired in whatever was going through his mind. He sat on the edge of her bed and without asking permission, Harley kneeled down and started working on the laces to his boots.

"I can do that," Coach protested weakly.

"I know. I got it," Harley told him, tugging the first boot off. She removed his sock, then attacked the other one. Removing both the boot and sock on that foot, she placed them to the side. She pulled him to his feet and tried to push him toward the bathroom.

"Go. Do your thing. There's a new toothbrush in the drawer to the right of the sink. I'll be right here."

Coach didn't move, just stood by her bed, and then took her head in his large hands and stared down at her for the longest moment. Finally, without a word, he kissed her on the forehead and trudged off into the small bathroom.

Harley climbed back under the sheets, which still held her body heat from earlier, and waited for Coach to reappear. Within moments, he did.

On his way back to the bed, he tugged off his shirt and dropped it in the middle of the floor, obviously not caring where it landed. His hands went to his belt and he made short work of removing his pants as well.

He left his boxers on, unusual for him, and crawled into the bed next to Harley. She was winging it, and wasn't sure what her next step should be, but as usual, Coach made the first move. He turned to Harley, who was lying on her back, and snuggled up to her.

It should've been weird, *she* was usually the one who curled into *him*, but this felt right. Coach's arm went around her waist and he buried his nose into the space between her neck and shoulder. He shifted, pulling her even tighter into him. One of his arms was still tucked up against his body and she could feel his fingers brush against her shoulder as he tried to merge his body into hers.

Harley moved her arm out from under him and curled it around his shoulder, holding onto his head. She covered his massive forearm with the other and lay still.

She wouldn't beg him to talk. She realized after her chat with Davidson, and some inner reflection as she sat at home and worried about where Coach was, that he'd tell her what was going on in his own time. He was an adult, with his own thoughts and feelings. It wasn't her place to force his feelings out of him, she needed him to be comfortable with her, and trust her enough to talk about what was bothering him when he was ready. It was enough for the moment that he was here with her, safe and sound. Harley knew she'd lay there in silence with him forever if that's what he needed.

Coach didn't move his head, but Harley felt his lips moving against her skin as he finally spoke a long twenty minutes later. He didn't preface his words with anything, just jumped right into a story as if she'd asked him what the weather was going to be tomorrow.

"My sister's name was Jenny. She was the sweetest kid you'd ever meet. Chubby-cheeked and bubbly. She never met a person she didn't like."

Harley held her breath. She already didn't like what she was hearing. Didn't like that Coach was referring to his sister in the past tense. It was the first time he'd done that. For some reason she'd thought his sister was alive and well somewhere, even though he didn't really talk about her much. Harley kept quiet, not asking any questions, and let Coach get the story out in his own way, in his own time.

"She followed me around incessantly when she was in elementary school. My friends thought it was annoying, but I mostly thought it was cute. I knew she idolized me, and I was okay with that. She was my little sister. I'd do anything to protect her."

Coach took a breath and paused, as if giving himself a pep talk to continue. Finally, he went on, his voice even softer than it had been before. He was almost whispering now. "One of my favorite memories was when I was in the seventh grade and she was in the fourth. I had an old tape recorder and we'd tape messages for each other and leave them outside our bedroom doors to listen to in the morning when we got up. We didn't talk about anything interesting, just what we'd been doing and telling silly stories. Crap little kids would find amusing and interesting. I don't know what happened to those tapes, but I'd give *anything* to have even one today. Absolutely anything."

Again, Coach paused. This time a longer one. So long, Harley wasn't sure he was going to continue. For all she knew, he'd fallen asleep. Then out of the blue, Coach asked, "Why does Dr. Pepper come in bottles?"

His voice was sad, the question totally incongruent to the topic of the tapes he'd been reminiscing about. Harley was confused, but went with it, not wanting to interrupt the flow of whatever was going through his head. "I don't know," she said softly.

"That's what Jenny said too," Coach recalled in a sad tone. "It's a joke. I knew she wouldn't get it, she wasn't old enough, but being twelve and full of hormones, I thought it was the funniest thing ever. I asked her that question in one of our taped conversations. She listened to it one morning, obviously having just woken up. Her answer was full of yawns and she sounded completely out of it. I warned her she probably wouldn't know the answer and that was okay. But she tried so hard to answer it…for me."

Harley's eyes filled as she felt a splash of wetness against her shoulder. Coach's tears. Each drop of liquid against her skin tore her heart in two. The man lying in her arms was hurting. Badly. She ruthlessly held her own tears back, breathing deeply through her nose. This was about Coach, not her. He needed her to be strong.

Coach acted as if he didn't even know he was crying. He didn't try to wipe his tears away. He only continued to tell his story in a heartbreakingly despondent tone.

"Jenny hemmed and hawed and finally said just what you did. 'I don't know, Johnny. If it didn't, it would just fall out. It has to be in bottles otherwise we wouldn't be able to drink it.' I remember laughing at her response."

Harley didn't move a muscle. Johnny. He'd told her once that he didn't go by his first name. That as far as the Army and everyone else knew, his name was Beckett.

Johnny.

It was what his beloved little sister called him.

And he was speaking about her in the past tense.

Her heart broke for the man in her arms.

The tears escaped her eyes even as she tried desperately to hold them back. This was about him, and Jenny, and the last thing she wanted to do was distract Coach and have him feeling as though he needed to console her. Her tears dripped down the sides of her face into the pillow beneath her head, soaking the fabric.

"The answer is actually, 'Because his wife died.'" Coach paused, as if waiting for Harley to get the joke.

It took a moment, but finally she grimaced at the horribly off-color joke and chuckled weakly, telling him without words that the meaning had sunk in.

"Yeah," Coach agreed, in the same forlorn voice, "Prepubescent boy humor. I obviously was in the jerk-off stage then, that's the only excuse I have for telling that awful joke to my little sister. But Jenny didn't get it. Even after I told her the answer in a later tape. She just told me it didn't make sense, not understanding what a wife and a soft drink and drinking out of bottles had to do with each other, and went on with a story about what happened to her on the playground at school that day."

"What happened to her, Coach?" Harley prodded in a gentle voice when he paused once again. She'd listen to him reminiscing all night, but she realized he needed to get whatever had happened to Jenny off his chest.

"Mean girls. That's what happened," Coach mumbled in a tired, sad voice. His tears had stopped, but Harley could still feel the dampness of them on her shoulder. "Middle school came and the girls Jenny used to be friends with turned on her. Said she was fat and ugly. Made fun of her. Tripped her in the hall and laughed when her books went sprawling. Gossiped about her to the boys in the school. Everything they could do to get under a shy, too-trusting girl's skin, they did.

"Then they went too far. One day a note appeared in her locker. It was supposedly from a boy. In it, the boy said he liked her and wanted to get to know her better. He told her he was shy and that he wanted to keep his identity a secret for the time being. Jenny ate it up. She loved having a secret admirer.

"In the note, the boy told her if she wanted to write him back to leave a note in the library inside a specific book in the history section. He said that no one had checked out the book in months, so it would be a safe place."

Coach paused for a moment before continuing. "I guess she got caught up in the romance of it all and didn't stop to think about what might really be going on. She opened up to this boy who she thought liked her. Telling him how sad she was that the other girls in the school didn't like her and picked on her.

"When she told me about the boy and how much she liked him, I cautioned her. Told her to be careful. She broke my heart when she told me that he was the only friend she had."

Harley couldn't hold back the gasp, somehow sensing what was coming. She wanted to jump out of the bed and beg Coach not to continue, but she didn't. It wouldn't make anything un-happen. She kept silent and let him finish the incredibly sad tale.

"Yeah," Coach agreed. "Jenny found out it was all a big trick when she overheard the girls laughing at lunch about something she'd told the boy the night before.

She realized for the first time that everything she'd confided in the boy, she'd actually told to the bullies who were tormenting her. It broke her. I tried my best to reassure her it didn't matter, that things would get better and she should blow it off, but she couldn't. She was too heartbroken, humiliated, and devastated."

Harley stroked Coach's arm soothingly. She really didn't want to hear the rest of the story, but knew Coach needed to tell it.

"I told her I was going to the library one night. It was a school night, and I know she didn't believe me, but I winked at her and she winked back. I knew Jenny wouldn't tell on me. I went over to a buddy's house and partied. I didn't get too drunk, I knew I needed to sneak back home, but it was a fun night. One of my best, and worst, memories of high school. The next morning, I got up for school. Jenny and I ate breakfast together. She seemed in a better mood. She laughed with me and I told her a little of what I did the night before. She seemed lighter, happier than I'd seen her in a long time. I was so relieved.

"We left for school. I was driving my own car and Jenny was still taking the bus, but she didn't end up getting on it that day. After waving at me as I drove by the bus stop, she doubled back and waited until my parents left for work, and then went into the house. She went through every cabinet in the house and collected as many pills as she could. She took them all, Harley. Every single fucking one. Aspirin, Tylenol, Benadryl, antibiotics, anti-nausea pills, even some sleeping pills my mom had for when she had horrible headaches and needed them to sleep."

The tears came faster down Harley's cheeks now. She couldn't stop them and she refused to take her hands off Coach to wipe them away. His voice was remote, as if he was telling a story about walking across the street instead of about his little sister dying.

"I got home from school first, as usual. I found her. She was lying on my bed, curled into a ball, clutching my pillow. She crawled into *my* bed to die, Harley. To this day, that haunts me. Maybe it was because she felt safe there, maybe it was because she wanted to apologize to me for doing it, I have no idea. She didn't leave a note or anything, but we all knew why she'd done it. She couldn't handle the humiliation of knowing she'd been tricked. She'd been dead for a couple of hours by the time I got home. Her body was cold and stiff. But I swear, she looked so peaceful. I've never seen her look so relaxed. At least not for a long time."

"I'm sorry, Coach. I'm so sorry," Harley told him with every bit of love she had in her heart.

"Yeah. Me too," he agreed, sadly. Coach hadn't moved from his position. If anything, he'd tightened his grip around Harley as he'd talked about Jenny's death, as if she was the only thing holding him together.

"We had a memorial for her at the high school," he went on. "Standing-room only. Lots of people stood up and said what a great person Jenny had been. What great potential she had. She was going to do great things...and all that shit. But she was only thirteen, Harley. *Thirteen.* She had her whole life ahead of her, but no one knew what she was going to do, no one knew she was going to be a great success. It's just something people say when a kid dies. Maybe she would've been the President, but she could've easily also ended up homeless and hooked on drugs, working at a fast food restaurant for the rest of her life or a dead-end job in a factory somewhere. But whatever she would've ended up doing, I wouldn't have cared. She was Jenny. My little sister. I thought she'd always be there."

Coach's next words finally fully explained why he'd disappeared after lunch that day.

"The worst part about that memorial was when I was leaving, I saw the girls who'd been tormenting her. The reason she'd been lying dead curled up on my mattress in my room the day she died. They came to her fucking memorial, as if they cared. When Jenny killed herself because of what *they'd* done to her. It was too much. I lost it. I started screaming at them that they'd killed her. It was their fault. I was hauled out of the auditorium pretty quickly, but not before I saw the confusion on their faces. They honestly had no idea that they'd done anything wrong. None. They killed my little sister and didn't even realize it."

Coach took a deep breath and came full circle to what had happened at the restaurant with the high school girls. "I will never condone bullying. *Ever.* When I heard those girls today, it all came back. I realized that all it would've taken was *one* person being Jenny's friend. Just *one* person standing up for her. *One* person putting themselves between her and those bitches. That's what I did today. I'm not sorry for what I said." The last was said belligerently.

"And you shouldn't be," Harley soothed though sniffles. "They deserved every word of it. I'm proud of you, Coach. And I love you. I know I said it earlier, but I'll say it again. I love you. You're exactly the kind of man I want to be around. You're tough as nails, but you also care. I don't think I've ever known a man with as much depth as you."

Harley paused for a moment, considering her next words and whether she should even say them right now, but finally bit her lip and went for it, wanting him to understand. "I'm not like your sister. Even though I was picked on growing up, and there were times that I desperately wanted a friend who would eat lunch with me, and laugh with me when the mean girls at my school started making fun of me, I never once thought about killing myself."

"I know you're not," Coach agreed immediately, showing her he knew her well enough to get what she meant. "You're tougher than Jenny ever was. You ignore people who want to cut you down. You live your life your way, and you have no idea what that means to me." Coach finally lifted his head and looked into Harley's eyes.

His own were bloodshot and his cheeks still held the evidence of his grief, but he didn't waver when he spoke to her from his heart. "I'll always protect you, Harley. From mean girls, birds flying through the sky, or whatever might come after you. But it does my heart and head good to know that you don't *need* me to protect you. I don't think I could handle it if you relied on me for everything. As much as I give you shit about it, it makes me proud that you don't want me to open your car door for you. That you can take care of yourself. I'd rather die than have you hurt because I failed, Harley."

"Oh, Coach. You won't fail me. I'm strong, and too old to worry about what others are saying about me. Screw them. I'm successful, I love what I do for a living, I have great siblings, and while I'm sad that my parents didn't get to see all the cool things I've done, I'm okay with everything that has happened in my life." She took a breath and continued.

"It took me a long time to figure this out, but everything happens for a reason. Everything. Ultimately, I believe to the marrow of my bones that I would never have met you if my parents hadn't died in that accident. There doesn't seem to be a connection on the surface, but every decision I made after that time, led me here. My schooling, my job, even my decision to be at that skydiving club the same time you were substituting for your friend came about because of the death of my parents. I know some people think that's a weird way to look at life, but in my heart, I know they led me to you. Coach, the only person I care about pleasing is you. If your friends decided to hate me tomorrow, I wouldn't care, as long as I have you."

A smile crept across Coach's face at her words. "I don't think you have anything to worry about there. Annie is already calling you Aunt Harley. Rayne and Mary have threatened to cut off my balls if I don't let you up for air and let them take you out on the town. And I punched Hollywood the other day because he looked a bit too long at your tits when you leaned over to hug Annie and the V-neck of your shirt dipped. You don't have to worry about my friends liking you."

Moving for the first time since he crawled into bed, Coach suddenly turned onto his back, bringing Harley with him, pulling her over until she was lying on top of him from chest to crotch. He moved his legs apart, and

Harley's own legs fell between them, bringing them closer than they were before.

She felt his hands at her lower back, pushing her into him. Harley felt his cock harden against her, but his words froze her in place.

"You don't think less of me?"

Harley knew exactly what he was talking about, and brought her fingertips up to his face and wiped away the last traces of his drying tears. "Absolutely not. I'd be even more concerned if you *didn't* cry."

He didn't comment, but Harley saw some of the tense lines around his lips relax. He'd been genuinely worried that she'd see him in a different light because he'd cried while talking about his sister. She leaned down and kissed both cheeks gently, trying to reassure him that nothing had changed about her feelings for him.

"I love you, Harley. I was a dick and told some bitch-face teenagers before I told you. I'm sorry. But know this—not a day will go by from here on out when you won't hear those words from me. The only time you might not is if I'm overseas on a mission, but I promise to make up for those times when I'm home.

"I love the fact you can get so engrossed in your work that you don't hear me come up behind you, but that also scares the shit out of me, because if I can sneak up on you, then so can someone else. I love the fact you don't wear makeup. I don't have to worry about sneaking a kiss and getting lipstick all over me, and I can carry you into the house and have my way with you without you having to jump out of bed to take that shit off your face so you don't break out. I love your clothes. You dress for comfort, and since most of the time that means no bra and pants with elastic waists, its easy access for me."

"Perv." Harley smiled at him, happy he seemed to be getting back to his old self.

"Yup," he agreed easily, obviously not offended in the least. "But most of all, I love you because of what's up here." Coach tapped her temple with a finger, then brought it down and traced her eyebrows. "You're smart, funny, compassionate, and somehow you were thrown into my path. I learned from Ghost. He was an idiot and let Rayne go, and it was only by the grace of God that they got a second chance. I wasn't about to let you go once I found you."

"I love you too, Coach."

They looked at each other for a moment, then Coach asked in a quiet voice, "Would you mind calling me Johnny sometimes? It's just that…now that I've talked about Jenny, it seems right, you knowing about her and using my real name like she did."

Harley could feel her chin wobbling, and the damn tears she'd managed to finally beat back minutes before returned. She loved this man so much, there was nothing she wouldn't do for him. "I love you, Johnny. You're the man I never knew I wanted or needed. I saw your looks, and didn't bother to see past them to the man underneath. I figured you'd be shallow and would only see a big nerd standing in front of you. But I swear, you had better say something right now that will make me laugh. I'm so sick of crying."

Coach chuckled and kissed her on the forehead before drawing her down into his arms. Even though Harley could feel him hard against her, she somehow knew he wouldn't make love to her. They were too comfortable and he was too…raw…for that right now.

"As long as you're crying happy tears, I'll take 'em. It's the other kind I can't stand."

"I know." Harley sniffed a couple of times, but breathed out a long breath as she got herself under control. "Can I tell Rayne and Emily that joke?"

She felt Coach's smile against her hair. "As long as you only call me Johnny when we're alone, you can do whatever the hell you want. If the guys find out my given name, I'll have to beat you."

"Deal." Harley knew he was kidding. As if he'd lay a single hand on her. No way.

"But not around Annie," Coach further cautioned.

"Of course not. She wouldn't understand it anyway," Harley told him in a sleepy voice.

"Don't underestimate that kid. She's smarter than any first grader I've ever met."

"Maybe I should start teaching her how to code."

"Maybe you should," Coach agreed.

Ten minutes later, Harley shifted to the side of Coach into a more comfortable position for both of them. She kept her hand over his heart and her head on his shoulder, copying the position he'd been in earlier. "Thank you for coming back. I was worried about you."

"I know. That's why I returned. I'd sooner rip out my own heart than make you worry unnecessarily about me."

"You can always take the space and time you need, but please, always come back to me."

"I will. I promise."

"Love you, Johnny."

"I love you too, Harley."

Chapter Twenty

HARLEY GROANED AS a beeping noise woke her up. She lifted her head and looked at her clock through bleary eyes. "What in the hell is that?"

"Sorry, Harl, it's my alarm," Coach told her after he'd shut off the offensive tone coming from his phone.

"Good Lord, it's only five-thirty. We didn't get to sleep until after three. What are you doing?"

"Work. Gotta go in for PT."

"Insane. Seriously. Go. Get. I'll get up in another six hours or so," Harley mumbled sleepily.

Coach laughed and kissed Harley on the forehead. He swung his legs out of the bed. "You're definitely not a morning person," he observed unnecessarily.

"Humph."

"I'll call ya later. Maybe we can do lunch?"

"If I'm up by then," Harley slurred, obviously on her way back to dreamland.

"Okay. Love you, Harley."

"Love you too, Johnny."

Coach stood on the side of Harley's bed in nothing

but his underwear and never felt happier. He never expected that doing a favor for Tommy would lead to finding the woman who completed him.

Once upon a time, Coach believed that he'd never be happy again. Losing his sister had torn his heart in two, but somehow, over the last couple of months, Harley had put it back together. She had done everything perfectly last night. Letting him talk about Jenny, not demanding to know where he'd been and what he'd been doing. She hadn't freaked out about him telling off the high schoolers. She'd been quiet and let him work through his history in his own way. He felt as if a weight had been lifted off him.

In the middle of telling Harley what had happened to Jenny, he realized that he finally forgave his sister for what she'd done. Her death had haunted him for a long time, but Harley had helped him crawl out of that dark hole he'd felt like he'd been in for most of his life.

And not only that, but she was absolutely right. He would never wish Jenny dead, but as a direct result of her taking her own life, he'd joined the Army. He was where he was today because of her actions. There was no telling what he'd be doing if it wasn't for what she'd done. In a roundabout way, he'd met *Harley* because of Jenny.

It was an amazing way to look at life, and he shouldn't be surprised that Harley realized it. If anyone had told him when he was in high school that eventually he'd meet the woman meant to be his because of Jenny dying, he would've beaten the shit out of them. But time, and crying in Harley's arms, had made it seem so clear.

Coach spared a thought for his friend Fish. He wondered what direction the man's life would go as a result of what happened over in the Middle East and losing part of his arm. He hoped like hell it would be somewhere good, like meeting the woman who was meant to be his, and not something like ending up drunk and homeless in a gutter somewhere.

Hearing his real name fall so easily from Harley's lips when she was mostly out of it meant so much…and the last step he'd needed to feel connected to Harley and to let the bitterness over Jenny's death go. He sent up a quick prayer to his little sister.

Thank you for sending Harley to me, Jenny. I miss you so much, but I'm at peace now. I love you.

He hadn't liked keeping his past from Harley, and felt like a weight was lifted off his heart. Coach loved Harley like he'd never loved anyone before.

It was…more.

All encompassing.

Healing.

Perfect.

Coach leaned down once more and kissed Harley

lightly on the lips before backing away and gathering up his clothes. He needed to run back to his apartment and grab his workout clothes before heading to the base, and he had just enough time.

Since they hadn't exchanged keys yet, Coach couldn't bolt her door, but he turned the lock on the knob and closed the door behind him, testing it to make sure it was secured. It was.

Coach drove back to his place with a smile on his face, feeling lighter than he had in years.

Later, even as he and his teammates were getting hammered at PT, he couldn't keep the smile from his face. Life was good.

COACH FROWNED AS he held his phone up to his ear for the fourth time that day.

"Still can't get ahold of her?" Hollywood asked, concerned.

Coach clicked the button to end the call, not bothering to leave another message. "No. It's now going straight to voice mail."

"She's probably just in the middle of working or something. You told us she gets that way. That once she starts working on a project, nothing short of a nuclear blast could tear her away."

Coach nodded distractedly. "Yeah, but this feels different. We…shit man, we had a moment last night. I know that sounds pussy-ish, but it's true. I…opened up to her about my past, and it was intense. She didn't get a lot of sleep last night, but it's two, she should've been up by now. Besides, I said I'd call her about lunch."

"Go," Hollywood ordered immediately. "I'll talk to Ghost and tell him where you went. You're not going to be able to concentrate until you see for yourself that she's all right."

"You sure?"

"Of course. Go. And call me later."

"Thanks, Hollywood, I will."

Coach didn't hesitate. He'd been battling the urge to go to Harley's place for at least two hours to make sure she was all right. As he walked to his SUV, he checked his texts one more time. Nothing.

The messages he'd sent her were there, but she hadn't responded.

Hey Harl. You up yet? We still on for lunch?
Get up sleepyhead! Lunch at 12:30?
You're worrying me. Please text me.

He'd started calling her after she didn't respond to the third text. After the first call, it went straight to voice mail, as if the phone was off or dead. Coach didn't think it would be dead; Harley was pretty good about keeping it charged. He couldn't imagine why she'd turn it off, unless she really was trying to get some work done without distractions.

As soon as Coach had the thought, he dismissed it. He knew Harley. Knew she wouldn't turn off her phone, especially after last night. She always had it on and next to her, just in case her brother or sister—or he—needed to get ahold of her. Not only that, but she'd been devastated for him after hearing about Jenny. She wouldn't do that, not when they'd sort of made plans for lunch.

Coach fretted the entire way back to her townhouse, frowning when he didn't see her piece of crap Focus in the parking lot. He'd asked Fletch to take a look at her car, but between their missions and general life getting in the way, he hadn't had a chance to yet.

Coach went up to Harley's door anyway, knocking loudly. She didn't answer. Wishing like hell he had a key to her place—that was the first thing on his agenda when he saw her again, exchanging keys, if only so he could make sure he could get inside her place in case of an emergency—he knocked again. Still no answer.

The older woman, Gretel, opened her door in the townhouse next door. "She's not there."

"Do you know when she left?" Coach didn't bother with any idle chitchat.

"Nope. Woke up this morning and her car was gone. Didn't hear or see anything." She tapped her ear. "Hearings not what it once was."

"Do you think Henry heard her leave?" Coach asked, looking toward the townhouse on the other side of Harley's, then back at Gretel.

Surprisingly, the older man's head popped up behind the woman's. "Sorry, young man, we were a bit occupied and didn't hear a thing."

Gretel blushed and smacked Henry on the shoulder. "Henry!"

Coach grinned, even though he was stressed. Good for them. It was about time they hooked up. From what Harley told him, they'd had the hots for each other for a long time. Harley would get a kick out of hearing they were finally together.

"Appreciate it. If you see her, will you tell her to please call Coach? I've been trying to get ahold of her. She isn't answering her phone."

Henry waved his hand. "Eh, you know these kids. Not worrying about calling people back. I'm sure she'll get in touch with you soon."

Coach nodded, but disagreed. Harley had always phoned him back when she'd missed his calls in the past. Every single time. The bad feeling in his gut intensified.

Coach sat in his SUV outside her townhouse and drummed his fingers on the steering wheel. He wasn't sure what to do next. Yes, they were dating, but she was also an independent woman. They'd even had this conversation last night. She had her own life and they didn't tell each other what they were doing every second of every day.

But Coach was worried about her.

He didn't think this was normal.

Just last night, this morning, he'd promised to protect her, and he had the weirdest feeling that she needed him right now.

Coach picked up his phone and dialed Rayne's number first.

"Hey, Coach, what's up?"

"Have you talked to Harley this morning?"

"Well, good morning to you too, grumpy," Rayne teased.

"Have you?"

Obviously reading the concerned tone in his voice, she hurried to respond, "No. The last time I spoke to her was at the restaurant when you guys left yesterday."

"Okay, thanks."

"Wait! Coach, is everything all right?"

"I don't know, but I don't think so."

"You'll let me know when you hear from her? Now I'm worried."

"Sure. Gotta go."

"Okay, later, Coach."

He hung up without saying 'bye, and dialed Emily's number.

"Hello, this is Emily."

"Hey, Em. This is Coach. Have you talked to Harley today?"

"Today? No. I called her the other day to chat, and we made plans to get together one night with Rayne and Mary. We also talked about going shopping for dresses for the Army Ball coming up, but haven't finalized anything yet. Why?"

"I can't get ahold of her."

"Oh, well, I'm sure she's fine."

"Yeah. Can you let me know if you hear from her?"

"Sure. Want me to call Fletch?"

"No, I'll be seeing him soon."

"Okay, talk to you later, Coach."

"Later."

Coach ended the call and immediately dialed Montesa. He was probably overstepping his boundaries, calling her sister when he'd only met her once, but the training he'd had was kicking into overdrive. The hair on the back of his neck was standing straight up and he had the same feeling in his gut that he had the one time they'd been in Afghanistan and they'd walked into an ambush. Luckily, Ghost had reacted immediately after hearing Coach's concerns and they'd all made it out of that clusterfuck with their lives.

"Hello?"

"Is this Montesa?"

"Yes, who is this?"

"It's Coach, Harley's boyfriend."

"Oh, hi, Coach. Is everything all right?"

"I don't know. Have you heard from Harley today?"

"Nope. She called yesterday, upset because she couldn't get ahold of *you*. What's going on? Did she find you?"

"Yeah, I had some shit go down with me yesterday, but I came back to her townhouse last night and we talked it out. We're good. But I can't reach her now. She was supposed to meet me for lunch."

"She's probably just engrossed in code or something."

Coach clenched his teeth. If one more person told him that, he was gonna lose it. "I'm at her place and her car's not here and she's not answering her door."

"Oh."

"I've called and texted her, but she's not answering."

"I'll see if I can get ahold of her."

"I'd appreciate that. You'll let me know if you do?"

"Of course."

"Thanks. I love her, Montesa." Coach wasn't sure why he was blurting out his feelings for Harley to her sister, but it seemed like the right thing to do. "I've known for a while, but as her older sister, I wanted you to know, and be assured that I'll do what I can to protect her."

There was silence on the other end of the line, before Montesa said, "Good. She means the world to me. She needs someone like you to stand up for her and to force her out of her house every now and then."

"You'll call me back if you hear from her?"

"Yeah."

"Thanks. Later."

Again, Coach clicked off the call without waiting for her to say goodbye. He immediately dialed Davidson's number. He was definitely pushing his luck now, but he wasn't going to stop until he'd found Harley.

"Yo."

"This is Coach, Harley's boyfriend. Have you heard from her? I can't find her and I'm getting worried."

"No. We don't talk every day. The last I heard from her was last week."

"Damn. Okay, if you *do* see or talk to her, will you let me know?"

"What's up? You have a fight?"

"No. I just…she's missing." Coach said the words that he'd been thinking for the first time, and they tasted like acid in his mouth. "I don't know where she is."

"Fuck. Okay, I'll try her cell and see if I can't get ahold of her."

"It's going straight to voice mail for me," Coach told Davidson.

"I'll swing by her place then."

"I'm *at* her place. She isn't here. Look, I don't want to embarrass her if she's just out doing errands, but I have a bad feeling about this. I'm going to drive around and see if I can find her car."

"Sounds good. I will too. You call Montesa?"

"Yeah, right before you. I didn't say that she was missing, but I'm sure I worried her."

"Good call on not giving her all the details. She *will* worry, but she'll hold tight until we have more info. I'll touch base later and we can compare notes."

"Thanks, Davidson."

"She's my sister. Of course I'm going to help."

Coach knew *exactly* how the other man felt. "Later."

"'Bye."

Coach sat for a moment in his vehicle, at a loss on who else he could call. Finally, he clicked on one more number.

"You find her?"

"No. Ghost, I need your help. And the team. And maybe that mysterious computer guy you know. She's nowhere. Car's gone, she's not home. Neighbors didn't see her leave, and she hasn't called her brother, sister, Emily, or Rayne. Something's wrong."

"Like Afghanistan wrong?" Leave it to Ghost to ask exactly the right question.

"Yeah."

"On it," Ghost told his friend and teammate immediately without asking for any more information. "I'll meet you at your place. We'll organize there and see if we can't do some sort of grid search. I'll call Rock and see if he can help us too."

"Rock? The sniper who works down in San Antonio now?"

"Yeah. He helped us with the situation with that asshole Jacks and Emily and Annie. Since he's a cop, he can help put out a be-on-the-lookout for her car."

Coach swallowed the bile that crept up his throat. "You think a BOLO is necessary?"

"I do. And I think you know it. Coach, if she got carjacked, or kidnapped, or even was in an accident, the car is key."

"I need to call the hospitals and the local cops," Coach said, realizing he hadn't done that yet. The thought of Harley in the clutches of a madman was more than he could process right now.

"Okay, do that, I'll call Rock, see what he thinks. Be at your place as soon as I can, Coach. We got this. We'll find her."

"Thanks, Ghost."

"No thanks needed, man. She's one of ours. We're closing ranks."

Coach clicked off the phone and put his head on the steering wheel in despair for a moment, before pulling himself together and finding the number to the local hospital.

Harley was out there somewhere, and he'd find her. Maybe she was just running errands and all his worry was ridiculous.

But he didn't think so.

No, he *knew* that wasn't the case.

"Hold on, Harley. I'm coming for you," Coach whispered as he waited for someone at the hospital to pick up the phone.

Chapter Twenty-One

Sixteen Hours Missing

"WE'VE BEEN ALL over this city, her car's not here," Beatle said in frustration, running his hand through his hair and pacing in front of the sofa at Coach's apartment.

"I put out some feelers in the seedy bars around the base," Truck told his teammates. "Said we were looking for a missing woman and if anyone had any information they'd get paid under the table, no questions asked." Everyone nodded. If anyone was going to have success at what he'd done, it was Truck. He blended in perfectly with his huge badass frame and his scar. No one dared fuck with him. Even the baddest of the bad respected him.

"Davidson called a while ago and said he hadn't had any luck either. He went out again this evening to see if he could find her car," Hollywood told the group.

"What about Tex?" Coach asked Ghost. "What's he come up with?"

"Nothing. I wasn't able to get ahold of him. Apparently his wife is having a baby and he's unavailable."

"Dammit!" Blade bit out, his frustration clear in his voice. "What about Tiger's friend? The computer geek down there in San Antonio?"

"Haven't asked her yet," Ghost said calmly, used to his team's outbursts and frustrations. He was obviously just as frustrated, but, as team leader, was better able to control it. Calling Penelope Turner was on his list of things to do, but since he'd been organizing the physical search for Harley, he hadn't had a chance yet.

Coach felt like he'd downed several energy drinks. He hadn't eaten anything since he'd realized Harley was missing, but the adrenaline in his body hadn't lessened over the last couple of hours. "What'd Rock say?"

"He put a BOLO out on her car. No matches yet," Fletch told the group of tight-knit men.

"What's our next step?" Hollywood asked.

"I'll call Tiger and ask her to get Beth on this," Ghost said decisively, moving it to the top of his to-do list. "We need to track Harley's phone and see where it last pinged. That will help narrow down the search area. Beth will also be able to track her digital footprint as well. Credit cards, ATM transactions, things like that."

Coach sat down on his couch and put his head in his hands. "Her phone's off. That's why it's going straight to voice mail. She drives that older piece of shit, so there's no GPS tracking in it. And you all know as well as I do that if someone snatched her, she could be a couple of states away by now."

"Maybe, maybe not. We have to try," Ghost told his friend in a stern voice. "We aren't giving up, you can't either."

The words were what Coach needed to hear, but he was frustrated. "I'm not fucking giving up, Ghost. I'm terrified out of my mind for her. Is she scared? Is she hurting? If someone took her, what do they want? Are they violating her? Is she even still alive? Too many people disappear without a trace in our world. I can't lose her, man. I can't!"

His words were all over the place, pain clear in every syllable.

"We won't give up until we find her, Coach. You know we won't," Ghost told his friend, putting his hand on his shoulder in support.

"I know." Coach said the words calmly, but everyone heard the terror in them.

Thirty-Two Hours Missing

COACH SAT ACROSS from the detective in the Temple Police Department. He'd come down to the station with Davidson to officially file a missing person's report. He only hoped that the officers would do something immediately, rather than playing the "she's an adult and is allowed to not talk to anyone for a few days" card.

Since Davidson was related to Harley, he was the one who was filling out the paperwork.

The detective had brought them into separate interrogation rooms to take their statements. That had been two hours ago, and Coach was still being grilled. He could appreciate that the boyfriend or husband was usually the first suspect in missing person's cases, but his patience was being tested. The only reason he hadn't lost his shit before now was because he knew his team was out there looking for Harley while he was stuck answering the same questions over and over.

"Tell me again what happened the night before Harley went missing," the detective ordered, his pen hovering over a pad of paper.

Coach sighed. He'd already told the guy twice what had happened, and knew the man was looking for inconsistencies to his story, but it still pissed him off. *He* knew he hadn't hurt Harley, but he needed to convince *this* asshole so he'd stop looking at him as the culprit and start the investigation.

"I was upset about something that happened that day and didn't get back to her place until really early in the morning. We talked it out, we went to sleep, I got up around five-thirty because I had to get to PT at the base. I don't have a key to her place, so I locked the doorknob, not the bolt, and left. That's it."

"And Harley was sleeping when you left?"

"Yes."

"What happened to make you upset?"

Coach clenched his teeth and tried to control his anger. "Nothing that has anything to do with Harley disappearing."

"You don't know that. Maybe whatever it was had a direct effect. Did you get in a fight with someone yesterday? Maybe that person came back to take it out on Harley. Maybe you fought with *her*. Was that it? Did you hit her? Maybe she left to get away from you?"

"No, dammit!" Coach swore, standing up and leaning over the table. "We did *not* fight. I love Harley. We admitted we loved each other for the first time last night."

"So what happened to make you upset then?"

Fuck. The man wasn't going to let it go. Coach had no desire to relive the incident, from yesterday or his childhood, but if he didn't, he'd never get out of this damn room. "We were having lunch and some high schoolers were making fun of some other girls. It bothered me. I told the teenagers off. That's it. No fight. Just some civilized words of advice for our younger generation."

"Hmmmm," the officer said, scribbling something on his notepad. "Were there witnesses to these 'words?'"

"Yes," Coach bit out. "Harley was there. And my friends, Ghost, Blade, Hollywood, Emily, Rayne, and

Mary. Not to mention the high schoolers themselves. And there was probably another random civilian or two who happened to exit the restaurant at the same time as well. Please. Harley is missing, and every minute you spend in here with me is another minute that you're not investigating where the fuck she is."

The detective leaned back in his chair, as if he had all the time in the world. "See, now, *you* say she's missing, but maybe she's not. She's an adult, she can decide to leave of her own accord. It's not breaking the law."

"Fine. She left of her own accord, but you still have a responsibility to see if you can find out where she is. Track her credit cards, check her phone, look at her bank records. If she left on her own, you can figure it out and I won't worry about her anymore." Coach knew *that* was a lie, but he needed this guy to stop dicking around and do *something*.

The detective finally stood up and put his notepad in his pocket. "You'll be around if we have any other questions? I'll also need to contact your commanding officer and CID."

Coach didn't give a shit if this guy contacted the Criminal Investigation Division on base, as long as he was doing something. "No problem. I'll write down my CO's information." Since Coach was still standing, he was now eye to eye with the detective. He needed to try to get through to the man.

"Please. I know I'm a suspect. I can live with that, but don't only look at me. I'm innocent. I wouldn't hurt a hair on Harley's head. I love that woman so much, I'm putty in her hands. Do what you have to do, but for the love of God, keep looking for her while you're investigating me."

"We'll be in touch."

The detective didn't look moved in the slightest by his impassioned plea. Coach closed his eyes for a moment. Fine. He'd done the right thing, the legal thing, and reported Harley missing through proper channels. He just hoped like fuck Beth, Penelope's friend, had more information.

Penelope Turner was a soldier they'd been sent to Turkey to rescue from ISIS. She was tough as nails and the entire team had been impressed with her. She lived in San Antonio and was a full-time firefighter now. In a weird coincidence, she was friends with Rock, who now went by TJ, their former Delta sniper contact.

It was all very convoluted, but Coach didn't care. Help was help and he could use all he could get right about now. Penelope's brother was dating a woman named Beth, who was a computer hacker, much like Tex was. Coach would've been suspicious of how they happened to know the right people at the right time, but he'd been a Delta Force soldier long enough to not look a gift horse in the mouth. He'd take every coincidental connection he could get, and give out as many markers as needed, if they could only find Harley.

Fifty-Three Hours Missing

"YOU WERE RIGHT, there's no active signal coming from her phone," Beth told the group of men via speakerphone as they hung on her every word. "I checked and the last signal pinged from the tower nearest to her townhouse. But I can't tell if that was while she was inside her place or when she was leaving. There's been no activity on her credit cards and the piece-of-shit cameras in her complex haven't been in operation for at least a year or more."

"So you have nothing," Coach grumbled in frustration.

"I wouldn't say that," Beth returned immediately. "I've been checking out traffic cameras around her place and I'm pretty sure I've identified her car on a couple. They're complete crap images, so I can't read the license plate, or see who was in the car, but it looks like a blue Ford Focus, with only one person visible in the driver's seat. That doesn't mean someone else wasn't crouched down with a gun making her drive, or that it's not her driving at all."

"Where were the cameras?" Ghost asked.

"One is at the intersection of Main and Fourth, the

other is farther down, at Main and Eighth."

"Which direction?" Hollywood asked that time.

"West."

Fletch turned to the others sitting around the table at the base. They'd moved their operation there with their CO's blessing, as they had access to more gadgets than at Coach's apartment. "Okay, so she left her place—"

"We don't know if she left voluntarily or if someone broke in and forced her to leave," Truck interrupted. "Coach didn't have a key to bolt the door, so it would've been easy to jimmy open."

"The police admitted that there weren't any signs of it being tampered with," Fletch continued, not irritated at all that he'd been interrupted. "And the bolt was locked when they got there to check it out. Her landlord had to unlock it to let them in. Since Coach said he only locked the knob, we have to assume she left home as usual that morning and locked the bolt as she left."

"We don't know where she was going," Blade observed.

"No, but she was driving west through town. Coach, can you talk to her brother and sister and see if they have any ideas about where she might have been headed?"

"Yes." Coach hadn't slept much, only twenty minutes or so here and there. Every time he fell asleep, he saw Harley's face and heard her pleas for help. When he asked her where she was, she disappeared in a puff of smoke and he woke up shaking and sweating.

The dream he'd had right before this meeting was equally as awful. They'd been sitting on a wall near the ocean when a tsunami came out of nowhere and swept Harley away. He'd been holding her hand as the wave tried to suck her under. He hadn't been able to hold on to her anymore, and as she was carried off by the water, she'd been screaming at him to help her.

"I'm still working on scanning the other cameras," Beth told them through the speaker of the phone.

"What about her phone records?" Coach asked, trying to shrug off the memory of his nightmare. "Did she receive any calls that morning or text anyone?"

"No, and don't ask how I know that. I'm breaking about forty-three FCC rules, but I'd do it again in a heartbeat. And I hacked into her home computer as well. Nothing stands out there either. Harley logged in at eight forty-two and deleted some emails. She checked her social media, but didn't comment or otherwise engage with anyone on there. She didn't go to any websites either."

The room was silent for a beat.

"How could she have disappeared without a trace?" Coach asked nobody in particular in an agonized voice. "She was here one minute, then gone the next."

"She's somewhere," Beth said soothingly from the other end of the phone. "We're gonna find her. I think her car is the key. It has to be. I'm going to spread my search area. I'll hack into the cameras at the Austin and DFW airports and see if the car ended up at either one. I'll also check the toll roads around the areas as well. No matter what, Coach, I'm not giving up."

"Thanks, Beth. I owe you," Coach said in a soft voice. As much as he hoped they'd find Harley's car, he knew it wasn't necessarily the key to finding her. If someone had taken her, they could've dumped her car and been hundreds of miles away by now. Thousands, if they flew her somewhere. But he had no idea who would want to kidnap her...or why. He had so many unanswered questions, his head was spinning. But he was grateful that he had such a great group of friends who would drop everything and work around the clock to do what they could to find Harley.

"No you don't," Beth returned a bit gruffly. "You don't owe me a damn thing. You saved Pen's life. She's one of my closest friends. I couldn't have made it down here in San Antonio without her. So this is making us even. Now, I g-gotta go. I'll be in touch."

The phone clicked off and no one commented on the break in Beth's voice. She was as affected by this as they all were, even though she didn't know Harley personally.

"We need to search the roads. Look for skid marks or broken guardrails. Maybe she was in an accident," Ghost commented.

"I called the hospitals, there were no Jane Does admitted from any car wrecks," Coach told Ghost.

"Okay, but still, if the cameras said her car was driving west on Main Street, we need to follow up on that."

"Me and Beatle can go," Blade said. "I'll drive so he can concentrate on seeing if he can catch anything out of the ordinary."

"Good," Ghost told them. "Pay close attention to the gravel on the shoulders too. Once you get out of town, some of those roads are raised. There are irrigation ditches and streams along a lot of them."

"Will do," Beatle reassured both Ghost and Coach at the same time. "If there's any sign of an accident, we'll investigate it."

"I'm going to see if I can get into her apartment," Coach announced, standing up. "I want to get a look at it myself. Maybe I'll see something that the cops didn't. I was there that morning, I might notice if something is out of place."

"I'll go with you," Truck said, his chair screeching on the floor as he stood.

"Coach, be sure you're back here at noon. CID wants to interview you," Ghost reminded him with a warning in his voice. "You can't miss it. It'll make you look guilty."

"I'll be there." Coach knew he *already* looked guilty, but didn't bring it up. It didn't matter. Coach didn't want to go through another interrogation, but he'd sit through as many as it took to get the cops off his back. He didn't hurt Harley. The faster the authorities understood that the better, and maybe the more re-sources would be spent looking for her rather than following him around, watching his every move.

HARLEY'S APARTMENT LOOKED just like it did when Coach had left the other morning. There were new dishes in the sink though, so Harley had gotten up and eaten breakfast. Coach looked into the trash can, seeing nothing out of the ordinary, although it did need to be emptied. There was no way he was going to touch it though. It would be one more way the cops would try to pin her disappearance on him...accusing him of tamper-ing with evidence if he brought the trash out to the Dumpster.

"I'm going to look around," Coach told Truck. His friend nodded and continued to run his eyes over Harley's things, as if memorizing the placement of every book and knickknack.

Coach wandered into her room and the sight of her

bed nearly took his breath away. The covers were thrown back as if she'd just been there. He could picture her sliding her feet to the side and standing up after finally awakening. Had she thought about him? Was she concerned about what he'd told her? Was she sad for him? The bed held no answers.

He looked at the bedside table. Her glasses weren't there, telling him that she had most likely put them on as usual when she'd gotten up. A part of Coach wanted them to be there. It would be *some* clue as to what had happened.

Wandering into the bathroom, Coach saw nothing out of the ordinary. Her towel was hanging over the bar next to the shower, her toothpaste and toothbrush were sitting next to the sink. Her hair dryer resting in its usual place. He opened the doors under the sink. Again, the trash can held nothing unusual. Some cotton swabs, a Q-tip, and a used tissue.

The sun was shining brightly into the room from the small window above the shower. It was as if she'd snapped her fingers and poof…disappeared. It was frustrating, and so damn depressing.

For just a moment, Coach allowed himself to feel despair. He was deathly afraid he'd never see Harley again. That he'd finally lucked out and found the woman meant to be his, only to have lost her in the next instant. It wasn't fair. For a minute or two the dark cloud that had followed him around for years after the death of his sister threatened to engulf him once more. He'd spent many months going through life in a haze, unable to get over the feelings of guilt, despair, and grief.

Taking a deep breath, Coach got himself back under control. Being depressed wouldn't help Harley, and it certainly wasn't helping him.

He gritted his teeth in newfound determination. No one was gonna steal his girlfriend out from under his nose. No way in hell. He and his friends were Delta Force. The most badass soldiers the military had. They'd find her or die trying. It was what they did, what they'd been trained for.

He walked out of her bedroom and back into the living area.

"Nothing," Coach told Truck.

"Yeah, it looks like she left to go out for errands or something."

Coach nodded, agreeing. "Her purse is missing, her glasses, keys and cell aren't here, and while I'm not an expert on what she wears, I don't see her usual sneakers."

"I'm gonna have Beth look into Jacks. I know he's in jail for what he did to Emily and Annie, but I don't trust the man. He hates us to the marrow of his bones. He could've had a friend kidnap Harley just to piss us off," Truck said evenly.

"Good idea," Coach nodded. "I should've thought about it. If that fucker has touched even one hair on Harley's head, I'm gonna kill him."

Instead of reacting to Coach's harsh statement, Truck looked at his watch. "You gotta get back to base. The MPs and CID are waiting."

"Yeah." Coach looked at his friend for a beat and finally said, "I didn't do this, Truck."

"What the fuck?" the other Delta spat. "Of course you didn't. Why would you say something like that?"

"I know the cops are gonna think it was me and I just wanted to tell you, man to man, Delta to Delta, that I didn't."

Truck put his hand on Coach's shoulder and said in a low, urgent voice, "Coach, I've spent more days than I can count in hell with you. We've fought next to each other; we've saved each other's lives several times over. I know you, man. I *know* you. You would never hurt someone you cared about. Ever. I've got your back. So does Ghost, Blade, Hollywood, Beatle, and Fletch."

"Thanks." It was all Coach could get out. He loved every one of his teammates like brothers.

"Come on, let's get you back to base."

The two men were quiet on the way back to Fort Hood. Coach lost in his thoughts about what could've possibly happened to Harley, and Truck worried about what was to come for his friend.

Seventy-Two Hours Missing

"THERE ARE REPORTS of you being involved in an altercation outside of the burrito place on Sanders Street," the Army investigator informed Coach. He was sitting across the silver metal table with another man. They both had their notepads out and had been asking him to repeat the events that led up to the time when Harley disappeared.

"It wasn't an altercation," Coach protested. "I had a conversation with a group of teenaged girls. Then I left."

"We went to the high school and with the assistance of the employees there, tracked down the young women you spoke with. And their story is quite different than yours." The other officer looked down at his notes, obviously having done his research, and read what was written there. "He was scary. He got in our faces and yelled at us, told us we were rotten and bullies. But we aren't. He told me that he hoped my dog died and that my future kids would get cancer." The officer looked up. "That sounds like an altercation to me."

"That's not what I said, and you can ask anyone who was there, but as I told you before, I *did* chastise them for being bullies. It was wrong, but I was emotional and not thinking straight."

"Were you emotional and not thinking straight

when you went back over to Miss Kelso's place later?"

Not liking the insinuation, but also not surprised by it, Coach tried to keep his temper under control. "I was emotional, but not in the way you're thinking. I went over to Harley's place because I knew she'd make me feel better, and I knew I had to explain why I said what I'd said that day."

"*Did* she understand? Maybe she was shocked at your behavior toward those kids. Maybe she said she didn't want to see you again and you lost it. Hit her a bit too hard. With your training, it'd be easy to do. I know you and your buddies know how to kill and not leave a mark. I wouldn't be surprised if you had connections that could help you get rid of a body as well."

Even knowing the man was egging him on, purposely trying to get under his skin, his words infuriated Coach. "I. Didn't. Hurt. Harley," he enunciated. "I didn't hit her. I didn't yell at her. I didn't do *anything* to her. I crawled into bed with her and we held each other. All night. I told her I loved her, and she said it back. We snuggled and fell asleep. In the morning, she was exhausted. When I left her place, she was sleeping."

"Did you have sex with her?"

Coach gritted his teeth and met the investigator's eyes. He so wanted to tell the man that it was none of his business and had nothing to do with whatever happened to his girlfriend, but knew he didn't have the luxury to tell him off. If he was going to be any kind of help to Harley, he had to keep his shit together. "No. Not that night. The night before? Yeah. But that night, we were both too tired and emotionally drained to do more than hold each other. Is there a law against sleeping now?"

Coach's snarky words didn't even faze the officer asking the questions. "No. But you could've been pissed she wouldn't let you fuck her. Maybe you did it anyway, and she got scared and ran."

"I didn't rape my girlfriend!" Coach yelled, finally losing it. "I *love* her. I would sooner stab myself in the eye than hurt her. I'm telling you exactly what happened, but you're not *listening* to me. I left her that morning, safe and alone, sleeping. We had plans to meet for lunch and I couldn't get ahold of her. That's it. That's all. Now she's missing and no one is doing *anything* other than trying to get me to admit that I did something to her. I didn't. I *wouldn't.*" His voice dropped until he was begging the two strangers sitting so stoically in front of him.

"Please. You have to believe me. I didn't do anything but spend the night next to the woman I love and leave her warm and sleeping in her bed. She's out there somewhere. She needs help, I can feel it to the very marrow of my bones. But you accusing me of hurting her isn't helping Harley. Time is slipping away and if you don't find her, she's gonna die."

"So…did you hurt her after your argument? Then panic because you knew what would happen to your career if anyone found out? Did you stash her in a motel somewhere? Immobilize her? Does she need a doctor? Is that why you think she's going to die? If you tell us where you put her, we can get her medical help, then she won't die, and you won't be charged with murder."

Coach put his head on the hard, cool table in front of him in defeat. If Jacks was behind Harley's disappearance, he'd succeeded in his mission to make his life a living hell. He'd won.

Regardless, it was obvious Harley was going to die, because no one would pull their heads out of their asses long enough to see that *he* wasn't the bad guy here. Coach had never felt so defeated and scared in all his life.

No matter that he'd been on more deadly missions than he could name.

No matter that his name was listed in files deep in the guts of the United States' war records.

He had more medals than he could ever wear.

But all of it didn't matter.

Nothing did.

Harley was going to die, and somehow he felt as if it was his fault because he couldn't find her.

Chapter Twenty-Two

Ninety Hours Missing

*T*HANK YOU FOR *tuning into KWTX Evening News Ten. Tonight's big story is of missing local woman, Harley Kelso. We've been reporting on her disappearance and the questioning of an Army sergeant about her whereabouts. This afternoon, we received this phone message from one of Miss Kelso's neighbors,*

"I'm calling about the disappearance of that woman. She lives across the way from me, and I don't sleep much anymore. And I have to say that something is very wrong here. I saw a big SUV pull up to her place really early in the morning, and then it left only a couple of hours later. The guy was huge, and I know I sure as hell wouldn't want to meet him in a dark alley. He had something to do with it. I know he did. Why would he leave so soon after arriving? It doesn't make sense. It's just really fishy and I'm willing to help the police with whatever they need to put him behind bars."

The Temple Police Department and Army investigators have interrogated the soldier, but so far no arrests have been made in the case. If you have any information about

Harley or her missing vehicle, please contact the TPD as soon as possible.

Coach didn't even look up at the television screen. He barely heard the newscast and didn't give a shit that he was being crucified in the press, and people he didn't know were fingering him. He'd never met the mysterious neighbor who had called into the radio station to accuse him.

He hadn't done anything to Harley. He knew it. His friends knew it. Hell, even her siblings knew it. Everyone else could go to hell.

Coach had been in close contact with both Montesa and Davidson since Harley had gone missing. Davidson had been on searches with the rest of the Deltas, and Ghost had been keeping him updated on what they found out, which was damn little. Montesa had hit social media hard, posting smiling pictures of Harley all over, urging everyone to report anything they saw, no matter how small they might think it was.

Coach's hands shook as he remembered the dream he'd had the last time he'd fallen asleep. He and Harley were skydiving again. She was strapped with her back to his front as she'd been the first time he'd met her. She was giggling and smiling as he pushed them from the plane. Then suddenly she was face-to-face with him and they were hurtling toward the ground. He went to pull the ripcord, but it wasn't there. He wasn't wearing a parachute at all.

Harley had looked up at him in the dream and said in a sad voice, "I'm gonna die, aren't I?"

He'd opened his mouth to tell her that wasn't true, that he was doing all he could to save her, when her eyeballs had started bleeding. The blood oozed out of her eye sockets and dripped to his face as gravity pulled the two of them toward the ground. He blinked, but couldn't see Harley anymore, only a red haze.

"I'm so scared, Johnny. I need you," were the last words she'd said, suddenly sounding like his sister, Jenny, before he'd jerked awake.

Running to the bathroom and throwing up hadn't been enough to wipe the memory of the horrible dream from his mind.

The last couple of days had been hell. He'd only slept in short spurts, and they had absolutely no new information about where Harley was. Blade and Beatle had found no signs of a recent car accident when they'd investigated and trolled Main Street all the way past Temple and into the countryside. There were still no unidentified bodies in the morgue or in the hospitals. The team had no new information from Beth either.

She'd investigated Jacks and had reported that from what she could find, the man hadn't had any contact with any of the men in his former unit. His days were taken up with meetings with his lawyer to discuss his upcoming trial.

Harley's credit cards hadn't been used and her phone was still dead.

At this point, Coach knew Harley could be as far away as California. Or someone could've snatched her away, changed the license plate on her car, and driven across the border to Mexico. He knew what happened to most of the women who went missing in Mexico, and it was extremely difficult to even think about. But even more horrific than the thought of her being kidnapped and used as a sex slave, was that she could be dead.

Coach wasn't an idiot, he knew the longer a person was missing the more likely it was that they were deceased.

Four days. She'd been gone for four days. It was an eternity. Very few people were found alive after so long. The few publicized cases were the exception, not the norm.

The guys were taking turns staying with him, and today was Truck's turn.

"What do you think happened to her?" Coach asked in a low, agonized voice. Truck might be big and scary looking, but Coach knew inside, he had a marshmallow heart. He was the first one to volunteer to sit with newborn puppies when the animal shelter was low on staff. He was the first one on the team to rush into situations where women and children were involved, and he had taken it upon himself to help out Mary, and the other women, whenever they needed it. He seemed to find Mary's caustic attitude endearing, rather than offensive. He might be easygoing most of the time, but at the same time, he was also the first one likely to take his knife to the throat of a terrorist threatening one of his teammates.

"Don't do this to yourself," Truck warned. "It'll bring you nothing but grief."

"I already have grief," Coach told him in a weary tone. "Do you think she was snatched?"

"Coach…"

He ignored the warning tone of his friend and kept talking. "I think that has to be it. I mean, otherwise why wouldn't we have found *some* trace of her by now? Even Tex looked after he got home from the hospital, and he found a big fat nothing."

Obviously deciding Coach was going down the pity road whether it was healthy or not, Truck went along with it. "They could've ditched the car in a lake or pond or something. It could be years before someone found it."

"But Harley would've fought them. I know it. There's no way she would sit back and let them take her easily. I just can't see it."

"Yeah, I agree. She'd probably try to leave clues, just like Tiger did over in Turkey."

"Her phone too. She knows all about how they can be tracked by the towers. She would've kept it on as long as possible, or even sent me a text. It doesn't make sense."

"The kidnappers could've taken it away from her and ripped out the battery," Truck countered.

Coach nodded. "I suppose there's always the possibility that she really did just up and leave. I wouldn't have thought it of her, especially since she's close to her siblings. But she could be planning on getting in touch with them in a few months, after the search for her has died down. Maybe she couldn't handle what I told her. Maybe I disgusted her when I let those teen girls have it at the burrito place. I kinda disgusted myself. I wouldn't blame her if—"

"She didn't leave you, Coach," Truck interrupted. "No way in hell. You guys might have been dancing around each other, figuring out the new relationship and all, but I can tell you with one hundred percent certainty, that Harley did not just up and walk away from her life. We've all seen the way she's looked at you over the last couple of months. She loves you."

Coach lifted his head to look at his friend, not caring that his eyes were full of tears for the second time in a week. "Then where is she, Truck? Where the fuck is she?"

Truck put his hand on Coach's shoulder. "I don't

know, Coach. I simply don't know."

Ninety-Six Hours Missing

"JOHNNY BECKETT RALSTON, you need to come with us. We have more questions about the disappearance of Harley Kelso."

"What? I've already told you everything I know!" It wasn't entirely unexpected, but the officers had still surprised him.

"Turn around, sir. Put your hands behind your back."

"Truck!" Coach bellowed as one of the officers grabbed hold of his biceps and turned him around. He didn't fight them, but yelled for his friend again. "Dammit, Truck!"

His teammate ran out of Coach's back hallway in time to see his friend being held securely by the arms by the two officers from the Temple Police Department.

"Call Montesa," Coach ordered brusquely. "She told me yesterday that she and her partner, John, would be there for me if I needed them."

"Done. Don't worry, I'll make sure you—"

"I don't care about me," Coach said over his shoulder as the officers led him down the breezeway toward the parking lot. "We both know I didn't do this. I don't care how many questions they ask me. Don't stop looking for her! I don't care if they keep me there indefinitely. Promise me. *Promise* me you won't stop looking for Harley until you find her!"

"Swear, Coach!"

Truck stood in Coach's doorway, fists clenched. He had no idea what the cops thought they had, or what new questions they thought they'd ask, because the team sure had dick. If the detectives had more information than Beth or Tex had been able to dig up, he'd be shocked.

Harley had literally disappeared out of thin air. If their computer hacker friends couldn't find hide nor hair of her, there was no way the cops had found anything to point toward Coach being responsible. Speculation and circumstantial evidence, maybe, but nothing concrete.

Truck hadn't met Montesa or her partner, but if she was anything like her sister, they'd make sure Coach would be treated fairly, and not kept in an interrogation room indefinitely.

In the meantime, he had to get word to the team that Coach had been detained for more questioning. Even being *suspected* of murder could hurt his Army career, and Truck wasn't about to let that happen. Coach was a damn good soldier, and an even better Special Forces Delta operative. The team needed him. Hell, the *country* needed him.

Whirling around to head back into Coach's apartment to grab his cell and wallet, Truck shook his head, worry furrowing his brows. Where in the world was Harley? He was afraid that finding her would be the only thing that might save Coach's ass at this point.

Ninety-Seven Hours Missing

ROBERTA HARRIS WAS running late, as usual. She'd dropped her oldest kid off at school, and then stopped by the grocery store to grab a gallon of milk and a few other essentials. Her kids ate like horses, and seemed to always be hungry. With her shitty luck, there were only two cashiers open and the self-checkout wasn't working. She had to wait behind a woman with two baskets full of food and a fistful of coupons.

She was going to be late dropping Ricky off at pre-school...again. She couldn't manage to get him there on time to save her life. Luckily the girls at the school were understanding. It was nine fifty-five and she had five minutes to get him checked in. Wasn't going to happen. She thought about abandoning the groceries and making a run for it, but decided against it. Ricky and Rob would be hungry after school, and this was one of the only times she had that day to pick up some food.

Thinking about her crazy schedule as she drove to-ward Ricky's preschool, and how she wished her husband hadn't been deployed for the third time, Roberta didn't see the brown coyote running across the road until it was too late.

She slammed on the brakes, but it didn't help. She heard a yelp and felt the car shake as the poor animal smacked into the front bumper of her car.

Shaking, Roberta pulled her car over to the side of the road. There was a guardrail along the edge, so she couldn't pull as far over on the shoulder as she would've liked. But she'd only passed one other car in the last five minutes, so she thought she was pretty safe to stop and check out her car. Looking behind her to make sure Ricky was all right, seeing him smiling and laughing, Roberta finally climbed out of the car to see what the damage was.

There were no other vehicles around at the moment as it was a deserted roadway outside of town. Ricky's preschool was a bit out of the way, but it had gotten great reviews, and Ricky loved his teachers. It was worth the commute to get him the best education she could. "The last thing I need right now," she grumbled, "is to have our insurance rates go up." She rounded the front of the car, relieved to see no dent and only a small scuff on the bumper.

Looking around, she didn't see the coyote she'd hit though. It wasn't in the road and it wasn't lying on the shoulder.

Worried now, Roberta hoped it hadn't slunk off the road to die in horrible pain. She headed to the side of the wide street to look over the guardrail. If the injured animal was there, she'd call the cops. Maybe they could come shoot it and put it out of its misery. She hated thinking of any creature being in pain.

Looking down the ravine to the small creek running alongside the road, Roberta gasped. She looked twice to make sure she was really seeing what she thought she was, and fumbled for her phone. Yeah, she'd definitely be calling the cops.

Chapter Twenty-Three

Ninety-Eight Hours Missing

OACH PACED THE small interrogation room. The police officers had not-so-politely shoved him into the room and told him to take a seat. As soon as he'd invoked his right to have an attorney present while being questioned, and informed the officers that a lawyer was on the way, they'd nodded and said they'd be back as soon as Montesa arrived.

He knew this ploy. The cameras were on him and the officers were analyzing his every movement. He'd seen enough crime shows to know that his actions right now could be scrutinized as much as the words that came out of his mouth. Everything he did could be a reason to put more suspicion on him.

Coach gritted his teeth and continued pacing. Every minute that went by was one more that he wasn't able to be out looking for Harley, or at least planning what he should be doing. He didn't really blame the cops for doing their job, he was the most likely suspect, especially with his background and since there was absolutely no trace of Harley, but it was frustrating as hell. She was still missing.

So he paced.

It was four steps to the right, a turn, two steps, another turn, four more steps, and then two more paces back to where he started. He'd lost count of how many times he'd circled the small room, but it hadn't even begun to calm him down. Coach wanted to know what it was the investigators thought they had on him, but he wasn't going to talk to anyone until John or Montesa got there.

Coach's stomach growled, but he ignored it. He hadn't eaten much in the last few days, he simply couldn't keep anything down. The few times his teammates had convinced him he needed to keep up his strength for Harley, he'd had a nightmare about her, and thrown up whatever it was he'd eaten. It was simply easier not to have anything in his stomach *to* throw up.

Just when Coach thought he was going to lose it, training on how to keep his cool while under interrogation by the enemy be damned, the door to the room popped open, making him jerk in surprise.

A middle-aged man who could only be Montesa's partner stood in the doorway with a look on his face Coach couldn't interpret.

"John Black?"

"Yes. Listen, something's happening."

"Yeah, the cops want to accuse me of something I didn't do," Coach told his lawyer in obvious irritation.

"No, I mean with your case. Something's happened. The police are running around as if a fire was lit under them and no one will tell me what's going on. I finally asked the secretary where you were being held, and she gave me directions to get to you."

"Harley?" Coach asked in an urgent tone.

"Maybe. I'm going to lurk out there and see if I can't get more information."

"Dammit! I need to get out of here."

"Unfortunately, that's not happening right this second," the other man told Coach sympathetically.

"Fuck." Coach pulled out a chair and fell into it, resting his elbows on his knees and putting his head in his hands. He stayed that way for a second, then pulled his head up and met John's eyes. "Go. But if it has anything to do with Harley, I don't care who you have to beat up to get back here, I *need* to know."

"Will do. If it was someone I loved, I'd want to know too." John turned on his heel and left the room, the door's lock echoing loudly in the small space.

There was absolutely nothing Coach could do but wait. If he was lucky, whatever was happening meant that Harley had been found. If he was *extremely* lucky, she'd been found alive.

Coach prayed harder than he'd ever prayed before in

his life. As much as he wanted to be with Harley, he'd be content for her to be breathing and in the care of someone else. His teammates would be on it. They'd take care of her until he could get to her.

Just in case, Coach crossed his fingers on both hands and said another quick prayer. "Please, let her be alive. We can deal with anything that happened to her as long as she's breathing."

Coach sat alone in the interrogation room for another ninety-three minutes, each ticking by slower than the last, before one of the officers who'd collected him from his apartment finally opened the door. His words stopped Coach's heart.

"We found your girlfriend."

Chapter Twenty-Four

C OACH SAT ON the hard chair beside Harley's bed in the ICU and simply watched her chest move up and down. It was the most beautiful thing he'd seen in his entire life.

He'd been released from the police station without so much as an apology after being informed that Harley had been found barely alive.

Thankfully, John had still been there and had driven him straight to the hospital. A nine-one-one call had come into dispatch right after Coach had arrived at the station. A woman claimed to be on the side of the road on Main Street, five miles outside of Temple city limits, looking at a car that was on its side. It was resting in the water at the bottom of the ravine and she'd claimed it looked somewhat recent.

The cops had gone to investigate and had found the Ford Focus…and Harley. She'd been unconscious, but alive. She was dehydrated, had a broken collarbone and arm, and a severe concussion. The medics on scene had told Montesa and Davidson that based on the fact she wasn't in acute organ failure because of a lack of water, it looked like she'd been conscious for the first few days and had been able to somehow get water from the creek to drink. It had saved her life. Her cell phone was found lying in the water next to her, useless.

Trapped by her jammed seat belt, and the fact that she'd been crushed up against the steering wheel, Harley hadn't been able to free herself. With her broken arm and collarbone, her mobility had been limited. She couldn't do anything but lie sideways in her wrecked car and hope someone found her.

The most pressing issue at the moment was that Harley was extremely dehydrated and they were concerned about her kidney functions. She was too weak for the surgery needed to repair her arm, so the doctors were waiting until she was more stable before deciding when they'd operate.

The machines around Coach beeped and hummed, but all he could see was Harley's chest moving. She was breathing, albeit with the help of machines at the moment, but she was alive. She hadn't regained consciousness at all yet, but Coach wanted to be there when she did. He wanted to be the first thing she saw.

"She wake up yet?"

The question was soft, but Coach knew it was Ghost.

"No, but she will."

"Of course she will. She's tough, Coach. No way she would've survived being out there for four days if she wasn't."

"Yeah."

"You need anything?"

Coach appreciated the fact that Ghost wasn't trying to talk him into leaving, or giving him any more platitudes. "No. Thanks though."

"Montesa and Davidson said they'd stop by in the morning."

Coach nodded.

"We checked that road. There was no sign of the accident," Ghost told him, knowing exactly what his friend was thinking. "Blade and Hollywood went out there after the ambulance left and double-checked. No skid marks. The guardrail was damaged, but nothing that would be noticed from the road itself. The only thing they could find was part of her front tire on the side of the road. The best they can figure is that she hit something in the road, there was some debris in the area that looked like it might've fallen off the back of a truck at some point. If she hit it, lost control of her car when the tire blew and overcorrected, she could've flipped the car. It's a long shot that she could've flipped it over the edge of the road without leaving a trace, but from the evidence, it looks like that's what happened.

"The ravine had a large gouge in it where the car hit,

but then it rolled back the other way and came to rest on the side near the road. It was invisible from the street above, from either direction. It was literally a miracle that woman hit the coyote where she did and stopped to investigate. Half a mile in either direction and she wouldn't have seen Harley's car at all."

Coach merely nodded again. It was a relief that his friends hadn't missed anything, but it still hurt to think about Harley being scared, in pain, and alone by the side of that road. Later, he'd find out the name of the woman who'd found the car and reward her. Right now all he could think about was Harley.

"I'll tell the nurse you're staying," Ghost reassured Coach.

"Thanks."

"The team'll be here in the morning. When her brother and sister visit, you can talk with them and get any other questions you have answered."

Coach didn't like the thought of spending even one minute away from Harley's side, but he knew her siblings needed to see her too. He wouldn't begrudge them that. If things had been different and it was Jenny lying in a hospital bed, he wouldn't want anyone to keep him from her. Coach turned to his friend for the first time. "Appreciate it, Ghost. I know it's been a long week, and even though I haven't said it, I'm glad you've been there for me."

"You'd do it for me and Rayne. Or Fletch and Emily. We all know it. I said it before and I'll say it again. She's one of ours. Now, try to get some sleep."

Coach didn't answer and Ghost obviously didn't expect one. He turned and left the room, the door snicking closed behind him with barely a sound.

Coach turned his attention back to Harley. She hadn't moved. Her lungs continued to be pushed upward by the pressure in the machines helping her to breathe. He hated to see her as helpless as she was, but damn was he thankful she was here. He'd honestly begun to think he'd never see her again. That someone had kidnapped her for whatever reason. He'd been sure it was somehow related to Jacks, but both Tex and Beth had said over and over that they didn't think the man had anything to do with her disappearance.

Coach was both relieved and horrified that Harley had been within five miles of her house the entire time she'd been missing. They should've had a helicopter search, or used dogs…or something. He shook his head, knowing better than to second guess the last week. Sure, they debriefed their missions all the time, trying to figure out what they could've done better, but this hadn't exactly been a mission.

He settled back into the uncomfortable chair, keeping his eyes on Harley's chest and his hand on her arm. He needed the connection. Needed to feel her warm skin. Coach let the rhythmic motion of the breathing machine lull him into a restless sleep.

Four hours later, in the dark of the night, Coach came awake with a start. Something had woken him up.

Harley.

She was jerking under his hand and making frantic gagging noises in her throat around the breathing tube.

Coach stood up, the chair screeching loudly before toppling over. He immediately found and pushed the call button for the nurse, then leaned over Harley until his face was inches from hers.

"Relax, Harl. I'm here. You're okay. You're in the hospital. You have a breathing tube down your throat, don't fight it. I called the nurse."

Her brown eyes met his and he could see the panic in them. Her eyes were wide and she was choking around the tube in her hysteria. He put one hand on Harley's forehead and the other on her cheek and leaned down even closer. His nose was touching hers now. Instead of being tender with her, Coach hardened his voice, wanting to pull her out of her panic to concentrate on what he was saying. "You're okay, Harley. We found you. You're safe. Hear me? I've got you. I'm here."

Remarkably, his words seemed to work. Her eyes stayed wide and frightened, but she wasn't fighting the tube anymore.

"That's it. Good girl. Stop fighting. Let the machine breathe for you. Just hang in there. The nurse'll be here in a second and she'll see what you need. I'm so fucking glad to see your brown eyes, Harl. You have no idea."

Her mouth opened like she wanted to respond, but Coach shook his head. "No, don't try to talk. Just keep your eyes on me. Okay? I'm right here. You are absolutely fucking beautiful. Thank you for fighting to stay alive out there. Thank you for coming back to me."

The nurse came through the door at that moment. "What's wrong?"

Coach didn't turn his head, keeping his eyes on Harley's. "She's awake. She panicked."

"Ah, okay, let me check her out."

Coach eased back, but told Harley, "Eyes on me. That's it. You're okay."

He didn't lose eye contact with her as the nurse checked the various machines around her.

"I'll call the doctor. I can sedate her until the doctor gets here or I can see if I can get authorization to pull it out now."

Harley's gaze pierced Coach's. Even without a word, he knew what she wanted. "Make the call and get the doctor to authorize you taking it out."

"I think we should—"

"No. She's lucid enough right now. Harley?"

She nodded vigorously.

Coach lifted his eyes from hers for the first time to look at the nurse. "Remove it."

Knowing the nurse would have final say, Coach stared at her, willing her to make Harley more comfortable. Finally, she nodded. "Okay, I'll be back as soon as I can."

Coach didn't watch her leave, but merely turned to Harley. "No problem, Harl. This is easy compared to what you just went through. Hang on a bit longer, okay?"

She nodded at him, and Coach's chest hurt at the trust he saw in her eyes. For the first time in almost a week, he felt the itchy feeling on the back of his neck dissipate. She was going to be okay. He'd make sure of it.

Chapter Twenty-Five

HARLEY SAT ON Coach's couch and smiled at everyone around her. She was so happy to be out of the hospital it wasn't funny. She knew she'd come too close to death. *Way* too close. She'd felt it as she lay pinned inside her car. The accident had happened so fast she hadn't even had time to hit the brakes. One minute she was driving along, lost in her thoughts and enjoying the warm weather, and the next she was stuck in her car in a couple inches of water.

She had a ways to go to get back to her old self, including gaining back the ten or so pounds she'd lost and getting her strength back to sit at her computer for hours at a time, but overall she was lucky—and knew it.

"I don't know how you did it," Emily told her. "I know I was scared to death when those guys kidnapped me and Annie. But I knew it was just a matter of time before Fletch found me."

"That's how I did it," Harley told the other woman. "I knew Coach wouldn't stop looking for me." She felt Coach squeeze the back of her neck, and smiled as she continued. "The first night was the worst. I thought someone would see my car the first day. But as the hours passed, and I could hear the cars zooming by over me, and no one stopped, I knew I was in trouble."

"It's almost creepy how your car landed in a way that you were invisible to anyone driving by," Rayne commiserated.

"Yeah. My phone landed in the creek when the car stopped rolling, and I couldn't reach it, not that it would've mattered, it was waterlogged anyway. I couldn't get out of the car because of the angle and my arm. All I could do was wait. After the first night, it weirdly got easier though," Harley tried to explain. "I think I designed at least three new games in my head, and I went over every single minute that I had spent with Coach. It was almost…calming."

"You should know, Harley," Truck told her in a gruff voice, "that we pulled every string we had to try to find you. There was a former SEAL in Pennsylvania trying to find you, along with a firefighter's girlfriend in San Antonio, a highway patrolman, who we just happen to know from the Army, down in San Antonio also doing his part. Not to mention all of us."

"I appreciate it. Every second," Harley said in a broken voice.

"You're one of us," Ghost told her, echoing what he'd told Coach more than once when she'd been missing.

"Has that asshole officer apologized to you yet, Coach?" Harley asked in a hard voice, obviously wanting to change the tone of the gathering away from a sad one.

"Heh, no. But I don't give a fuck. I knew I hadn't hurt you. My friends knew it. I didn't give a shit about what anyone else thought."

"I can't believe they wanted to blame you. Assholes," Harley said to no one in particular. "It pisses me off. There's no way you would ever hurt me. I hate that you might've gone to jail," Harley pouted.

"Fat chance," Montesa scoffed. "They didn't have any real evidence. The police chief was feeling pressure to do something after all the press, and since they didn't have any leads, they decided to concentrate on Coach."

Harley smiled at her sister's staunch defense of Coach. She loved that both her brother and sister approved of him. It was important to her. "Thanks, sis."

"You know it."

"I got a call from Fish this morning," Truck told the group, unexpectedly.

"Really?" Ghost asked.

"No shit?" Hollywood exclaimed at the same time.

"Yup. Apparently Tex called him and told him what was going down. He was pissed the hell off. But the weird thing is that I think it was the best thing that could've happened," Truck said as he chuckled.

"How in the fuck was Harley disappearing a good thing?" Coach asked in a low, lethal tone, his grip around Harley's nape tightening in his agitation.

Without seeming to be concerned about Coach's anger, Truck explained, "He'd been moping around the hospital. Not caring about doing his physical therapy and getting better. The fact that he couldn't do anything to help look for Harley, or to assist in the investigation, pissed him off. He's been doing everything he can recently to get better and get released."

Coach calmed down. "Is he chaptering out of the Army then?"

Truck nodded. "Yeah. Says he's gonna move to Idaho to get away from people for a while."

Ghost shrugged. "Can't say I blame him much. People suck most of the time."

"That's not true," Rayne protested. "I think all of you guys are pretty cool."

"Present company excluded of course," Ghost elaborated with a smile, kissing Rayne on the side of the head.

"He says if we ever need him, he'll be here in a heartbeat. And he means it. The man was gutted when he lost his team. He needs us, and I for one have no hesitation in calling him if we need backup. Just like with Rock, it can't hurt to have a brother on the outside to have our backs," Truck said almost absently.

"And he'll have ours in return," Coach said fervently.

Choruses of "absolutely" and "of course" were muttered amongst the Delta Force operatives.

"So, when are we going out?" Harley asked the group of women gathered around her, trying to change the subject and lighten the mood. "We were gonna have a girls' night out, and we didn't get to yet. And I still need to get a dress for the Army Ball."

Emily, Rayne, Mary, and Montesa all started talking at once. Arguing about when and where they should go.

Coach held a hand to his mouth and whistled, stopping the chatter and getting everyone's attention. "How about we let Harley fully recover before we start talking about going out and getting drunk? Not sure that's in her best interest at the moment."

"Coach, I'm fine—"

"You just got out of the hospital this morning."

"So?"

"How about this. When you can sit up without falling asleep, eat an entire order of Hunan spicy chicken, and play a marathon game of *This is War* with me, like we did on our first date, then you can plan this girls' night out with my blessing and make plans to go shopping."

Harley looked up into Coach's eyes. He was sitting

next to her on the couch. Actually, "next to her" probably wasn't the right description. She was practically in his lap. He had his arm around her shoulders, rubbing the back of her neck, and his other hand was holding hers, resting in his lap.

She would've protested, but she saw the worry in his eyes. It looked like he'd aged ten years since the morning she'd disappeared. Yes, she had been the one hurt and missing, but *he'd* been the one who had clearly suffered.

He'd told her late one night in the hospital, when she couldn't sleep because of the pain in her arm that he'd dreamed about her pleading for him to find her. Harley didn't know exactly how the spiritual thing worked, but it was obvious, at least to her, that the coyote, which mysteriously was never located, had been instrumental in making sure she'd been found. Harley had wondered more than once if it was somehow Jenny or her parents who had intervened and lent a hand in the search for her. Whatever the case, Coach had certainly done everything he could to find her...including almost getting arrested.

"Okay, Coach. When I can realistically reenact our first date, then we'll plan our night out."

"Thank you, Harl."

"Okay, visiting time is over," Emily declared. "Annie is probably driving her gym teacher nuts by now.

She was nice enough to babysit her long enough for us to get Harley settled, but if I know my daughter she's probably made her teacher recreate the obstacle course she loves so much in the backyard."

Everyone laughed, but no one disagreed. Emily was probably right. Annie was a handful, but everyone loved her.

"Since we're all here, I have something to say," Fletch said suddenly.

Everyone turned their eyes to the man, who suddenly looked nervous.

He turned to Emily and took her hands in his. "Everything that happened to Harley made me realize how short life is, and I might've adopted Annie, but I haven't officially made *you* mine yet. Miracle Emily Grant, will you marry me?"

Harley's hand came up to cover her mouth and tears gathered in her eyes. She couldn't believe Fletch was asking Emily to marry him right now, in front of them all.

Emily didn't make him wait for her answer. "Of course I will!"

"Soon," Fletch demanded.

Everyone chuckled, including Emily.

They put their arms around each other and she looked up at him. "Any day. Any time. Name it, and me and Annie will be there."

"Soon. I don't want to wait."

"I'll work on it." Emily paused a moment before asking, "Can we invite that guy, Fish? And Tex? And maybe your SEAL friends?"

"I don't see why not," Fletch told her. "I can't guarantee they'll be able to make it, depends on when it is, but we can certainly ask."

"Good," Emily said with satisfaction. "I'd like to meet some of the men you work with. To thank them for having your back."

The couple stared at each other for a moment, then kissed. It was a long, passionate kiss. Harley glanced over at Coach.

He was looking at her, and not at his friend.

"Are you all right?" Harley asked softly.

"You're safe and back in my arms. I'm perfect," Coach replied.

She smiled at him, then closed her eyes in contentment. She opened them again as she heard everyone congratulating Fletch and Emily and gathering their belongings. Harley hated to see everyone go, but she was exhausted. Coach was right, it would take a while to get her stamina back.

"Thank you all for coming over," Harley told everyone as they got ready to leave.

Each of the men came over and kissed her on the cheek, much to Coach's chagrin, and the women merely waved.

"Truck, can you give Mary a ride?" Rayne asked, not so innocently. "Ghost and I have some errands we need to do on the way home."

"I don't need him to—"

"Sure. No problem," Truck interrupted with a grin.

"Dammit, Rayne," Mary began, but Rayne simply ignored her.

"Thanks, Truck. We'll see you later. 'Bye!" Rayne waved and pulled Ghost out of the room before her best friend could protest further.

Harley laughed as Mary huffed and crossed her arms. It was amusing to watch the…relationship…if that was the word, between Mary and Truck. He was a big man, he towered over the smaller woman, but Mary didn't put up with any shit from him. It was almost as if she protested too much, however. It would be fun to watch those two in the future. If Harley was the betting sort, she'd put money on Truck. He had a certain gleam in his eye when he looked at the other woman.

Fletch and Emily came over to say their good-byes.

"Congratulations you two," Harley told them earnestly.

"Thanks," Emily replied, her smile stretching from ear to ear.

"When you're feeling better, you can help Emily plan the wedding, sound good?" Fletch asked.

"Okay, but I'm not sure I'm the best person to ask. I only own one dress and I suck at decorating. But I'll give it my best shot," Harley said honestly.

"It's going to be laid-back," Emily told her firmly. "A quick ceremony, then a big party. Nothing fancy or stuffy. So all I really need is someone to make sure I don't go overboard." Hugging her briefly and carefully, Emily said, "I'm glad you're all right."

"Me too," Harley responded, feeling Coach squeeze her hand.

"See you tomorrow," Coach told Fletch.

The couple left and the others followed suit until it was only her and Coach.

"How are you doing, Harl?" he asked in a low voice.

"I'm good."

"No pain?"

"I didn't say that. But it's not bad."

"Not good enough," Coach told her as he suddenly stood, cradling Harley.

Instead of protesting, which she probably would've done in the past, she simply laid her head on Coach's shoulder as he easily carried her into his bedroom.

"I love you, Harley."

"I love you too, Johnny." Her words were soft and full of love.

"Move in with me?"

"What?"

"Move in. I can't imagine not being with you every morning, or coming home to you each night."

"Don't ask because you feel guilty, or because you're scared if you let me out of your sight I'll disappear again. It was a freak thing, Coach. It won't happen again."

"I'm not asking because of that. I can't deny that I'm going to worry about you incessantly. You're gonna get sick of me texting and calling all the time to check on you. But I'm asking because I missed you. The thought of never seeing you again ate at my soul. Life is short and I don't want to spend mine without you."

"Shit, Coach. How can I say no to that?"

He smiled with an almost evil grin. "You can't."

Harley smacked him in the shoulder as they settled on the bed. "You manipulator."

His smile disappeared and he leaned over her until she lay back on the bed. His face was above hers as he said, "I love you. I want to spend my life with you. I'm not trying to manipulate you in any way. If you're not ready, you're not ready. It's fine. But I want to marry you. And not because Fletch asked Emily tonight. I—"

"Yes. I'll move in. Or you can move in with me. I kinda like my place better."

"Deal."

"Thank you for not giving up on me. I know you weren't the one to find me, but it wasn't because of lack of effort on your part."

"Damn straight. Oh, and you should know something."

"Yeah?"

"Hollywood is picking up your new car tomorrow."

"Coach!"

"Don't 'Coach' me. It's gonna be a Highlander, just like mine. It has GPS technology so if you're in a crash, the service calls the cops automatically. They can find you with a touch of a button. Give this to me, please."

"Okay." Harley nodded. "To tell you the truth, it'd make me feel better too. But I'm not letting you pay for it."

"Too late."

"No. No way."

"How about a wager?"

"A bet? What kind?"

"We play a video game of my choosing. If I beat you, you won't say anything else about the car. If you win, I'll let you pay me back for half."

"That's not a deal. If I win, I pay for all of it."

"Nope, take it or leave it."

"Fine." Harley yawned and blushed. Dang it. She was still so tired all the time. "What game?"

Coach moved off her and reached for her shoes. He removed them, then gently helped her out of her sweats and T-shirt. He tucked her under the sheets, careful not to jostle her arm. She settled on her good side, her cast resting on a pillow in front of her. She heard Coach stripping and snuggled into him when he curled behind her.

"*Bejeweled*."

Harley tried to whip her head around, but he kissed the back of her head, keeping her in place. "*Bejeweled*? That's not a real video game."

"Too bad."

"You suck," Harley told him with a grumble. "I hate that stupid game."

"I know. And I've been practicing."

"Figures."

They were silent for a while before Coach whispered in her ear, "You're everything to me, Harley Kelso. You scared me, and I don't scare easily. I love you."

"I love you too, Johnny. When I get this cast off?"

"Yeah?"

"I want to recreate our first time."

She felt Coach smile into her hair.

"Deal. But I have a feeling you're not gonna be able to wait that long. Starting tomorrow, we'll get creative."

"I like the way you think." Harley couldn't stop smiling. She had it all. A great career, a man who loved her, loving siblings, and now a whole new set of friends. Life was good.

"Good night, Harl."

"Good night, Johnny. Good dreams tonight, yeah?"

"Oh yeah. Nothing but from here on out."

"Agreed." Harley fell asleep within moments, safe in the arms of her man.

Epilogue

HARLEY MOANED AS Coach hovered behind her. She was on her knees on their bed, her hands resting on the headboard, her legs and Coach's hands on her hips holding most of her weight. Even though her collarbone and arm had been declared healed that day by their doctor, Coach hadn't wanted to put any of her weight on them.

"Coach, please, I'm dying here."

"You want me?"

"Yes!"

The word was hardly out of her mouth when Coach pushed inside her with one hard thrust. She bent over, arching her back, taking him even deeper. Harley loved when Coach took her from behind. The position made it seem as if he was so much farther inside her than when they did it any other way. She groaned loud, knowing Coach loved to hear her.

"Oh my God, that feels amazing."

Coach thrust lazily in and out of her, taking his time. Harley tried to push back against him, but he held her hips still, so she couldn't do anything but take him at his speed. She felt one of his hands move down to where they were joined and gently rub against her clit.

"Coach, seriously, quit fucking around. Please. I need you."

He pulled out and Harley moaned in complaint. Before she could say anything, he flipped her and crouched over her.

"You've been on the pill for a month and half, yeah?"

"Uh huh."

"I want to take you bare."

Harley stilled. After all this time, they still hadn't made love without Coach wearing a condom. He hadn't wanted to take the chance of getting her pregnant, especially when she was still recovering from the accident. She'd started on the pills before it had happened, but since she'd missed so many while she'd been missing and in the hospital, he'd refused to ditch the condoms.

"Really?"

"Yeah."

Harley's breaths sped up. "Yes, please. I can't wait to feel you."

Coach reached for the condom covering his erect cock and peeled it off. He dropped it off the edge of the bed, not caring where it landed.

Harley reached out a hand and stroked him, loving

how he felt hard and soft at the same time. Without breaking eye contact, she brought her hand down between her legs and inserted two fingers into herself, making sure to coat them with plenty of her juices. She then brought that hand back up to his dick and stroked him.

"Harley," Coach moaned, his head falling back for a moment.

"Gotta make sure you're sufficiently lubricated since you don't have the condom."

Her words made Coach smirk, but he didn't say anything, merely brushed her hand away from his length and braced himself over her once more.

He picked up a pillow and shoved it under her hips, raising them so she was tilted up toward him. Notching his cock against her wet folds, he pushed himself between them, not entering, but making sure her juices coated him instead.

"I know I've said it before, but I would move heaven and earth to keep you safe. If you disappear again, nothing will keep me from finding you. I don't want to live my life without you, Harley. I love you. Will you marry me? Become Mrs. Johnny Ralston?"

"Yes." There was no hesitation in her words at all.

Coach pushed into his fiancée until he couldn't go any farther.

They both breathed out in ecstasy.

"Does it feel different?" Harley asked.

"Yeah. Fuck yeah." And Coach moved. "It's amazing."

It was obvious that being inside her bareback was exciting for him, because Coach thrust into her again and again, harder and harder, each thrust making Harley's tits bounce up and down on her chest.

"Unh, I'm not gonna last. Make yourself come," Coach ordered, lost in the pleasure of the skin-on-skin contact.

Without hesitation, used to masturbating in front of Coach by now, Harley frantically rubbed her clit as he took his pleasure.

"Harl, God. Please say you're close."

"I'm close, just a little…more…"

Harley felt the orgasm swallow her up, but did her best to keep her eyes on Coach. His teeth were bared and the veins in his neck were standing out in stark contrast to his normally smooth skin. He grunted and made noises she'd never heard from him, before thrusting inside her as far as he could go and holding himself still.

When he finally looked back down at her, Harley was smiling up at him, running her hands over his chest soothingly.

"I'm thinking you like taking me without a condom."

"I'm never using one again," Coach said, completely straight-faced.

Harley smiled wider. "Okay by me."

Coach eased down next to her and drew her into his arms. "You'll really marry me?"

"Yes."

"When?"

Harley shrugged. "Whenever."

"Cool. We'll figure it out."

"I gotta warn you though, Montesa is going to want to go all out."

"Damn," Coach swore, but smiled as he said it, letting her know he was teasing. "Here's the thing. I want you protected. I want you to have all the benefits that come with being married to an Army guy. What would you think about us having a civil ceremony so I can file the paperwork with the Army...then we can take our time in planning a huge shindig?"

Harley smiled. "Can we keep it a secret?"

Coach quirked an eyebrow at her in question.

"I'm not ashamed to be married to you, but I don't think Montesa or Davidson would understand and—"

"Of course we can," Coach said immediately, understanding where she was going. "My commanding officer will know, and probably the guys too, but I'll swear them to secrecy. I won't even let Ghost and Fletch tell Rayne and Emily. That work?"

"Yeah. That works. Would you be offended if I didn't change my last name?" Without giving him a chance to comment, Harley went on, trying to explain. "It's just that it means a lot to me with my parents gone. Any kids we have would be Ralstons, but I've been Harley Kelso for so long it seems weird to change it now."

Coach leaned down and kissed her tenderly, then said, "I don't mind. As long as you're legally mine, you can call yourself anything you want."

She smiled. "Will I get a ring that everyone will think is an engagement ring but is really a wedding ring?"

"Fuck yeah. The biggest one I can find so everyone knows you're taken."

Harley rolled her eyes at that. "It's not like men are beating down my door, Coach. I think you're safe. I love you. So much."

He sighed in contentment, and Harley groaned when his length slipped out of her. His hand was immediately between her legs, playing in their combined juices.

"Hmmmm, I hadn't thought through *this* part of ditching the condoms," she remarked dryly.

"I love it. I'm not going to freak you out right now, but I want to see it."

"See what?"

"See my come dripping out of you."

"Okay, yeah, that's gross."

Coach merely smiled back at her.

"How come you don't think that's gross?"

"Hon, you have no idea what's really gross. I see stuff all the time in my job that's not fit for anyone's eyes. Trust me, Truck holding Fish's artery between his fingers while he carried his ass out of the desert and bled all over him? Gross. This? The result of both our pleasure? Nope. Not gross at all."

Harley harrumphed, but relented. "I gotta get up. I'm not sleeping in a wet spot."

Coach kept his hand over her folds. "Stay. Just for now."

"You like that."

"I do."

"Okay then. Coach?"

"Yeah, Harl?"

"I love you. Thank you for not giving up on finding me."

"Never. I love you."

HOLLYWOOD STARED AT the invitation to the annual Army Ball. He hated it. *Loathed it.* He'd been to every one since he'd joined the Army, but every single one was torture. This year it was being held in Austin, Texas. They'd rented some high-rise building and it was on the top floor.

He knew he was good looking, but when he put on his dress blues, women seemed to lose their minds. His teammates would roll their eyes if they knew how much he hated being hit on all the time.

It was part of the reason why he'd signed up for the stupid online dating site. Rayne gave him crap about it, but it was one of the only ways he felt he could get to know a woman and have even an inkling that she was attracted to him because of who he was, rather than what he looked like.

The picture he'd used on the site was an older one. He'd been fishing with one of the guys and was wearing jeans and a long-sleeve shirt. He had a ball cap on and it'd been pulled low over his face. He looked like any other guy...just about.

Over the last few weeks, he'd been talking to a woman online. He liked her. She seemed to like him back. But the last few times he'd talked to her, he'd gotten the feeling that she was hiding something. It was stupid; of course she was. They'd met online. It wasn't as if she was going to open up and tell him all her secrets...just as he wasn't telling her everything about himself. But it was a gut feeling that it was more than just an average reticence to tell a stranger you met on the Internet everything about you.

Hollywood wanted to ask her to the Army Ball, but wasn't sure she'd say yes.

Her name was Kassie.

She lived in Austin.

She was younger than him.

And she was scared and hiding something from him.

It was only a suspicion, but somehow he knew it was true.

Hollywood took a deep breath and made a decision. He'd never get to know her better if he didn't bite the bullet and meet her in person. The ball was a perfect plan. There'd be lots of people around, so she'd feel comfortable, she'd see that he was a soldier who had a lot of friends, and who could be trusted. It sounded like the perfect first date—so why did he feel so nervous?

KASSIE ANDERSON LOOKED down at her phone in trepidation as it dinged in her hand. She was hoping to hear from Hollywood again, but was also afraid of what he'd say. She was in over her head, was weak, but didn't know how to get out of the situation she'd found herself in.

Seeing the email wasn't from Hollywood, Kassie wanted to shut the phone off and ignore it, but she couldn't. She knew it. She clicked the email open, not surprised by what she read.

Jacks is pleased with your progress. Time to step it up. Report back ASAP.

Kassie wanted to throw up.

Her ex-boyfriend wasn't going to leave her alone. Ever. She'd thought that when he'd gotten arrested for kidnapping and assault, she could finally relax. That she was done with him. But she'd been deluding herself. It didn't matter that he was behind bars. He had enough friends to keep tabs on her. If she didn't do what he wanted, she'd pay.

Her phone made another dinging noise. Another email.

This was the one she'd been expecting from Hollywood.

Hi Kassie. I don't have long, so I'll keep this short and sweet. We've been talking long enough now for me to know that I really like you. You're funny and sweet and I'd love to meet in person. I don't want you to feel threatened though. There's an Army Ball in a few weeks. It's a dress-up thing, and it's being held in Austin. I thought maybe you might want to meet me there. We could see if the chemistry we have online transfers to face to face. If so, great, we can go from there. If not, no harm, no foul. What d'ya say?

~ Hollywood

Kassie read the email twice, her eyes filling with tears.

Hollywood didn't deserve what she was doing to him. The shit thing was, she honestly liked him. She did feel the chemistry between them. What had started out as a revenge thing at the request of her ex had turned into something else entirely.

She wanted to tell Hollywood no. That she didn't want to see or talk to him anymore, but that was impossible. Jacks was holding all the cards.

She slowly typed out a response, hating herself with every word.

I'd love to. I can't wait to meet you. ~ Kassie.

Look for the next book in the *Delta Force Heroes* Series, *Marrying Emily*.

To sign up for Susan's Newsletter go to:
http://bit.ly/SusanStokerNewsletter

Or text: STOKER to 24587 for text alerts on your mobile device

Discover other titles by Susan Stoker

<u>Delta Force Heroes</u>
Rescuing Rayne
Assisting Aimee – Loosely related to Delta Force
Rescuing Emily
Rescuing Harley
Marrying Emily (Feb 2017)
Rescuing Kassie (May 2017)
Rescuing Bryn (Nov 2017)
Rescuing Casey (TBA)
Rescuing Wendy (TBA)
Rescuing Mary (TBA)

<u>Badge of Honor: Texas Heroes</u>
Justice for Mackenzie
Justice for Mickie
Justice for Corrie
Justice for Laine
Shelter for Elizabeth
Justice for Boone
Shelter for Adeline (Jan 2017)
Shelter for Sophie (Aug 2017)
Justice for Erin (Oct 2017)
Justice for Milena (TBA)
Shelter for Blythe (TBA)
Justice for Hope (TBA)
Shelter for Quinn (TBA)

Shelter for Koren (TBA)
Shelter for Penelope (TBA)

SEAL of Protection
Protecting Caroline
Protecting Alabama
Protecting Alabama's Kids
Protecting Fiona
Marrying Caroline
Protecting Summer
Protecting Cheyenne
Protecting Jessyka
Protecting Julie
Protecting Melody
Protecting the Future

Ace Security
Claiming Grace (Mar 2017)
Claiming Alexis (July 2017)
Claiming Bailey (TBA)

Beyond Reality
Outback Hearts
Flaming Hearts
Frozen Hearts

Connect with Susan Online

Susan's Facebook Profile and Page:
www.facebook.com/authorsstoker
www.facebook.com/authorsusanstoker

Follow Susan on Twitter:
www.twitter.com/Susan_Stoker

Find Susan's Books on Goodreads:
www.goodreads.com/SusanStoker

Email: Susan@StokerAces.com

Website: www.StokerAces.com

To sign up for Susan's Newsletter go to:
http://bit.ly/SusanStokerNewsletter

Or text: STOKER to 24587 for text alerts on your mobile device

About the Author

New York Times, *USA Today*, and *Wall Street Journal* Bestselling Author Susan Stoker has a heart as big as the state of Texas, where she lives, but this all-American girl has also spent the last fourteen years living in Missouri, California, Colorado, and Indiana. She's married to a retired Army man who now gets to follow *her* around the country.

She debuted her first series in 2014 and quickly followed that up with the SEAL of Protection Series, which solidified her love of writing and creating stories readers can get lost in.

If you enjoyed this book, or any book, please consider leaving a review. It's appreciated by authors more than you'll know.

CPSIA information can be obtained
at www.ICGtesting.com
Printed in the USA
BVOW06s1226281016
466302BV00017B/326/P